Viking Legend

Book 10 in the Dragon Heart Series
By
Griff Hosker

Content

Viking Legend i
Chapter 1 2
Chapter 2 13
Chapter 3 21
Chapter 4 31
Chapter 5 40
Chapter 6 55
Chapter 7 66
Chapter 8 79
Chapter 9 89
Chapter 10 98
Chapter 11 111
Chapter 12 124
Chapter 13 132
Chapter 14 141
Chapter 15 152
Epilogue 162
Glossary 164
Historical note 167
Other books by Griff Hosker 170

Viking Legend

Published by Sword Books Ltd 2015
Copyright © Griff Hosker

The author has asserted their moral right under the Copyright, Designs and Patents Act, 1988, to be identified as the author of this work.

All Rights reserved. No part of this publication may be reproduced, copied, stored in a retrieval system, or transmitted, in any form or by any means, without the prior written consent of the copyright holder, nor be otherwise circulated in any form of binding or cover other than that in which it is published and without a similar condition being imposed on the subsequent purchaser.
A CIP catalogue record for this title is available from the British Library.

Cover by Design for Writers

Dedicated to Sam Polito one of my American readers who passed away recently, his wife said he was 80 and had enjoyed life.

Viking Legend
Chapter 1

There had been a time when we had allies in many corners of the world. We had been favoured by the Emperor of the Romans, the King of Wessex had been an ally, we had traded with the Welsh and earned their trust, we had traded with Amalfi and we had even had an alliance with Duke Seguin I Lupo of Vasconia. Now we heard that the Duke had been deposed and his land swallowed up by the Holy Roman Empire. The Emperor who had favoured us and his sons had been usurped and the other allies had turned upon us. The King of Wessex saw us as implacable enemies and even the Welsh had shunned us even though we had bled and died in their cause. We were now an isolated island surrounded by many enemies. To other people, this would have seemed a disaster. We cared not. My people were wealthy and our warriors were undefeated. We were a land of pagans surrounded by the followers of the White Christ. I was Jarl Dragon Heart of Cyninges-tūn and I was the Wolf Warrior.

As the snow left our land and we prepared our drekar for the sea I was as happy as I had been since my wife, Erika had died. I had thought I would end my life alone as Ragnar, my former master, had done but the Norns had other plans for me. I had rescued the illegitimate child of King Arthfael Hen ap Rhys. The King had shunned her and she had returned with me to my home by the Water. My daughter had spoken with my wife's spirit and it seemed that Brigid of the Welsh was to be the woman who would share my bed with me. *Wyrd.* And I was happy. It had been some years since I had enjoyed the company of a woman and in the long winter nights, my bed had seemed cold and lonely. I had comfort and peace in my hall which was home once more.

Now that our thoughts turned to the sea and to revenge. I had a young man from Lang's Dale serve with me. His name was Magnus but he had earned the nickname Foresworn for he had betrayed our people. He had cost warriors their lives and he had been banished by me. My men said I should have had him killed; perhaps they were right. While I had been fighting in the south he had raided the lands of Jarl Sigtrygg, one of my oathsworn and killed some of his people. My warriors, the Ulfheonar, wished to sail the seas to seek him and end his life. I should have killed him when he betrayed me but I am not of Norse blood and such ruthlessness does not sit easily with me. Perhaps the blood of the old people of the land had affected my decision. The next time I met him then he would die.

I said goodbye to Brigid as I left on my horse with Aiden to visit my ship. It had been some years since I had had to say goodbye to someone who had shared my bed. Brigid was totally different to Erika and I found the experience of bidding her farewell strange. She kissed me, embraced me and gave me an enigmatic smile. "I will see what changes I can make to your home while you are away."

I frowned, "I do not like change and I will only be away for one night."

Viking Legend

"Then I cannot do much can I?"

Aiden and I rode with Haaken along the road which bordered the Water. Haaken was married and now had two children. He laughed at me having witnessed the farewell. "You are tamed, Wolf Warrior! She will be fitting a ring through your nose before too long!"

Aiden said, "Do not listen to him Jarl Dragonheart. You have not been this happy and content for years. When you are in a contented state then the spirit world is happy and nature is too. Did you not notice that the winter was mild and we had no deaths? Our animals prospered and babies were born healthy. That is not luck that is due to your state of mind. Even though this Welsh Princess is a follower of the White Christ she has brought balance to your life. You have brought balance back to nature. This is good, this is *wyrd*."

I could see that his words had made Haaken think. My second in command nodded thoughtfully as we rode south to the sea.

I changed the subject. "And have the spirits told you where Magnus the Foresworn is hiding?"

"Not yet but it should be beyond our wit to make a good guess."

Haaken snorted, "If we are to take the '***Heart of the Dragon***' to sea to seek him we need more than a good guess. There are too many enemies out there for us to try to stumble upon him."

Aiden enjoyed a challenge such as this and, as we neared the forest road he began to tell us where he thought our enemy might be. "He came by sea and we did not pass him when we returned from the land of the Welsh. Therefore, he is either in Hibernia, Mann or north of here. If the Jarl sails first to Mann we can see if his ship is there. Sigtrygg's people said it had a red sail in mockery of yours."

"And Mann is not a safe place either." Haaken knew of the treachery which abounded in our former home.

"But think, Haaken One Eye, if Jarl Dragonheart sails around the island it will show the Vikings there that he does not fear them. They know the legend of the sword; let them fear the legend that is Dragonheart."

I nodded, "I fear not those on Mann. Aiden is right. As for Dyflin, it is time that we found out exactly who rules there. Sihtric Silkbeard is dead. Who knows, we may have allies there. We did trade with some last year. It may be that we can find friends there. Perhaps this is a good thing." Haaken nodded. What I had said had made sense. "And then Aiden, if Magnus is in neither of those places where would we search?"

"We would sail along the coast north. The islands of Orkneyjar have many places where a drekar could hide. And it would be good to see if the people there are willing to trade. Their seal oil is valuable and we have weapons and iron which they need."

My galdramenn's words made both Haaken and me silent as we pondered them. Aiden had an ability that all the gold in the world could not buy. He could see beyond the world around him. Sometimes it was through the spirits and sometimes... well I know not how he saw what he did. He had always been an enigma. Taken as a hostage when a child he had chosen to stay with me. Perhaps the gods had made that choice. I never ignored his advice.

When we reached the shipyard where the shipwrights and Erik Short Toe worked on my drekar I saw that it was drawn out of the water on the bank and the weed which had gathered on her hull during winter was being removed. Her strakes were being caulked to ensure they were watertight and the sail was being examined for damage.

Erik grinned when he saw me, "I wondered when you would come. The sea calls eh, Jarl Dragonheart?"

"The sea calls indeed Erik. When will she be ready?"

"By the time you return with a crew, she will be in Úlfarrston chafing at the bit."

"There is no hurry. I will visit with Coen ap Pasgen this night for I wish to speak with him." I looked around for Siggi and his knarr. "Where is Siggi?"

"He sailed to Sigtrygg. He wished to try out his new sail."

"Good. I would have him sail with us."

"So, you go to trade and not to fight."

I smiled, "Perhaps both. Remember, Erik, the wolf is a cunning creature. In a world of enemies, we have to use every weapon at our disposal."

Coen ap Pasgen was the headman of Úlfarrston. His father had been our oldest ally. He had recently died but Coen was a stout friend too. He had sailed with us before now. They were farmers and traders rather than warriors but we had made their defences strong and improved their skills with weapons such that few would think they were sheep to be shorn. Because they were not Vikings they were still able to trade further afield than we did. The Saxons would all trade with them for they were of the old people, the ones who had lived in the land when the Romans had left. Some called them Welsh but they were not.

He and his sons were at their ship when we reached the settlement. His face told me that he was pleased to see me. Winters here could be harsh and we often went months trapped in a world of ice. "Jarl Dragonheart, it is good to see you."

"And you, my friend. Could we impose on your hospitality this night? I need to speak with you."

"Of course." He turned to his son, Coel, "Go and tell your mother we have three guests."

The youth ran off. "A fine boy and he has grown."

"They do. Why it seems but a short time since your son, Wolf Killer was but a child and now he rules as a jarl. Time passes us all by."

I pointed to the wooden walls of his settlement. "Your father built those walls. They are a measure of how time makes us all stronger if we use our skills well." He led us towards his hall. "Where will you trade this season?"

"Wessex and Mercia both demand as much stone and metal as we can sell them. I was going to ask you if we could buy some of your surplus. There is

Viking Legend

great profit in it." He hesitated, "I know that you and the Saxons are now enemies. I would not wish to offend you."

I put my arm around his shoulder, "You do not. It is good that you trade with my enemies. We profit and you profit. Trade is trade." We entered his palisade and those within waved at us. To them we were not the wolves from the sea, we were friends. "That is one of the reasons I have come here. There are too many ports closed to us now. You will have to be our eyes and ears. I would have you bring us news of the world outside. I need to know the way the world moves."

"We can do that." He waved over a slave to take our ponies. "Come we will wash and then I will broach a new barrel of ale. A visit from Jarl Dragonheart is a reason to celebrate."

The visit proved illuminating. I discovered that the men of Wessex were on the rise. King Egbert had conquered the lands of On Walum. That did not surprise me. The king there was weak. We had bloodied his nose before now. He was now fighting the Mercians. We had fought them before and they were not a match for the men of Wessex. King Egbert was an implacable enemy. My son had stolen his young bride, Elfrida, some years earlier. Hitherto we had been beyond his greedy grasp but if he defeated Mercia then he would be our near neighbour. That information was worth storing. Coen, however, could add little to our knowledge of the whereabouts of Magnus the Foresworn. It seemed that following his abortive raid on Sigtrygg, he had disappeared. I wondered if he had tried to sail west to the lands beyond the seas. There were legends and stories of a wonderful land there with no winters and fine game; where gold and silver lay on the ground to be picked up. I did not believe in such a place but Magnus might.

As we made our way home the next day and discussed where he might be Haaken said, "Perhaps he sailed off the edge of the world."

I said nothing but looked at Aiden who closed his eyes. We were passing the start of my Water and there the power was great. Old Olaf and his mountain seemed to increase my galdramenn's skills. He opened his eyes, "He lives still. I can feel his malevolence."

"Then he is near."

Aiden smiled, "You are becoming skilled, Jarl. Aye, he must be close or I would not sense him so quickly."

"Haaken when we reach Cyninges-tūn tell the Ulfheonar that we sail soon. Find out if there are others who wish to join in this venture."

"Aye, Jarl."

"And do we gather trade goods?"

"Yes, tell Scanlan that Coen ap Pasgen will be buying stone and metal and tell Bjorn Bagsecgson that there will be opportunities for profit for him too."

Bjorn was our blacksmith. He was the richest man in Cyninges-tūn for he was skilled in the art of sword and armour making. It was he who had forged my sword but, as he admitted, it had been the gods who had made it the mighty weapon it was.

Viking Legend

Three days later my drekar slid through the water towards Mann. We could have taken many times the number of warriors that we could carry. Haaken and Snorri had sifted through those who wished to come. We wanted the best. Siggi was still in Úlfarrston loading with trade goods. When we had scouted Mann we would return and escort him to Dyflin. We would not trade with those on Mann. They were untrustworthy.

Cnut, who had been one of my oldest friends had died and his son was one of the crew of the Heart. This would be his last voyage as a sailor for he had said that he wished to be a warrior like his father. When Haaken began to chant the song of my sword I saw Cnut Cnutson swell with pride. The chant always helped us to sail faster for it spoke of how the sword had become magic. It was the stuff of legends. The rowers became as one when we chanted. It was always the first chant we used. My men were superstitious and this always acted as a good omen.

> *The storm was wild and the gods did roam*
> *The enemy closed on the Prince's home*
> *Two warriors stood on a lonely tower*
> *Watching, waiting for hour on hour.*
> *The storm came hard and Odin spoke*
> *With a lightning bolt the sword he smote*
> *Ragnar's Spirit burned hot that night*
> *It glowed, a beacon shiny and bright*
> *The two they stood against the foe*
> *They were alone, nowhere to go*
> *They fought in blood on a darkened hill*
> *Dragon Heart and Cnut will save us still*
> *Dragon Heart, Cnut and the Ulfheonar*
> *Dragon Heart, Cnut and the Ulfheonar*
> *The storm was wild and the Gods did roam*
> *The enemy closed on the Prince's home*
> *Two warriors stood on a lonely tower*
> *Watching, waiting for hour on hour.*
> *The storm came hard and Odin spoke*
> *With a lightning bolt the sword he smote*
> *Ragnar's Spirit burned hot that night*
> *It glowed, a beacon shiny and bright*
> *The two they stood against the foe*
> *They were alone, nowhere to go*
> *They fought in blood on a darkened hill*
> *Dragon Heart and Cnut will save us still*
> *Dragon Heart, Cnut and the Ulfheonar*
> *Dragon Heart, Cnut and the Ulfheonar*

I saw that Karl was carefully watching all that Erik did. He was another of the ship's crew. Karl was the former ship's boy who now wished to be a sailor. He was old enough to be a warrior but he stayed by Erik's side. Soon I would need to do something for him. He had learned all that he could from Erik just as Erik had when Josephus had captained my ship. Perhaps Karl could captain a small knarr. We had two we had captured. A knarr was easier to sail than a drekar. He had served me well. I knew that he had done a good job training Cnut Cnutson.

Erik shouted, "Karl, take in the sail. Haaken you can stop rowing. There is Mann ahead."

Our former home was just a short way away across the sea from us. I went to the dragon prow and leaned out to view Hrams-a where my mother had been slain. It had fallen into disrepair of late and the tower where my sword had been struck by lightning had long since fallen. There were no drekar in the small bay and I waved us south. We would not raid. There would be nothing worth taking from it these days.

Duboglassio was a different matter. This was fortified. We had our shields along the side. It showed all that we were a warship and warned them to stay clear. As we passed the port I saw that there were two threttanessa in the harbour but neither had a red sail. Two such ships would not worry us and we continued south. There were two more ports on the island. One on the south of the island, and the former home of my wife's brother, Erik on the west coast.

The one at the south which had first been ruled by Olaf the Toothless and then latterly Rolf, who had been one of my jarls, had one drekar in the harbour. It was as large as mine but it did not have a red sail. Nor was it ready for sea. I saw men still scraping the hull. That left Erik's old port. My brother-in-law and his evil wife had long since died. I knew not who lived there now. We would soon discover that information.

The wind was with us and my men lined the sides to watch the small port hove into view. Eystein the Rock pointed to the headland. There was a tower. "Jarl, it looks like they are making a signal."

I shaded my eyes and saw that he was right. The tower was new. "This may mean danger. Prepare for battle."

We all wore our armour but our helmets were stored in our chests as were our wolf skins. The wolf skins were symbolic. We did not need them for disguise when on our drekar but they marked us for who we were and they frightened our enemies when we ventured ashore. More than that they inspired those who were not Ulfheonar. It was seen as a great honour to fight alongside the wolf warriors. We did not don our red paint for our faces. The arming of my warriors was a precaution only. The ship's crew all strung their bows. We learned that the effect of a few arrows could be devastating.

I saw the fort they had built on the small knot of land attached to the land by a thin strip of earth. It protected the harbour well. The idea to build it there had been that of Prince Butar. He had always planned well. We kept well out to sea. It was as well that we did for two drekar suddenly raced from the harbour; alerted, no doubt, by the watch tower. They had their mast on the mast fish and were just using their oars. That was why we had not seen them

Viking Legend

earlier. They came at us like sharks. However, we had the wind with us. We would use that advantage.

Erik's voice carried down the drekar, "What would you have us do, Jarl?"

"Take us further out to sea. Arm yourselves and prepare to repel an attack." I walked down the gangway to Aiden who held my helmet and wolf skin.

Haaken was already dressed for war, "Think you it is Magnus Foresworn?"

"I do not know. That is why I will allow them to close. If it is then we will fight if not we will discourage them and sail for Siggi."

Haaken shook his head, "It does not do to run away from a fight, Jarl Dragonheart."

"You have known me long enough to know I run away from nothing. What would be gained if we fought them?"

"Honour! Glory!"

"And we would lose warriors. If we won then our enemies would lie in the sea with their treasure lost forever."

Aiden fitted my helmet and had attached my wolf skin, "The Jarl is right, Haaken. We do not throw away lives needlessly. Erik can outrun them."

"But they will be encouraged to attack us closer to home."

He could not see my face but I was smiling. It was the smile my enemies called my wolf smile. "And where is a wolf at its most dangerous? It is when it is in its den. Let them come. Their way home will be marked by their whitening bones."

The two drekar were racing towards us. Erik skilfully put the steering board over. We were tantalisingly close to the prows of the two ships. Had they not been rowing they might have loosed arrows at us. "Karl, can you see Magnus Foresworn?"

Karl was at the masthead with Cnut Cnutson. His voice came down to me, "I do not see him Jarl and the rolled sails are not red."

"Use your bows to discourage them. Go for the helmsmen."

Snorri and Beorn the Scout picked up their bows and joined the boys in releasing arrows. The two drekar were just fifty paces away and the range was close. I saw that the arrows had struck home immediately. One of those with the steering board was pitched over the side when he was struck by two arrows. His falling body made the drekar veer to the right. The two ships were so close together that a collision was inevitable. The oars on both drekar were sheered as they struck. The arrows continued to fall. I saw that the drekar on the steering board side of the one we had hit was lower in the water. Its strakes had sprung. They would be lucky to get back to land. I saw the two captains shaking their fists at us. My men laughed as they took off their helmets. We would not be fighting this day.

We spent a night in Úlfarrston. Erik had discovered that one of the ropes on the rudder withy was weak. He was annoyed with himself for he had allowed the shipwrights to look to that. He was angry until I pointed out that it was better for it to happen close to home rather than at sea. "We are watched over, Erik. The spirits have given us this chance to make our ship whole before we face unknown waters."

He smiled, "You are right, Jarl. It is just that I want our ship to be perfect."

"She is. This delay does not hurt us. We have a night on land and we can be across the sea by late afternoon. It has happened for a reason."

We left the next morning with our drekar repaired. Siggi's ship was heavily laden and slowed us down. She carried timber, stone and iron. All were valued by the Hibernians and I hoped that we would make good trades. We had traded with Hakon the Bald the previous year. He had seemed quite happy to do so but he had served with Rorik and Magnus Klak in his youth. He might have reformed but I was still suspicious of him.

We sailed to Dyflin without shields on the side. We were going to trade. As we approached the river I had Karl and Cnut keep a good watch for a red sailed drekar. They reported none. There were longships in the river but they had their masts stepped. They were not yet ready for sea. We had left our home earlier than most ships.

We tied up first as the stubby knarr edged its way in to a berth. Already Viking merchants were making their way to the ship. My name was known and our goods were valued. There had been a time when we would have had to fight our way in but this time it seemed we were welcomed. I let Siggi and Aiden haggle with the merchants. I awaited Hakon the Bald.

He looked the same as he came towards me. He was slightly heavier. I think his days of going a-Viking were long gone. He embraced me in a bear hug, "Jarl Dragonheart! It is good to see you." He nodded towards my knarr. "I see you have come to trade. Do you have any of that fine wine from Frankia on board?"

"Sadly no. I fear I have worn out my welcome there. The Emperor of the Franks does not like me."

Hakon laughed, "I know! I heard he has put a price on your head. He has a price on every Viking but there is a bounty of a thousand gold pieces for your head and wolf skin."

I smiled, "I hope that you do not try to collect such a bounty Hakon the Bald."

He looked offended, "I am insulted, Jarl! I thought we were friends!"

"And we are. And as a friend, I would ask if you have seen Magnus the Foresworn. He has a ship with a red sail."

He nodded, "*'**The Red Snake**'*. Aye, she was in a week since and just before winter the time before."

"Where did he go? I seek him. He raided one of my jarls."

"I think he sailed north to the islands close to the land of the Picts. He had been raiding further south, towards Wessex. I do not think he prospered."

"How so?"

"Egbert's men were waiting for him. He raided last year and was successful. He had two ships then. One was lost close to Wessex." He leaned in, "He has a large crew on his '***Snake***'. He picked up most of the crew of the drekar he lost. He is a dangerous young man. He is unpredictable."

"Yet you showed him hospitality."

He smiled, "He paid well. He must have had some success on his raids for he paid for everything with gold. You, I welcome you as a friend. He paid for his welcome." He stroked his beard. "I did hear him say that the King of Northumbria was paying for warriors but that seemed unlikely. As you say he is not to be trusted. Who knows which of his words are the truth and which falsehoods? Will you stay?"

I knew that Hakon was as two-faced as a Roman coin, "No my friend. When we have traded then I return to my home with the profits."

"Yours is a rich land. You should keep watch that no one tries to take it from you."

"Many have tried. Their bones help our crops grow well."

He laughed, "That is what they say of you jarl. You are a good friend but a relentless and ruthless enemy. Fear not, I covet not your land. This suits me. If I had more of that Vasconian wine then it would be perfect."

Normally we would avoid sailing at night but I wanted to escort Siggi east as soon as possible. We left at dusk and kept the setting sun behind us. We used Siggi's ship as a navigational aid and, when we saw the coast loom up we bade them farewell and headed north along the coast of my land. The wind still favoured us and we made good time. It was late when we pulled in at the river close to Thorkell's Stad. Arne was my jarl there now. His was a lonely land for the Picts and the Scots who lived north of him were fond of raiding as were the Hibernians. He had to keep a good watch on the coast and the river. Although it was late his sentries spied us and we were welcomed into his hall.

"Welcome, Jarl Dragonheart. This is an unexpected visit. I hope it does not mean there is danger. We have prospered over the winter."

"No, my friend. We are hunting Magnus the Foresworn and we heard that he was heading north to the islands."

"Does he have a red sail with a dragon upon it?"

"Aye?"

"My fisherman spied him some many days ago. He was hugging the coast and heading north."

"He did not land then and raid? He knows the land for he and his family lived up Lang's Dale before I banished him."

"No, Jarl. He did not but we are ever watchful these days."

"I will be sending goods with Coen Ap Pasgen to trade. If there are any goods which you need then let me know."

"We need for little but if there is any seal oil then we would appreciate that."

"I will have Siggi find some for you."

We left the next morning. The night with Arne would be the last hospitality that we could expect. The jarls who lived in the islands were unpredictable. They spent much of the time squabbling and fighting amongst themselves. At other times they would join forces and raid the men of Strathclyde. I could see why Magnus the Foresworn would seek an island of his own. He could become powerful in the thousands of islands which dotted the coast. A cunning young man he had the ability to take advantage of a power struggle between others. The problem would be finding him in the myriad of islands which lay off the coast.

As we passed the land of the Scots I joined Aiden and Erik at the stern. "Now we begin the game. Where do we start Aiden? What do the spirits say?"

He smiled, "I have to be closer to our enemy before the spirits can aid me but Erik and I have been discussing where he might go." He unrolled one of his maps. He was skilled at making charts. "This chart has many gaps in it. We sailed here only once but there are four or five large islands. Some are almost as big as Mann. I do not think he would choose one of the larger ones. Perhaps we need to visit Ljoðhús. It is a large island and the King of Norway is said to have some influence there. We could try the port on the island. The jarl there might be able to give us information. However, we know not if the jarl is friendly or not."

I had had trouble many years earlier and fought a hothead who had lived in the islands. My name was known, "It is a starting place. Set course for Ljoðhús, Erik."

It was getting on for dusk when we saw Ljoðhús. It was a large island and there was a stockade and palisade around the huts. They knew how to defend. The question was, against whom? I saw three drekar bobbing in the bay as well as three small knarr. We were arriving without shields but that did not guarantee a good welcome. I made sure that we came in slowly so that, by the time we had stopped, there was a group of warriors to meet and greet us. I had no doubt that my ship was recognised but I had made many enemies in my life and I did not know if one of them was here. At least Magnus' ship was in the harbour.

I stepped ashore flanked by Aiden and Haaken. The warrior who approached me had a long scar running down his face. It looked as though it had been coloured when it was healing for it was a bluish-purple colour and his arms were covered in warrior bands. He had fought, successfully, it seemed.

He held out his hand, "I am Thorfinn Blue Scar." He gestured towards my drekar. "From your sail, you must be Jarl Dragonheart, the Ulfheonar."

"I am."

"I see that you come in peace but you come uninvited to my island."

"I did not know that you forbade visitors. Is this the King's will?"

I noticed a frown appear, "The King is far away in Norway and he trusts me to watch out for his interests here in Ljoðhús."

"Then I am a timely visitor. We are looking for trade with this land. You have fine seal oil and seal skins."

"We do. But what can you offer in trade?"

Viking Legend

"We have timber." I waved a hand around the island which plainly had no trees. "I can see that you have a shortage." He nodded. "And we have stone."

"We have stone aplenty."

"And there are the metals, iron and copper as well as weapons."

That convinced him. I saw his eyes widen when I mentioned them. "You have, as I recall, a sword touched by the Gods. Are all your swords as magical?"

"I would be foresworn if I said so and I only speak the truth. The sword was made by my smith and it was a powerful weapon before Odin touched it. Now it is magical. I cannot promise the same for all Bjorn's swords. But they are the finest swords this side of Frankia. Some would say in the whole world but that would be boasting."

I was watching the reaction of the others and they were impressed. I think that Thorfinn Blue Scar was trying to remain impassive but he failed. He nodded, "Then you are welcome. We would dearly like to trade for fine weapons. Ask your warriors to come ashore and we will show them Norse hospitality."

Viking Legend

Chapter 2

The warrior hall was very long and could accommodate a large number of warriors. Now that he knew what we had to trade Thorfinn softened a little and became more welcoming. "What has happened to your other trading partners?"

I smiled; the stories of my exploits in the Holy Roman Empire and Wales, not to mention Wessex were the stuff of legends. He had heard of my battles. "Let us just say that I have upset one or two former friends. I am my own man and I bow the knee to neither king nor prince."

I saw him bridle a little. I think he thought I was insulting him. "The King gives me free rein here."

"I am sure he does. It is just that I could not do what you do. We are different. I am not Norse-born. My blood is that of the people of Britain and Saxon." I shrugged. "It makes me who I am."

We sat at his table and his thralls brought us foaming ale. "I hear your son stole the daughter of the King of Wessex and you took the daughter of the King of the Welsh."

"Exaggerated stories. Both ladies were unhappy. We merely gave them transport to a place of safety."

He laughed, "You must have balls the size of a bull."

I laughed, "I fear no man that is true."

"So, when do you want the trading to begin?"

It was a little brusque but I did not mind. Trading was incidental. "As soon as I return home I will send my knarr. She carries far more cargo than I can. I did not want to send her here unannounced. I did not wish to offend you or risk pirates."

"I keep my waters safe."

It was the opening I had sought. "That is good for I seek a pirate who might have raided you. He used to be known as Magnus Slender Leg and he has a drekar with a red sail. Now he is Magnus the Foresworn and he is not to be trusted."

He nodded, "I know of whom you speak. He has called in before now offering his sword and his crew. You said used to be known as. What did you say his name was now?"

"Magnus the Foresworn. He and his men betrayed me after they had sworn to follow me."

Thorfinn clutched his hammer of Thor. No one would contemplate fighting alongside such a man unless they were desperate. "He has two islands which he uses. As no one lives on them I allow him to use them but I have little to do with the man. Now that you have told me his true name then I will close my ports to him. Such nithings are beneath contempt."

"Where are these islands?"

"You will have passed one on your journey north, Dyrøy, deer island. It is a large island but save for a few deer there is little to make a man farm there.

Viking Legend

The land grows little but bracken and heather. The other is not far from here, Bjarnarøy, it is on the other side of this island. But he is not there."

"Then he will be at the other island, further south."

"He could be. I will ask Thorgeir the Clumsy. He has a stad which overlooks Bjarnarøy. He will know." He waved over a barrel of a man. I saw that he only had three fingers on his left hand. I guessed at the reason he had been thus named. "Jarl Dragonheart seeks Magnus Slender Leg although his real name is Magnus the Foresworn. Do you know where he is?"

Thorgeir had already drunk much and his speech was not clear. "He is not in the islands. I heard that he was going to sail to Norway and offer his sword to the King of Norway." He shrugged, "Although why the King should want a runt like him is beyond me. But he seemed full of such tales. To hear him you would think that every king wished for his sword. He even said that he was a friend of the King of Northumbria, Eanred."

"There you are, Jarl. Perhaps he has fled your wrath. You have a reputation for vengeance and pursuing your enemies to the ends of the earth and beyond."

I nodded, "Those who hurt me and mine do not live overlong."

He laughed, "You may not have Norse blood but you have a Norse heart. Stay this night. I warm to you."

I had intended to follow Magnus but it seemed it would be a fruitless journey. We would leave the next day and return home. "Very well. I will just go and tell my ship's crew that we stay."

I went with Aiden back to my ship. I waved Erik over for he had anchored in the bay. He and his crew used a couple of oars to bring her over. "We are staying the night, Erik. I shall send some food for you and your crew."

"You need not, Jarl. We spotted a beach across the bay. It is better sheltered than here. I think they do not use it because it can only accommodate one drekar but we saw some seals. Who knows we may even hunt one. I like seal meat. We will camp there. We will be safer for it is in the lee of the island. I smelled a change in the wind."

I peered in the direction he had pointed, "I cannot see the island."

"No, Jarl. It is hidden by that ugly little rock of an island, they call it Sgeotasaigh."

"If you are certain?"

"Aye. I think we will be safer. We will be here by dawn. Fear not." Erik was close to his crew. He had more crew now. We normally carried and the eight of them, mainly boys, were a tightly knit band. They would be safe. With Karl and Cnut Cnutson, he had a crew he could rely upon.

Thorfinn feasted us well. Neither Aiden nor I tried to match him and the men in their drinking and we were rewarded with much knowledge about the King of Norway and those who lived on these islands. It seemed that the Scots and the Picts had begun to flex their muscles and there was a warlord called Alpín mac Echdach who was carving out his own kingdom on the mainland. He had been raiding some of the smaller islands and taking the people there as

Viking Legend

slaves. As I listened to Thorfinn speaking of how he would easily defeat him I could not help smiling for this Pictish warlord sounded a little like me. He was making his land safe for his people.

We all slept together in the huge warrior hall. It had been some years since I had done so. I was used to being alone. Aiden helped me off with my armour and I slept with my sword next to me. I slept badly that night. Perhaps it was the fact that I had not found Magnus and that it was unlikely I would in the near future. Or perhaps it was the mass of heaving, flatulent Vikings who surrounded me. Whatever the reason I rose, well before dawn, and went outside to make water. Aiden ghosted next to me.

I glanced at him as he too made a steaming stream into the sea. "You could not sleep either?"

"No Jarl, there is something amiss. My sleep was disturbed but there were too many in the hall for my thoughts to be clear."

I had learned not to ignore Aiden's premonitions. "Danger here or at home?"

"Here, Jarl Dragonheart."

I was about to go back into the hall when a figure hauled himself out of the water. It was Leif Siggison, one of Erik's ship's boys. He spluttered as he drew himself onto the stones, "Jarl Dragonheart, the captain sent me. There are ships heading here. You cannot see them for the island is in the way but they look to be warships." I looked at his dripping form. "I came in a small boat but it capsized yonder in the rocks. Luckily I can swim."

I peered into the dark and thought I saw a pennant fluttering white against the dark night. It was a ship. "Viking?"

He shook his head, "No, Jarl, Scots or Irish. We could not tell."

"You have done well. Aiden, see to him." I ran back into the hall and began banging my sword against my shield. "Awake, there is danger!" It was my men who reacted first.

Thorfinn stood and angrily shouted, "Who commands in my hall!"

"I do! There are ships coming across the bay and they are filled with armed men." I knew not if the latter was true but I guessed that they were.

"Is this some kind of trick?"

"If it is then what have I to gain save humiliation and embarrassment?"

He turned to one of his men. "Go and see if it is true."

I shook my head and said, "My men, arm yourselves and form up outside. We will be ready to fight whoever comes this way."

I grabbed my mail and donned it. I had no time for my wolf skin but I jammed my helmet on my head. As I left the hall I was nearly bowled over by the warrior Thorfinn had sent to investigate. "It is true, Jarl, and they have fired our ships!"

As the men of Ljoðhús donned their armour I went outside and looked across the bay. The three drekar and knarr were afire. Had Erik not moved my ship then it too would have been destroyed, *wyrd*. I saw the five enemy ships. They were shorter and tubbier than our ships; they were more like large knarr.

15

Haaken and Snorri appeared next to me. "I want us in two lines. Put the new men in the second line."

Snorri nodded and turned to give the orders. Haaken said, "Do we fight?"

"Of course, we do. We are guests. We owe it to our host."

"I thought we would. It is good to know the woman, Brigid has not changed you."

I looked at him in surprise, "Your wife did not change you. I was married for many years to Erika, remember."

"Aye, but Brigid is young and you are sporting some grey hairs. I wondered if it might have changed you."

I laughed, "Then you do not know my heart, Haaken. I am surprised."

Thorfinn and his men emerged, "I am sorry I doubted your word, Jarl Dragonheart. Whatever the outcome this day I am in your debt." The burning drekar illuminated the advancing ships. We could see the warriors crowded on their decks. "Picts and Scots!"

"You recognise them?" He nodded. "How do you wish to fight them?"

"We meet them at the edge of the sea. They will be hampered by the waves and the sand when they try to land."

I nodded, it was a good plan.

He raised his sword. "Forward, we take no prisoners! I want their heads along the beach as a reminder of their folly!"

Our spears were still on my drekar. My warriors had swords only. They would have to do. It was a sloping shingle beach which bordered the wooden jetty. Thorfinn sent his archers to the jetty while we began to spread out along the beach. I could now make out the half-naked warriors who crowded the bows of each of the five ships. Each ship appeared to have a leader who wore a helmet. I saw no armour. That was a good thing. Although the ones who leapt ashore first might be the only ones who were lacking mail.

One ship was moving faster than the others and it headed for the jetty. The others all headed for the safer approach of a wide shingle beach. The twenty bowmen who were standing on the jetty began to shower the deck with arrows. The lack of armour amongst the men on the ships and the shortness of the range drove the ship towards the beach which was safer than the wooden jetty. The jetty would be safe and the archers there could continue to pour death into the flanks of the Scots. As we watched them approach, ever closer, I realised that but for Erik, we would have been surprised. Thorfinn kept no watch upon his bay. We would have been slaughtered where we slept. *Wyrd*.

As luck would have it the boat closest to me ground upon the shingle and the sea was filled with reckless warriors who jumped into the surf and raced towards us. Thorfinn had been correct. They struggled towards us. Their legs sank into the shingle and it took more steps to reach us than it should have. It looked to take twice as much effort to move a short distance. The shingle and the sea would sap the energy from their legs.

The first ones ashore made it to our shields quickly for they were barefooted and had no mail. They threw themselves at our shields screaming ancient war cries. They were easily slain but allowed those slower ones with mail to begin to clamber up the beach and meet us sword to sword on the level sand and shingle where we stood. Their leader had a hammer and a shield. He roared some unintelligible words at me and launched himself towards our line. He brought his hammer from a long way back. His feet were still in the soft, slippery shingle. Had we fought on dry land then I might have been in trouble but the treacherous shingle conspired against him. I angled my shield as the blow came. He slipped slightly and the blow slid harmlessly down the side of my shield. I brought my sword overhead too but I had my feet firmly planted. I caught him across the neck. The blood spurted and sprayed the men adjacent to the leader.

There was a roar of anger as the men around him saw their leader die. I knew then that those close to him were his oathsworn and they would either kill me or die trying. Haaken and Asbjorn the Strong flanked me. Our shields overlapped. The warriors who tried to get at me threw themselves recklessly at our blades. Their swords clattered and clanged off our shields and our helmets. We sliced, hacked and stabbed at the sea of Scots who flooded from the surf towards us. I felt a blow on my knee as a dying warrior tried to hurt me with his last act on this earth. His sword struck my long byrnie which came below my knees.

The rising sun behind them showed their reckless courage for bodies were floating away on the ebbing tide. Suddenly a spearhead was thrust from behind the man I was fighting. It found a tiny gap between the sides of my helmet and the tip pricked my face. I brought my shield up sharply and the head broke on the sharp edge of my shield. The metal head fell at my feet. It had barely penetrated but blood flooded freely down my face. I judged that we had taken enough. "Ulfheonar! Forward! Drive them into the sea!"

The warriors behind us pushed against our backs with their shields. We, in the front rank, struck with our swords and then punched with the bosses of our shields. The line fell back and, as their feet struggled for purchase, many of them fell into the surf. They died like stranded fish. We moved forward. I now understood their difficulty for my legs sank almost to my knees in the soft stony sand. The ebbing sea sucked the dead bodies away from us. I felt my arms and legs ache from the effort.

"Switch!"

This would be a test of my new men. As my Ulfheonar turned and stepped back, most of my newer warriors took our places at the fore. It was a move we had used before. It gave fresh arms, legs and eyes to the fight. I watched with pride as my warriors who wore no mail yet but aspired to be warriors like us finished off the crew of the Scottish boat which had been closest to us. I was proud for none of the enemy returned to the boat. Three other Scottish raiders were slipping away west for the fight was over. There were so many bodies in the sea that I felt as though I could have walked across them. It had been a great slaughter.

Viking Legend

As my new warriors began to strip the arms and valuables from the dead closest to them I looked to see if any had fallen. Audun Arneson lay dead. He was a new Ulfheonar but he had died with a sword in his hand. He was so new that he had not yet been given a golden wolf as the rest had. I would have to make restitution to his family. When a man fought in my Ulfheonar then I cared for his family too. It was part of the bond. The rest of my men looked to have survived intact. Two of my newer warriors lay face down in the surf. This had been their first and their last raid. It was a chance all men took.

I saw warriors all along the beach finishing off the wounded who lay in the sea. Dawn's early light shone off the bloody water and metal helmets. It was a grim sight. Thorfinn Blue Scar strode down the beach towards me. I took off my helmet to greet him. The cool morning air felt good. He held his arm out for me to clasp it. "Thank you, Jarl Dragonheart. I see that the stories of your sword and your men are not exaggerated. Although few in number they truly have the courage of the wolf." I nodded. He pointed to my face, "Ah, you now have a scar upon your face. I have some blue ink if you wish it to look like mine."

I remembered the spear thrust I had suffered. I held my hand to my face and it came away bloody. "Thank you but no, I think one Jarl called Blue Scar is enough. I am happy to be the Dragonheart."

"And the name is truly earned. Come, we will eat while my men clear the beach. I am glad that you stayed the night."

"As am I." I turned to the Ulfheonar closest to me, "Snorri, have some men go to Erik and fetch over my drekar."

His thralls had prepared food and we ate in the hall while we awaited my drekar. Thorfinn Blue Scar insisted upon rewarding us. He brought out a golden torc from a chest he kept in his hall. It was an ancient piece of gold. I had seen others just like it. they came from the tribes who lived in the north of the land before the Romans had come.

"It is said that this torc was worn by a warrior queen of a tribe called the Brigante. My men found it in the cave of a witch on the island of Grimsay. She began to curse them and they killed her. I would not give such a gift away for it was a curse. But you have a galdramenn. Perhaps he can divine if it is cursed."

I handed it to Aiden. For my own part, I was not afraid for it was not the torc which had been cursed but the warriors who had killed her. Aiden examined it and closed his eyes as he did so. He held it tightly to his chest. A slight frown crossed his face. "There is no curse in the torc, Jarl. But the torc has many tales to tell."

Thorfinn Blue Scar nodded, "That is the advantage of having a wizard, Jarl. I envy you not only your sword but the warriors and men you have around you."

"We are brothers all."

"I can see that." He looked through the door of his hall and said, "I see your drekar approaches. Farewell. Consider me an ally and a friend now. We will trade, as I promised and I will ensure that any news of your traitor reaches you. I will gather the oil and the seal skins for the arrival of your knarr."

I clasped his arm, "May this be the beginning of a long friendship, Thorfinn Blue Scar."

As we headed south Aiden was much taken with the torc. "This needs the minds of both Kara and myself. Perhaps Elfrida too. This was worn by a woman and her spirit resides within. It is ancient and has stories buried deep within it."

I left him to it. Haaken approached me, "We made little from the fight, Jarl. We might only have lost one Ulfheonar and two warriors but we do not go back rich." He waved an arm at the new men. I could see that they were not as happy as they might have been. Those who had never sailed with me before looked especially unhappy.

"Would you have us raid?"

He brightened, "I could do with something stirring for a new saga. If we spy out something suitable then why not?"

I nodded. He was right. "Erik keep us close to the coast and have Karl and Cnut Cnutson keep an eye out for a place to raid."

Aiden placed the precious torc in his chest and brought his charts over. "I only have a little information about the places here in the islands. There was a monastery here, on the island of Hí but it was raided by Vikings and the monks fled to Hibernia." His eye was drawn to a red dot on the chart. "Ah, that is interesting. Alt Clut."

"What is that?" Haaken joined me as we looked over Aiden's shoulders.

"It is a castle which is high on a cliff. I have heard the name before. You remember that wizard we heard of, Myrddyn or Merlin, he was there once."

I nodded, "He as something to do with the warlord was he not? The one who was one of my ancestors?"

"Aye, he was. Well, I read in some of the writings we found in Ynys Mon that he stayed there and they were attacked by the men of Northumbria. He used magic to defeat them. It is said he flew from the tower and their enemies fled in fear."

"That does not mean there will be treasure there. That is just a story, Aiden. I cannot believe that a man could fly."

I looked to the south east, "True Haaken but perhaps we were meant to go there."

"But you go for a legend! A story of magic!"

"You of all people should know the value of such stories. Your sagas will be sung long after we are in Valhalla. Does that mean they are not true? Was not my sword touched by the Gods yet will men believe that in the future? I would see this rock and this castle. We will be cautious but I believe we were meant to visit."

Erik said, "What course do I sail?"

Aiden suddenly jumped as though he had been stung. "We are meant to go there, Jarl." He jabbed the map with his finger. We have to sail south, then north and then east. But we have to sail close to Dyrøy. It is one of the lairs of Magnus the Foresworn."

Even Haaken could not argue, "It is *wyrd*!"

We reached the island of Dyrøy just after noon. It was as Thorfinn had said, a desolate and bare island. We saw a settlement and we pulled ashore. It was deserted. The bones which littered the ruined huts could have been animal or human. Importantly, there was no sign of a palisade or a ditch. Magnus must have chosen it for its isolation.

I turned to Aiden. "There is a large rock there fetch it over." As he did so I said to Haaken, "We will leave a message for Magnus the Foresworn. Mark on the stone that Jarl Dragonheart was here and no place is safe for him. Tell him we will hunt him down."

Haaken used his seax to carve out the runes on the flat piece of stone. He had almost finished when the blade slipped and cut into his palm. Blood flowed over the message. Aiden nodded approvingly. "We could not have left a better message. It is written in blood. He will understand our meaning now."

The whole crew set to rowing with more heart once they heard what had happened. It was obvious that Haaken had been meant to cut his hand. It was no accident. The Norns and the Gods were on our side. None now feared what we might find. Whatever danger we faced they would deal with it. The younger warriors were particularly excited. This was the sort of story they had heard when growing up. They would be in a saga which might become a Viking legend. That guaranteed a warrior's immortality. Even if they died their names would live on in the stories which would be told.

We did not reach the mouth of the River Clut until after dark. We only knew it was the river when one of the ship's boys risked a handful of water. It was not salty. The chart was not clear and we were wary of grounding but Aiden found a channel which ran north. We were seeking somewhere to hide. We passed a small huddle of huts around a small church just a short way up this wide water. It looked to be silent and no one saw us. We pulled around a bend in the river. Snorri and Beorn the Scout slipped over the side while the rest of us pulled the drekar under the shelter of some large willows which overhung the fresh water.

"Do we camp, Jarl?"

"We will wait, Erik, until our scouts return."

The two of them were away for a short time. "There are eight families who live in the huts. We heard no dogs. They have a church."

"Then we camp here. We eat and get some sleep. When dawn breaks we will take this village and then find out who commands in this Alt Clut."

As the men headed ashore I looked south. I was looking beyond the river all the way to Wyddfa. The threads of my life all headed back to that mountain. The Norns had spun a strong web. I could not escape my destiny. Even when I was not seeking out my past, my past found me. Magnus the Foresworn would have to wait.

Viking Legend
Chapter 3

Leaving just my ship's boys and Erik to guard my ship we slipped down the river using the greenway which ran alongside it. Snorri and Beorn took four younger warriors to get around the far side of the tiny hamlet. The huts were so near they were almost in the water and I wondered if they suffered flooding. The greenway we used certainly felt soggy. Perhaps the advantages of being close to the river and the fishing outweighed the risks. We moved in a thin line. Ahead of us were archers with bows strung and arrows nocked. They would silence any dog which gave the alarm. The wind must have worked in our favour for none made a sound. As I passed the church I saw that it was made of stone. That promised riches within.

My men surrounded each hut and waited for my signal. I lowered my sword and they entered the roundhouses. There was noise then but the appearance of so many fierce warriors soon subdued them. When they were brought from the huts they stood in terrified family groups. The men placed themselves before their wives and children as though they might protect them.

I waved Aiden forward. He spoke their language. It was the same one he had spoken as a child. "Find the headman and bring him here."

It did not take long for the headman was not afraid of us. Hatred burned in his eyes. "Ask him his name?"

The man said something after Aiden had questioned him. "He says his name is Riderch and he is not afraid of you even though you have the eyes and skin of a wolf."

"Good. Tell him I will not harm any here if he answers my questions."

The man stood dumbly defiant. I sighed, "Ask him who rules at Alt Clut."

The man looked confused. I do not know what questions he thought we would ask but that one patently did not seem to conflict with his honour. He spoke.

"Owen the Bald."

I smiled and that seemed to confuse the man even more. He jabbered a whole sentence at Aiden.

Aiden could not keep the smile from his face when he told me what he had said, "He says that when Owen the Bald and his men return from Dùn Èideann then he will teach us who rules this land." He tapped his charts. "It is over fifty miles from here and is on the east coast."

"Good then tell him that we will be gone by then. They can return to their huts." I turned to Eystein Finnison. He had fought with me before and was a sound warrior. "Eystein, I want you and the new warriors to guard these prisoners. I will take the Ulfheonar and scout this Alt Clut."

He looked disappointed, "Aye Jarl."

"Have some of your men search the church. See what treasures lie within."

Viking Legend

Just then we heard a cry from the woods to the east. A short while later Beorn the Scout appeared. "The priest from the church tried to fetch help. Leif Bjornson ended his life with an arrow."

I frowned, "It was a priest! He could have been taken."

"I know Jarl. I think he became over-excited. Snorri has chastised him."

"Aiden, stay here until we have found the castle. I will send Beorn for you when we have seen where it lies."

We followed Beorn. I trotted off at the head of my warriors. We found Snorri and the young scouts. I could tell which one was Leif. His nose was still bleeding. I glared at them. "Go back to the village. Eystein commands." They loped off eager to be away from my baleful stare. "Lead on Snorri."

It was less than six miles to the castle and I stood in awe as I saw its position. It rose atop two huge mounds of rock. It seemed to me that the gods themselves had decreed that it should be built there. The two mounds both had dwellings and buildings on the top and were joined by a wooden bridge. I knew then that it would be able to withstand any assault. You would need to be a mountain goat to scale the sides and that left just the main entrance. A narrow twisting path which passed a wall and palisade. An attacker would have to endure arrows and stones before he could try the gate. Haaken shook his head, "That will not be an easy place to attack."

"And we will not attack it. But we shall gain entry." I saw that a road twisted its way up the side of the mounds. However, I also saw that they had a wall which ran from the river along the side up to the top. If we could scale that lower wall, at night, then we could find our way in. "There, let us see if they have guards upon the wall."

We made our way towards the wall. There was undergrowth less than thirty paces from it. While the base was made of stone the wall above it was wooden. We could climb it. There was a tower at the lower end and a second one halfway up. We were patient and we watched. There were sentries. It seemed that they walked the walls. I did not have Aiden's hourglass but it felt like an hour between the visits of the sentries. We could easily slip over during the hours of darkness.

"Beorn fetch Aiden, Eystein the Rock and some food. We will rest up here and keep watch."

It was a pleasant place to wait. We were shaded by the trees and, with our sentries out, we were safe from observation. By the time Aiden and Beorn returned we had confirmed the length of time it took for the sentries to move around the walls. I did not doubt that we could have gotten over during the hours of daylight but it did not seem worth the risk.

Aiden gave me some of the food he had brought from the village. "I managed to find out more information. Owen the Bald is returning in four days' time. He was attending a wedding. He is not a king but he is related to those who are. We found some candlesticks in the church, fine linen and a holy book which we should be able to sell."

Viking Legend

"Good." I ate and I drank. It gave me the chance to think about the castle above us. I could see, through the trees that the stone parts were old. It looked as though the wooden palisades had been replaced. "Tell me, Aiden, what do you think we might find in this castle?"

"I am not certain. However, it looks as old, if not older, than many of the Roman forts we have found and we always found treasure in those."

"And this wizard; what do we know of him?"

"I have read his name in many places. It seems he lived for over a hundred years." I frowned. Aiden shrugged, "I know that seems unlikely, Jarl Dragonheart, but we both know that magic can be powerful. If he was so powerful then perhaps there is some remnant of it here."

"You hope to find his writings!"

He smiled, "That I would. I have learned much but neither Kara nor myself have been trained by a wizard or a witch."

"Do not necessarily wish for that. Remember Angharad!"

"That is precisely why I hoping for some writing. Angharad came from the same place as the Myrddyn. It was close to Wyddfa. If we were to find it then we would have more power."

"But surely this Owen the Bald or whoever ruled here when Myrddyn was alive would have the writing if it existed."

"They might have it and not know of its significance. When we found that box with the writing in it last time it was hidden. The box was cunningly concealed below the ground."

"You are hoping we have enough time to search."

"If the Ulfheonar can capture and hold the castle then while you take the treasures I can search for my treasure; the book of magic which I hope lies within this castle."

We were both silent. I had learned much about my mysterious ancestor but I still had the need for more. I knew he had died protecting the old sword which I had found but I did not know from whence the sword came. I had found the scabbard for the sword and I had found the tomb of the wizard. I still needed to discover why they had come to me. I was in no doubt now that the Norns were weaving their webs once more and I was the fly who was stuck in the middle.

As soon as it became dark we headed for the curtain wall. Asbjorn the Strong and Eystein the Rock held the shield and my two scouts leapt lithely, to climb the wooden wall. They disappeared and we waited. A low whistle told us it was safe and we all ascended. We had plenty of hands to haul up the last two. Of Snorri and Beorn there was no sign. They would have scurried along the wall to intercept and eliminate the sentries.

I led the way up the walkway on the wooden wall. The palisade sloped and followed the contours of the rock. Ahead I could see the lights in the hall. They were not bright but they gave us an idea of the distance we would have to travel. I almost slipped on the pool of blood which marked the place where the first sentry had died. When I reached the door to the castle proper I saw that it was open. With sword drawn, I stepped through. A hand came to arrest me. It was Beorn. He held a finger to his lips and pointed. I saw, further along the internal wall, a shadow moving towards a sentry who was staring out to sea. Even though I was expecting it I was surprised by the speed with which Snorri despatched him.

The castle had a stone and wooden building attached to the wall. I could see no more sentries. We descended to the courtyard and ran for the main door. If it was locked then we were in trouble. It was not. As we stepped inside we felt the heat from the fires whose smoke we had smelled. We could also hear the sound of laughter. The garrison was enjoying the absence of Owen the Bald.

I stepped aside to let my scouts in first. This was where they excelled. We could all move silently but my two scouts could move like ghosts. I left Ulf Olafson to guard the main door and the rest of us headed towards the source of the noise, the hall. We came to some stairs and I waved my hand for two of my Ulfheonar to ascend. The rest of us went purposefully towards the hall. Although I could not understand the words I understood what was going on. It was a drinking contest. We had similar ones at home. I heard the ascending voices as someone was drinking. When he had succeeded there was a cheer.

I had heard enough and I waved Snorri and Beorn forward. Haaken and I followed. As we stepped into the hall it was like a moment frozen in time. There were a dozen warriors around a table. Another six lay in heaps on the floor. They turned as we entered. We must have terrified them with our wolf cloaks and red eyes, our black mail and our long swords. Snorri and Beorn lunged forward and three warriors fell to their blades in as many strokes. I turned and hacked Ragnar's Spirit through the middle of a stunned warrior. In less time than it took me to walk across the room, they were all dead. They had been either drunk or asleep. They were paying the price for having poor sentries.

"Snorri, see if there is anyone else in the castle. Haaken, gather the treasure. Aiden…" My galdramenn grinned and hurried off.

We moved swiftly and worked together. Time was now of the essence. As I passed Eystein I said, "Go and find the main door which leads to the west. Have it guarded for us."

"Aye Jarl."

There were some treasures to be found in what I assumed was the chamber of Owen the Bald. He had a richly decorated sword as well as a small holy book. Although the book was small it was richly decorated. I had an eye for such things and I put it in the leather satchel I found. There were other, smaller items such as two daggers and a small crown. It looked too small for a man and I wondered if this Owen the Bald had had a wife. He had some well-made clothes which looked to have come from the Holy Roman Empire.

There being nothing left of value I returned to the hall. My men had gathered the treasure from the chamber and my other men had returned with goods taken from the upstairs chambers. I handed the satchel and the clothes to Asbjorn. "Take these. Haaken, lead the men back to the village. I will fetch Ulf and we will find Aiden."

Haaken nodded, "A good haul, Jarl Dragonheart, but not the fantastic treasure such a castle suggested."

I nodded, "You are right but we have suffered no losses and we have found Magnus' lair while travelling here. It is good." They left and I shouted, "Aiden!" I received no reply.

There was no hurry and I returned to the gate we had used to gain entry. Ulf was hurrying towards me. His voice was urgent when he spoke. "Jarl. There are riders approaching. I heard them and I ran to the wall. It looks like this Owen the Bald has returned early. The gate to the east is still barred and it should take them some time to climb the walls."

"We need to find Aiden!"

We both ran inside shouting, Aiden!" at the top of our voices. There had been no hurry but now there was.

"Ulf, bar this door. It will delay pursuit!"

While my Ulfheonar barred the gate and placed a table behind it I ran down the stairs to the lower floors. It was the only place I had not seen and I assumed that Aiden was there. I stood at the top of the stairs and shouted, "Aiden, we must leave! Now!"

He came hurrying up the stairs clutching a small wooden chest. I felt the hairs on the back of my neck stand up. It was like the bone we had found in the hidden room in the Roman fort. "I have found it I…"

"Tell me later! The Scots have returned."

The three of us ran to the main gate which was wide open. There was little point in shutting it and we ran towards the village as fast as we could. When I was younger I would have this easy. Even a year or two earlier and it would not have been a problem. Now I was older and I had suffered many wounds. I was the one who was holding them up. I knew we had over ten miles to go. I wondered how long it would take our enemies to break in. It would take time to get into the castle and then the main hall was barred. I thought that we had, at most, half an hour. Then they would have to get their horses through the castle and find us. The gaping gate told them our direction. They would catch us just beyond the village.

My armour weighed down heavily upon my shoulders. My shield seemed like a body on my back. Even my wolf cloak felt like it was dragging me back. My legs burned and I found it hard to breathe. I had not practised enough over the winter. I had enjoyed the company of Brigid too much. I was paying the price for a comfortable winter. When I smelled the wood smoke from the village I almost cried out in joy.

Haaken and the others had puzzled expressions on their faces as we ran in. I said, breathlessly to Aiden, "Tell the villagers they are free and if they wish to live they should run to the castle!"

Viking Legend

He opened his mouth as though to question me and then smiled. He nodded and began shouting to the villagers. Haaken was equally surprised. "Have you lost your senses, Jarl?"

"We are being pursued. Our enemies came back early. Perhaps the villagers knew that he was due back today. This way he will have to stop and question the villagers. It will buy us a little time."

Riderch shepherded his people along the road. They had women and children with them and they did not run. That suited me. We now had all of my boat crew and, if we were caught we stood a chance. We ran but this time we did not run flat out. We kept a measured pace. I was still the slowest but this time I found I could breathe. I glanced over to Aiden who ran next to me. He clutched the wooden chest as though his life depended upon it. I hoped it was worth it. If we were caught by horsemen before we reached the drekar then we would lose irreplaceable warriors.

I heard the distant sound of hooves pounding along the greenway. They were coming. They would catch us. I could see the ship but it was some distance away. It was just the mast which I could see and the ship's boy shape on the cross tree.

I stopped, "Turn. We will ambush them."

My Ulfheonar knew what to do but some of the newer warriors looked confused. Snorri and Haaken quickly pushed them into position along the side of the track. "Aiden, get to the ship!"

He nodded, "I will, Jarl. This is worth it, believe me."

"I hope so."

I forced myself to breathe more slowly. I took out my sword and swung my shield around to the front. I could hear the hooves louder now as they thundered towards us. I was in the middle of the line. Asbjorn and Eystein were at the rear. They would attack when the horsemen neared them. It meant we would all attack together.

The Scots were so intent on catching us that they galloped hard and recklessly down the greenway track. I saw that they did not wear mail but all carried a spear and a shield. Everyone wore the same style of helmet. These were the best warriors that Owen the Bald possessed. Was he with them I wondered?

I heard a shout and a scream from my left and a horse whinnied. "Now!" Stepping forward through the bushes I swung my sword at the nearest horseman. His small round shield did not stop my sword from hacking deep into this leg to the bone. He fell screaming and was trampled beneath the next horse. I just managed to turn and take the spear from the next rider on my shield. Ulf Olafson brought his axe down and it bit into the shoulder of the horseman. Some of my men had slain horses and the track was filled with fallen horses and men. Other riderless horses milled around.

"Keep at them!" We had the advantage that we had mail and when their spears did strike they did not kill. I horse reared I lifted my shield and ran beneath his flailing hooves. I rammed my sword deep within him whilst

Viking Legend

pushing with my shield. The beast toppled backwards mortally stricken and the rider fell to his death. I was covered in its blood and intestines. A fallen warrior tried to rise. I swung Ragnar's Spirit sideways and my blade bit into his neck.

I heard a trumpet and the horsemen retreated. I suspected it was to give them time to reform. "Back to the ship!" We had some way yet to run. If we had to we could turn again but this time we would not be able to ambush them.

As we ran the trees and the bushes began to thin. I saw the water close to our left. Then I heard the horn behind us. It was a different call from the previous one. They were coming. We had not made the ship. When I heard the hooves thundering I shouted, "Turn! Shield wall!"

The Ulfheonar gathered around me and formed a wedge behind me. The newer warriors waited behind them. I heard Snorri shout, "Archers, have your bows ready!"

The horsemen would be ready for us this time. I saw them appear. They were four abreast and were coming a little slower. They were keeping tight together and they held their lances before them. This would not be easy. The narrow lane meant that we had six of us in the front rank and I felt the reassuring press of the shields of those behind us. I was mindful of the spear which had found a chink in my helmet and I pulled up my shield so that just the top of my helmet and my eyes peered over the top.

I saw the tips of the enemy spears wavering up and down as they came towards us. I realised that they had not fought this way before. "Brace and hold!"

The spear struck but with not as much force as I had expected. I saw why. The horsemen of the east of Miklagård used stirrups. These did not and the men were thrown from their saddles. The horses banged into our shields and we were pushed back a little but then they stopped. I yelled, "Push!" and the sudden weight of heavy mailed men against the small horses made them turn in panic and run towards the other advancing warriors. As I stepped over a fallen horseman I stabbed down with my sword. Then we heard the clatter of arrows as they fell into the disorganized horsemen. Shouts and screams told us that they had found their mark.

Suddenly I was aware of a dark shape to my right. I glanced over and saw that Erik and Aiden had used the wind to bring down my drekar. Arrows now flew from the decks too. It was too much for the horsemen who fled.

"Check the Scots for weapons and treasure!"

All around me my men, new warriors and Ulfheonar alike, ignored my words and began banging their shields with their swords and chanting, "Dragonheart!" over and over. We had defeated horsemen and, as I looked around saw that none of my men had died although some sported wounds. I raised my sword in acknowledgement and they all roared a cheer. I had no doubt that the departing horsemen rode faster fearful that we would follow and wreak even more revenge upon them.

Viking Legend

I did not tarry in my departure. We quickly loaded the drekar and sailed towards the sea. We could see, through the trees, the Scots who were reforming close to the village we had captured. I had no doubt they would have seen my ship and my name would be known. The villagers would have told them of the warrior with the wolf upon his shield. Had I wanted anonymity then I would have slain all of the villagers.

As we made our tortuous way out to sea I took off my helmet and cloak. I saw Aiden peering into his box. "Look at your treasures later. Take off my mail." He was like a child forced to leave a new plaything and he came over to me to help pull the byrnie from me. Normally I would have waited a while but the run down the hill and the fight had exhausted me. The mail felt like I carried the world about my shoulders. I needed sleep.

When the mail was removed I felt so much cooler and as light as a cloud. "Thank you, Aiden, now you can return to your book of magic. Perhaps you can find a spell to transport us home in an instant."

He shook his head. "It is not that kind of magic. It is the magic of healing and of using my powers better. The parchments in the box are worth more than all the treasure we have ever found."

I patted the hilt of my sword, "Worth more than Ragnar's Spirit?"

He grinned, "Possibly."

I nodded, "Then you have treasure indeed."

The inland waters through which we travelled as Erik twisted and turned back to the west were gentle. I lay on my wolf skin and closed my eyes. Soon I was asleep. I dreamed.

There was a castle high upon a rock. It was not Alt Clut for the sea was on the wrong side. I saw many fierce guards on the wall. I looked to my right and saw Erika and on my left was an old wizened man with bright blue eyes. We flew high into the air and the sentries saw us not. They flew me through a wall into a large hall and there I spied Magnus the Foresworn. He was with Saxons whom I knew not and they were feasting. My escorts disappeared and I began to lay about me with Ragnar's Spirit. No matter how many Saxons I slew Magnus was still safe beyond my reach laughing. I hacked and cut until my arms would cut no more. As I dropped to my knees Magnus pushed me and I fell into a deep hole in the floor of the hall. There was water there and it consumed me. I fell, down and down, deeper and deeper.

"Jarl! We have reached the sea!" I looked up into the face of Cnut Cnutson. "You were shouting in your sleep, Jarl Dragonheart. I was afraid."

"Fear not Cnut. When I sleep I am safe. Your father's spirit and the others who have died already watch over me." I smiled, "I feel safer asleep than awake!"

He shook his head, "I watched you and the others today. How could you stand and face such enemies? I thought they would have ridden over you all."

"When you become a warrior, you will trust in two things; your sword and the men who stand with you in the shield wall. Then nothing can harm you."

Viking Legend

Erik Short Toe chuckled, "You forgot the third thing, Jarl, you trust in a leader with the heart of a dragon and the sword of a god."

"The sword does help, Erik. How is the wind?"

"We need not row for a while but the rocks around here are treacherous." He pointed to the sun setting in the west and the stormy clouds gathering. "Do you wish me to find shelter for the night or risk running south?"

He looked at the masthead and the dragon's tail which fluttered from it. "If we head south and west we will have sea room. Let us risk running."

He smiled, "Let us hope that we have not used all of our luck up on this voyage."

I walked to the prow. I saw that most of my men were sleeping. They had earned their rest. My own sleep, while short, had refreshed me and I needed to think of the dream. I had learned that such dreams were not literal. I would not fly into a castle but it had given me an insight. If the spirits spoke true then Magnus was in the west for the sea had been on the other side of the castle. As I thought about the Saxons it came to me that they might be from Northumbria. That would make sense. There were hints that Magnus knew of King Eanred. That King of Northumbria was my implacable foe and Magnus would be drawn to him. *'The enemy of my enemy is my friend.'* That was too far a journey by sea. I looked aft and saw Aiden curled around a small chest, asleep. I would need to speak with Kara and Aiden.

"I have my saga now, Jarl."

I turned and saw Haaken, "Aye it was a good fight and all the better that we lost none."

Can I confess to you, Jarl, that I thought we would be trampled beneath those horses' hooves? It came to me that although I would be dying with a sword in my hand that would not be a glorious death."

I laughed, "Me too. Yet now that I think about it horsemen are only dangerous to us when we flee. If we stand then it is only their horses that are a danger. Those horses were little bigger than ponies. We were level with their muzzles were we not?" He nodded. "If they ever learn to use the stirrups they have in Miklagård then we are in trouble. Yet we could have held them off had we had our spears."

"Aye, you are right." He pondered my words for a moment and then said, "Erik told me that you dreamed."

"Aye. I will need to speak with Kara and Aiden to divine its meaning."

"But it involved Magnus the Foresworn."

I looked at him sharply, "How did you know?"

He shook his head, "I do not have second sight, Jarl, but I have stood next to you for over twenty summers and I know how you think. The Foresworn is an itch that you cannot scratch. He is the will o' the wisp who flits out of sight. Until he is dead and his head adorns your spear then you can never be settled."

"You are right. When we reach Cyninges-tūn we will begin to choose the next Ulfheonar. Even Snorri is becoming older. I watched these young men.

Some will never be more than a farmer with a sword but others look to have skills we could use. I will have Snorri and Beorn cast their eyes over them. This summer we will test their mettle so that they can hunt their wolves this winter."

"And Magnus?"

"We will have hunted him and slain him before a wolf dies."

I stood at the prow long after Haaken had left me for sleep. I held my hand on the intricately carved dragon head and I stared at the sea. It would ever be my destiny to fight my enemies for they were all around me. My allies such as Thorfinn Blue Scar were rare and could not aid me. I would ever be reliant on my own men and my own sword. I was content. I was beholden to no man. I had said to Thorfinn that I did not bow my knee to a king. As I looked to my left I saw the sun slowly peer from the mountains and hills of home I vowed that I never would. The land of Cyninges-tūn was my own and it would remain so until I died.

Viking Legend
Chapter 4

It was mid-morning when we pulled next to the jetty at Úlfarrston. Siggi's knarr was there. The tower had warned them of our arrival and Coen ap Pasgen and Siggi awaited us. We bumped gently into the wooden jetty and I stepped ashore. I saw the anxious looks as the two men looked to see if we had suffered casualties. I shook my head, "We did not find Magnus the Foresworn. He has fled. We will seek him another day."

There was relief from both of them.

"Siggi, you need to sail to Ljoðhús. The jarl there, Thorfinn Blue Scar, is now a friend and wishes to trade with us. They need timber, copper and iron. He has seal skins and oil awaiting us. Aiden and Erik will give you the instructions."

He shook his head. "Remember Jarl that I came from Orkneyjar. I know the island if not the Jarl. But I will ask advice nonetheless."

I turned to Coen. "We have a Holy Book. It is worth coin. I would have your captain sell it the next time he is in Lundenwic. You can have half of the proceeds."

"You trust me to give you your fair share?"

I stared at him. "Your father and I trusted each other his whole life. If I cannot trust you, his son, a man who has fought alongside me then it is a sad world."

"I am sorry Jarl. Forgive me, you are right."

We packed the goods we had captured on pack ponies we kept at the port. I spoke with Asbjorn and he went back to the drekar. He packed one pony himself. As I led my men back to my home I reflected on Coen ap Pasgen's words. It was sad that there were so many men who did not keep their word. It made honest men doubt each other. I had never betrayed anyone in my life. The betrayals I had suffered did not make me doubt my friends but look at strangers with suspicion until I came to know them.

The pack ponies behind us stretched further than I had expected. The Scots had been poor enemies but Alt Clut had yielded more than we could have hoped. The young men who had been on their first raid would receive more treasure than they could have dreamed. I would have to see the family of Audun Arneson; they would want for nothing. The thought of treasure brought my mind back to the golden torc. It would be interesting to hear what Kara thought of it. The Norns wove complicated webs. This one went back beyond the Romans. It was hard to picture such a world. Had they lived here in my water-filled world? Did their spirits wander the hills?

The fishermen on the Water alerted Kara, Brigid and our families that we were on our way back. The gates of the settlement were wide open and we were greeted like heroes. It was ever thus. Wives, parents and children flocked to welcome their heroes home. I saw Audun's parents. I would save them the anguish of watching everyone trooping in and then discovering that their son was dead.

I walked towards them. Arne his father held his wife tighter and nodded his head, "Your son is in Valhalla, Arne Liefson. He died with honour and he was buried as a Viking. We return his sword and armour to you." Asbjorn walked over with the pony he had packed. "I will bring you his share of the treasure and know this for so long as you live the Ulfheonar will watch over you and you will want for naught."

Arne's wife wept but I saw pride in the fisherman's eyes. "It was Audun's proudest moment when he donned the wolf cloak. I know he did not serve long but few men get to live out their dreams. I am happy."

I left the grieving couple and wondered how my family would view me when I died. I was not arrogant enough to believe that I was immortal and that one day my sword would not be fast enough or my armour strong enough and on that day I would go to Valhalla. I would see my family and I would see those who had died before but I would not know what others truly thought of me.

For the first time in many years, I was welcomed with a kiss. Brigid ran towards me and, throwing herself into my arms kissed me hard. I was taken aback. My Ulfheonar cheered and I saw, as she released me that the whole of Cyninges-tūn was smiling. Kara inclined her head with that look on her face. It was the look which said, '*See, I told you so*'. She knew me well.

"You are safe!"

"I am. And you are well?"

She smiled, "I am more than well. I am with child. You are to be a father."

"Truly?"

"Of course. Why did you think there was another?"

"No, but… I am no longer a young man."

She shook her head, "Men! Of course, you are a young man!"

"You did not see me as I tried to run with my warriors. I am getting older."

She touched my heart, "Not in here. You are only as old as you want to be. When your son is born you will need all the energy you had when Wolf Killer and Kara were children."

"A boy?"

"I believe so. I know not why. When Kara and I used your sweat hut after we knew I was with child the picture of a boy came into my head. It will be a son."

Wyrd.

Kara greeted me with a kiss on the cheek. "I see you have heard the news."

"Aye." I hesitated and my eyes were drawn to the other side of the Water where my former home had been and where my wife lay.

Kara saw my look. "Mother knows and she approves. This is a good happening father. Through your blood courses greatness. It is in me and it is in Wolf Killer. It needs to be in others. I can never see myself having children but you can have more. Brigid is fertile; you will have many more."

Viking Legend

I looked to see if my daughter's words embarrassed her but she looked pleased. I could never understand the way women's minds worked. The two of them hurried into Kara's hall. They would divide the fine linens and cloths we had brought back, equitably.

It was good to be back in my home. Here I was respected by all and I was comfortable with my life. Although our raid had not gone the way I had anticipated I was content. I went to my hall where I could take off my armour. Uhtric, my thrall, took the armour. He would clean and oil it. The sea was hard on mail. I had the finest mail for Bjorn Bagsecgson had cunningly mixed charcoal with the iron so that the mail was darker and also stronger. Even so, it needed care after each journey. I laid my sword to one side. I would sharpen that myself. Along with my seax, they were my two most important weapons. I looked up at the wall where the sword I had found in the cave hung. Old and a little worse for wear it was my most tangible reminder of my ancestor who had wielded it in battle.

I was about to order Uhtric to light the fire in my sweat hut when Brigid entered. "The sweat hut will be ready by the time we sail across, Jarl."

I looked at her with my mouth open, "You have second sight too?"

Laughing she said, "No. I had it lit for Kara and me. Your sister deferred to you. I will join you there." She cocked her head to one side. "You do wish to cleanse yourself do you not?"

I nodded, almost dumbly, "Aye the blood and the sweat cling to my body still and I have the need to let my mind wander."

She was intrigued, I could see that but Brigid was unusual in that she could remain silent and not question too much. Besides she knew I would tell her what was on my mind eventually. There had been a time when I would have sailed across the Water by myself but now I was ferried by Einar Long Thumb. He was the grandson of my blacksmith and worked in the forge. However, one of his tasks was to fetch some of the charcoal which the charcoal burners made close to our former home across the Water. He travelled back and forth when he was not toiling at the bellows.

Brigid and I sat in the middle of the small boat. "We hear you found a great treasure in the land of the Scots, Jarl Dragonheart."

"The Allfather was kind to us. Who told you?"

"Everyone said there was a fine golden torc and a book of spells. Soon Aiden will be the greatest of wizards."

I smiled, "Aiden is a good enough galdramenn for me and I do not think it was spells that he found."

"I am sure I heard that he found a spell to help make him fly."

Both Brigid and I laughed. She was a Christian and did not believe such things. She believed that a man could be crucified, killed and then walk from a tomb three days later but a spell to make a man fly was impossible. I had spoken with Aiden and knew that the parchments contained magic but not the type that Einar thought.

Viking Legend

He held the boat as we clambered ashore. Tying it to a tree he said, "I will fetch the charcoal and take it back to grandfather. I will return here and wait."

"You need not. I can signal you."

He smiled, "It will be easier waiting here than suffering the sharp edge of grandfather's tongue. He has high standards!"

He was right. Although he could afford to let his sons and grandsons work the smith Bjorn was there before the others and left when they had gone. He was proud of his work and he was the reason our mail and our weapons were respected and feared. I prayed that his sons would be as diligent as he.

We stripped off and entered the sweat hut. It was coming up to the right temperature. We sat opposite one another and Brigid waited for me to begin speaking. She knew that I liked to sit there first with my eyes closed and let the spirit of my wife come to me. Sometimes Erika did and sometimes not. Nonetheless, it was pleasant to sit in the heat and enjoy the sweat cleansing the grime from my body.

I opened my eyes. "When will the child be born?"

"After the harvest and before midwinter." She smiled, "Perhaps around Christmas. That would be good."

I shook my head, "We do not celebrate Christmas."

"The nuns, Macha and Deidra do. Kara allows it."

"We call it Yule and it has nothing to do with the birth of the White Christ."

"But it is similar. We both welcome the end of the short nights and the beginning of new life. The difference is we celebrate the birth of the son of God. It would be good for our son to be a celebration of that."

"Perhaps."

I had learned not to argue with Brigid about her religion; no one won.

"What other treasures did you bring back? The fine cloths and linen were most welcome."

"There was a golden torc. You heard Einar mention that. I am hoping that Kara and Aiden can divine whence it came. The Viking who gave it to me said that it belonged to an ancient queen."

"Your daughter's power frightens me a little."

I smiled, "She knows your thoughts?" She nodded. You will get used to that. Aiden can do the same." She seemed satisfied. "Come let us bathe in the Water."

We found that bathing in the water between hot sessions made us feel better and cleaner. By the time we were done, our skin would shine. Einar was fishing from the bank. He waved at us as though there was nothing strange about two naked people bathing.

When we returned to the hut the heat was almost overpowering. This was when it did the most good. I could feel my body glowing as it was cleansed. "You have spent some time with my people. How do you like them?"

Viking Legend

"They are good and honest people. They have been kind to me while I have been learning your language. I know that I am lucky to be here. Had I remained with my father I would have been little more than a slave."

"It is good that you are here and I am happy." That was about as romantic as I ever got. I did not have words like Haaken.

That night Kara had prepared food for me in my hall. Aiden joined us and the four of us enjoyed a fine meal. I still had a little of the wine we had brought from Vasconia. We would now be reliant upon Coen ap Pasgen's ships to bring such wine. After the meal, Aiden brought out the torc. He and Kara both held it and closed their eyes. Brigid looked as though she would speak but I held my finger to my lips. At one point Kara frowned.

They both opened their eyes together. "There is death connected with this torc. The Queen was murdered. She died with an unborn child within her."

We all looked at Brigid. Her hand went to her crucifix. She mumbled something, I think it was a prayer.

Aiden said, "I saw a sword." His eyes went to my wall. "That sword."

Wyrd.

Aiden and I finished off the wine and we sat in silence looking at the torc. It was obvious now that we could not sell it nor melt it down. It was connected to me and to the sword. I suspected, but I could not work out how, that it was also connected to the parchments which Aiden had brought.

Brigid broke the silence, "Is this not just an accident?"

Kara put her hand on Brigid's, "No my sister. This is the work of the spirits and the Norns. Jarl Dragonheart has been chosen. He is not Norse and yet he is a Viking legend. He is not of one world but of many. His threads reach back beyond time itself to the ancient peoples and their beliefs." She pointed to the torc and then to the sword. "Those were made before your White Christ walked the earth. We do not say your beliefs are wrong but ours are older. But you need not fear. You and your baby will be safe."

"How do you know?"

"The spirits have told me."

Later that night as we lay together, Brigid hugged me so hard that I thought I would break. "I am afraid."

"If Kara says you are safe then you have nothing to fear. I am content. This is just another part of my life… but now it is our life and you are part of it."

I really wished to travel to my jarls and see how they had fared. I had not seen my son for some time either but Brigid was still more than nervous and Kara advised me to stay close to home for a while. Aiden and Kara spent many hours poring over the parchments and even Kara was impressed. "The wizard gives advice on cures for ailments and diseases which now result in death."

The two of them and some of Kara's women took to travelling the land finding the herbs, leaves, roots and barks they needed to make their medicines.

After a month Brigid said, "Jarl you should go and make the journey. I am settled now. I was afraid but I have thought about this and I have spoken to

Deidra and Macha. They are not afraid and they, too have told me that Kara has a power which they cannot explain. It is enough. I trust you and your daughter."

I took only Aiden with me as I rode from my home. I headed first to the south for I wished to speak with Sigtrygg. He needed to know what had happened. It had been his land which had been attacked. I would then visit with my son, Windar, Ketil and finally Arne. I would be away some days but my jarls needed to see me and speak with me.

Sigtrygg had learned from the attack and now had a walled town with a double ditch. He had built towers across his land and he trained all of his farmers. He had been the finest warrior to have followed my wolf banner and he was a good leader. "When you find this Magnus let me know, Jarl for I will come with you and end his life."

"I will. And if your warriors wish to raid with me I will be honoured to take them with me."

He nodded, "When I have built up my treasure Again I will have Bolli make me a drekar. It will not be as large as yours but we will build one."

The journey to my son's home was pleasant for there were now more farmers living between the two strong jarls. My grandson, Ragnar, was growing in leaps and bounds. He and his mother had brought Wolf Killer and me closer together. We had drifted apart and it was still not the same as it had been but it was better. He, too, was intrigued by the torc and the connection. "I cannot see how these threads join but I agree with you, Jarl Dragonheart something binds them." He and Aiden were as close as brothers, "Aiden, are there no writings that you can find?"

He gave me a curious look. "I have heard of a book by a Roman writer called Tacitus. It concerns the man who conquered Britannia, Agricola. If I could find that book then we would know more."

"Where would we find one?"

"Miklagård."

"That is a long way to go for a book."

"If there is another on this island then it will be where there was a Roman fort. Lundenwic?"

"Egbert would dearly like to get his hands on me and he knows you too."

"Then that leaves Caestir and Jorvik."

"Again I am known in Jorvik and Caestir has been laid waste by us too many times. I fear this is one book that we will never see."

Our next visit to Windar was sad for he was now a bloated and corpulent old man. He had never been much of a warrior but he had been a good leader. Since his son Ketil had taken over the northlands he seemed to have forgotten how to be a leader. I did not tarry long but headed, instead for Ketil. He was the most exposed of my jarls. Unlike Arne, he had no river for protection and he was close to the Northumbrians and the Scots yet he was a brave and clever leader. He kept a close watch on his land.

Viking Legend

He had inherited a Roman fort which he had made stronger. It afforded him a fine view of the lands to the west. He proudly showed us around. As it was late we stayed with him and we told him of our finds and our journey.

"I miss the adventure of the sea but I am content with my land and my people. When my young men are stronger we will raid to the west for the Saxons are becoming weaker."

I advised caution, "The only treasures they have in Northumbria are the slaves and the holy books of the White Christ."

"Then I will take what I can." He was confident. He quaffed his ale. He looked at the horn and frowned. "Have you seen my father?" I nodded. "It is hard for me to see him as he is now. I always looked up to him."

"A man cannot change his nature Ketil. He is still your father. He is getting old. Let his last days be happy ones."

Arne too had made a stronger wall and I was happy that my land was now encircled by strong walls. We headed south over the col and the Grassy Mere towards the Rye Dale. "I think Ketil will make a good jarl of Windar's Mere when his father goes to the Otherworld."

"He would but does Windar's Mere need a strong leader? It is one of the safer parts of our land. In all the time we have lived here it has suffered but one attack." Aiden shrugged, "I am no war leader jarl. Perhaps I am wrong."

I laughed, "No Aiden you are right. I should think of the good of all of the people and not individuals."

The realisation that I had, however accidentally, strengthened our borders made me feel quite contended as we rode down the fertile Rye Dale. We paused to speak with Audun Thin Hair at the col. He always had fine beer and he was a good listener. He knew the mood of the farmers in the valley. His son, Leif had grown and was now a man. He stood and listened as we spoke.

"The farmers are happy, Jarl. The crops grow well and we are safe, however..." he hesitated.

"Go on Audun, speak."

"There are many young men who are restless. Many of them tried to go with you on your last voyage but you took but one drekar. They do not wish to be farmers; they want to be warriors. I fear that if they cannot go with you then they will seek others to lead them and leave this land. We cannot afford to lose such young men. I am sorry, I have spoken out of turn."

"No Audun, you were right to speak as you did." I looked at Leif, "You wish to be a warrior too?"

"I wish to know what is within me, Jarl. I want to stand in a shield wall and hold a sword in my hand. Perhaps I will only be one for a short time but when I return to the farm and have a wife and children then I will know that I can protect them."

I understood then the need for my young men to have the opportunity to test their mettle. This suited me for I had many journeys yet to make.

My feelings of contentment disappeared when I entered my walls for a large crowd had gathered before my hall. I saw Kara speaking with them.

Viking Legend

When they saw me they became silent and parted so that I could approach. I saw two angry young men facing each other. They were no more than fifteen summers old. Both were being restrained by my Ulfheonar. I dismounted and handed the reins of my pony to Aiden. Turning to face the crowd I smiled, "Thank you for this welcome! It was unexpected."

I saw scowls flash across the faces of the two young men. I recognised them now as Olaf Grimsson and Rolf Eriksson. My daughter allowed the briefest of smiles to flicker across her face. "This is not a welcome for you, Jarl Dragonheart, father to our people but it is good that you have returned. Here we have a dispute. The two young men both wish to take the daughter of Thord the Shepherd, Hlif."

"And where is this Hlif?"

"Her father keeps her in his home on the fells. He says she is too young to marry." Lowering her voice, she added, "She is not yet thirteen summers and she is his only child. His wife died two winters since."

I stared at the two young men, "It seems to me there is not a problem here. Unless, of course, Hlif wishes to disobey her father and marry one of you. Is that the case?" I nodded to my men so that they released the youths. I did not think the dispute would continue whilst I was present and I was right. They stood glowering at each other. They remained silent.

Behind me, Kara said, loudly enough for all to hear, "Hlif is happy to stay with her father and to obey him."

"Then there is no problem, is there?"

Rolf pointed an accusing finger at Olaf. "I am happy to wait for I know that she will choose me when the time is right but Olaf here wishes to fight for the right to her hand. I was going to oblige him."

I now had Audun Thin Hair's words in my head. This was what he meant. When young men did not have the chance to vent their anger in battle they turned it amongst themselves. This was my fault. I had not led them as I should have. "We are one people! We do not fight amongst ourselves. It is not our way and I forbid the two of you to continue this dispute. If you do so then I will banish you both." I saw the mothers of the two youths grip the arms of their husbands who stoically stood. "I will speak in my hall with the two youths. This thing is over." It was not really a thing. I had not formerly convened one and only I had spoken but I wanted all of them to understand how seriously I took it. "Haaken one Eye would you join me?"

Kara and Brigid had entered my hall and they stood by the table. I took off my sword and laid it, symbolically, along the table and then I sat at the head of the table. Kara and Brigid flanked me. I knew the effect this would have on the boys. They came in, somewhat fearfully. It was rare for others to enter my hall. Haaken followed them and I saw him nod when he saw the sword. It was a symbol of my power. Kings had crowns and titles. I had Ragnar's Spirit and that was all that I needed. He came to sit next to my right hand.

I allowed the silence to grow uncomfortable. When I spoke it was softly. Even so, they both started as I did so. "This dispute has upset the harmony of our home. I am not happy. When I am not happy our land becomes disturbed. Do you wish the crops to fail and the animals to decline?" They shook their heads. "Perhaps I should go away eh? Then the disharmony would pass. Would that solve the problem or would you two still bicker and squabble? Would your wishes still cause division in my land?" They hung their heads. I knew that I had won but I did not leave it there. I pushed the sword further down the table. "You are both young men. Have you chosen if you wish to follow your fathers yet?" Rolf's father was a farmer. He raised cows on the lower fells. Olaf's father was a fisherman. "Speak."

Rolf shook his head. "I am the younger brother. My elder, Erik Eriksson is the farmer."

"Olaf?"

"I do not like fishing."

"But you are comfortable on a boat?"

His eyes widened, "I would be a sailor."

"And Rolf what would you be?"

"I would be a warrior. I would follow your banner and your sword."

"Will you hear my judgement then? And will you obey for I cannot have disputes upsetting the land? I meant what I said, I will banish you if I have to." They nodded. "Good. Until such time as Hlif is ready to choose then you both put her from your mind and you will take the hand of friendship now." They hesitated. "Do it for I have yet to finish." They clasped hands but there was still enmity in their eyes. "You, Olaf, shall become a sailor. You will accompany me to my drekar and Erik Short Toe will discover if you can be a member of his crew." He nodded, eagerly. I saw the disappointment on Rolf's face. "And you Rolf can begin to train as a warrior. You will serve in the warrior hall as a servant until my warriors can train you. Until that time, you will learn to sharpen swords and clean armour." He too nodded, eagerly. "Good, now go. I had done."

They ran out together, both keen to tell their friends of my judgement.

Haaken smiled, "You have grown wise. That was masterful."

I shook my head and told them all of Audun and his warning. "The peace in this land means we have many such as Olaf and Rolf. Unless we do something, this will become commonplace and may result in bloodshed. We are rich. I would use those riches. I will go tomorrow to see Bolli. I will have a new drekar built. We will take the young untried men and we will raid."

Kara came over and kissed me on the top of my head. "That is why you are Jarl. You are not only a great warrior you are a great leader." She nodded, "The spirits approve. This is *wyrd*."

Viking Legend
Chapter 5

I had a drekar and my son, Wolf Killer, had one too. My son was more occupied with his own land and his family rather than raiding so his drekar was rarely used. It was not mine to command and so I would have a smaller one built to accompany '***The Heart of the Dragon***.' It would not need to be as big. My own ship was one of the largest and we had yet to see a bigger one. Bolli would be able to build one in a relatively short time; if he had the men. Haaken, Aiden, Kara and I worked out the best way to do that.

I sent word to all those who lived under the shadow of the Old Man of Cyninges-tūn that I was looking for thirty young men to become warriors. While they assembled I rode down to Bolli's shipyard accompanied by Olaf. When I reached the yard he and Erik were repairing the withy which had caused us problems.

"This is Olaf Grimsson. He would be a sailor."

Erik frowned, "He is a little old to begin to learn the skills."

Erik could be blunt. "He has some skills already. His father is a fisherman and I wish this to be so." Erik bowed his head in acceptance of my decision. "Have Karl begin to teach him."

Erik waved over Karl and after a brief conversation took away Olaf. I had no doubt that he would first be given all of the tasks which Karl and Cnut Cnutson did not wish to do. Cnut, too, would be eager to leave the drekar and become a warrior. He would make sure Olaf could replace him. Alone with Bolli and Erik, I went to the heart of the matter. "I wish a threttanessa to be built and to be built quickly."

Bolli nodded, "That will take more men than I have."

"Do not worry. I will bring thirty willing workers in the next few days. They are to be the crew."

"Good for if they work in the building of a ship then its heart will be stronger and there will be a bond."

I turned to Erik, "I will get you some more ship's boys. Could Karl captain a drekar?"

He looked across to where Karl was beginning to instruct Olaf. "Aye. He sailed that trader back from Vasconia. He could not operate alone but if I gave him some of my ship's boys he could." He seemed pleased that his apprentice was to be thus rewarded.

"And Cnut, he is ready to be a warrior but if he sailed on the new drekar on its first voyage he could help Karl."

"Aye, they work well together."

"Good then make it so. I will bring the gold for the drekar when you have decided a price Bolli." I clasped his arm as a sign that I would pay. I held it for a little longer than was necessary. "I want this to be the fastest drekar ever built."

He grinned, "Aye Jarl!"

Viking Legend

We had more than enough young men who were willing to both work on the ship and then serve whoever commanded. We had thirty-four of them. I went down for the first week to watch them working together. I was relieved to see that Olaf and Rolf were getting along. They were doing different tasks but each one was doing something they wanted to do. Hlif had just been the collision point for two frustrated young men.

I spent time with my Ulfheonar and Aiden discussing who should command the new drekar. We had many warriors who had sailed with us and raided but none of us could agree on a suitable captain. It would be my ship for I would be paying Bolli for it but we needed someone who could be decisive and control a crew of, largely, young men. I noticed that Asbjorn and Eystein remained silent during these discussions.

"Asbjorn; have you nothing to say." There was a slight hesitation which I knew meant he was reluctant to speak his thoughts. "Come I know that you and your friend Eystein are amongst the younger members of the Ulfheonar but your views are welcome nonetheless."

He shifted uncomfortably. Karl Word Master smiled, "He is seeking words which he knows might offend."

His friend, Finni the Dreamer said, more seriously, "Perhaps he has other words in his heart."

"Come Asbjorn, you have your comrades putting words into your mouth. Answer the Jarl." Haaken often acted as the one who spoke for the Ulfheonar.

"I would captain the new drekar."

He blurted it out and that made Haaken smile. I was taken aback. I had thought he enjoyed the life of the Ulfheonar. He lived in the warrior hall and was as stout and doughty a warrior as any.

Eystein the Rock added, "And I would serve with him. Sorry, Jarl"

I nodded to help me gather my thoughts. Asbjorn, now that he had found his tongue could not stop. "I love being Ulfheonar and wearing the wolf cloak. There is no greater honour than serving in the shield wall with you. But, Jarl Dragonheart, I would be you. I know that would be but a pale shadow but I would hope to lead and inspire warriors as you do. When I saw the young men working in the forest this week felling trees I wanted to train them as you trained us. Eystein and I would still be Ulfheonar. We would still protect your back and be your oathsworn."

"But you would follow in the other drekar. I understand." I glanced at Aiden for confirmation of what was on my mind. He nodded. "It is good. I was silent, not because I was disappointed but because I wished to weigh up the words you spoke. You shall be the captain of the new ship and Eystein will be your warrior chief. Know that the captain is Karl the Sailor." They both nodded. "Then that is settled."

Haaken asked, gloomily. "And what of the Ulfheonar? We now have a mere ten to follow you."

Snorri laughed, "I can remember the time when there were but eight of us and that included the Jarl. There are many warriors who can follow the

Viking Legend

Ulfheonar. Wearing the skin of the wolf is not for all warriors. Perhaps this was meant to be. I say that we use those who would go a-Viking and they shall be our crew."

Surprisingly all agreed and so we took on no more Ulfheonar, at least not for a while. When we invited other warriors to join our crew we had the same problem we had had with the young warriors. We had too many. The difference was that we could accommodate the extras on my much larger drekar. We would have rowers to spare and that was something we had never had before.

Bjorn had repaired my helmet. The scar which had resulted from the blow was still angry but it would not be a blue scar! He felt guilty that his well-made helmet had allowed a blow to get through. "It was the gods testing me Bjorn." He touched his hammer of Thor. "We will be needing more helmets soon enough."

"We need them now, Jarl. Those who voyaged with you came back and invested their treasure wisely in good helmets and good swords." He smiled, "Trade is good." We walked out of his forge and along the Water. "We have come far since I watched my father at the forge and you followed Prince Butar and went a-Viking."

"Aye old friend, it has been a long journey."

He spat into the Water. "You sound like your life is over, Jarl."

"Not but I see all these young warriors and most are far younger than even my son. I feel like a grandfather."

"Prince Butar never grew old. And look at Old Ragnar. I barely knew him but he lived, half blind and crippled until you came to care for him. Look on each day as a new one. Each dawn brings a page for you to write upon. The legend of Dragonheart grows."

"The legend, like the sword, can be a burden sometimes."

"You were chosen Jarl. Embrace it."

I returned, ten days later, to see how the work progressed. The shape of the hull could be clearly seen. The new crew had to make the strakes and the planks under the close and stern supervision of Bolli and his shipwrights. They were hard taskmasters. That was good for the young warriors. It would make them stronger both in body and mind. They would need all of those skills when they went to sea.

I drew Bolli to one side. "You know your drekar better than any man alive. Tell me what this one says to you."

He smiled, "It is just a skeleton, Jarl, but I can tell that she will be light and she will fly. I am confident that she will be faster, under sail, than *'Heart'*."

I nodded. My ship was incredibly fast. "Will that be a problem for her crew? Will she be hard to control?"

"She will need a firm hand. I hope that young Karl has the hand and eye for it."

Viking Legend

"You know as well as I do Bolli that a drekar picks its captain. If Karl is not up to the task then we will find another. He knows that better than any." He nodded. "Tell me then. When will she look like a drekar?"

"She will be ready for the water in a month. After that…"

"That depends upon the crew, I know. And have you begun to carve the prow?"

"I have." He pointed to a large object which was hidden by a cloth. No one would be allowed to see it until Bolli fitted it to the drekar. It was the way of shipwrights. At least I had a time in my head. The time the drekar was ready would determine the place we would raid and blood our young men and our ship.

Aiden and I sat, one warm evening watching the thin high clouds above the Old Man. "Where would you suggest we raid, Aiden? I know that you have thoughts upon this."

"My heart is ever drawn to Wyddfa. I know the cave of the wizard is lost but there may be clues about his power in the land and the buildings."

"That would please you but how would it help me and my warriors?"

"Grain. We have rye and barley only. The holy island is like a huge granary and it seems to me that the launching of the ships and the voyage south will coincide with the harvest. The men will be in the fields and the crops ready for reaping. We know the island and we know the mettle of the warriors. There are no easy battles, I know that, but there are some which are better for untried and untrained warriors to experience."

I was not totally convinced. We had been to that particular well many times before. "I am not sure."

"The alternative would be to attack the Mercians for they too have good grain." He looked at my face. "They might be awaiting us."

"I would have Kara and you speak with the spirits and divine what I should do."

"I could twist their words to suit my purpose."

"You could, but you will not. Remember I have powers from my mother and I know that you are true to me."

"Aye, since you rescued me from my father I have ever been your man. I would not be what I am today were it not for you."

As it happened there was a full moon that week and the two of them took the potion whose ingredients Aiden has discovered in his parchments. They sat by the Water all night. When they returned, the next morning I was both excited and intrigued. I hoped they would have communicated with my wife's dead spirit but speaking with the dead was not a precise method. Sometimes it worked and sometimes it didn't.

They both looked drawn and tired. Brigid had prepared food and drink for them. They sat at the table in silence and looked at each other. I could barely contain myself but I knew that I had to wait until they spoke. It was Kara who broke the silence after drinking a horn of beer. "The spirit of the dead Queen came to us. She was a striking woman." Aiden nodded. This was not what I had asked them to discover but I knew better than to interrupt. "She ruled this land for a long time and she was murdered by a witch. Her spirit is restless. She has left work unfinished."

Aiden took up the story. "Your mother's spirit joined us. She told us that a voyage to her homeland would bring us great fortune. In her hands, she held a blue stone and it sparkled." He nodded towards my sword. "It was the same blue, perhaps even the same stone as the one in your sword."

"And the Queen's spirit had one too. It was around her neck. The blue stone has powerful magic, father. I thought so before and now I know it."

I smiled for I had my answer, "And did your mother's spirit come too?"

They both looked at Brigid and Kara said, "The child will be a boy. She is happy for you... both."

I could not contain myself and I hugged Brigid. I would have another son and I had not offended my dead wife's spirit.

Aiden and I threw ourselves into the expedition. The support of the spirit world would guarantee success. Added to that was the fact that I now knew that my sword was even more powerful than it had been before. It explained why I could defeat young, stronger warriors. It was the sword which made me invincible. I was not immortal but it would take a mighty host to fell me.

We went down to the shipyard to see the finished ship. When the drekar was launched we watched as the lithe little drekar slipped swiftly through the water. It seemed to float higher than any other I had ever seen. Bolli had outdone himself with the prow. The dragon had the look of a warrior and Haaken said, "It looks like Odin and he seems to be blowing."

We all took that to be a good omen and the name came naturally, Karl's ship was *'Odin's Breath'*. And she was the fastest drekar afloat. Perhaps the gods had faster ones but here on earth, it was *'Odin's Breath'* which outflew every other vessel. Asbjorn, Eystein and Karl spent many days with their crew to make sure that the ship was balanced and that the crew were in the right places. When they were satisfied they told me they were ready to sail.

Many families came to Úlfarrston to see us off. There was a happy atmosphere as mothers and wives said goodbye to sons and husbands. Fathers looked on proudly remembering their glory days. Coen came to me with a small chest. He looked happy. Opening it he showed me that it was filled with silver. "This is your share of the money from the Holy Book. The men who bought it did not ask whence it came but merely asked if we had more."

"Good, then we shall seek them on our travels." I handed the box to Bolli. "Take your payment for the drekar and give the rest to Brigid."

"Aye Jarl. And I have a commission from Sigtrygg Thrandson for a drekar built on the same lines as *'Odin's Breath'*. "

I lowered my voice, "If he does not have the funds for it I will pay."

"He is a good man. I do not mind waiting for payment. When he raids there will be great rewards."

I tapped the small chest, "I have more than enough."

Viking Legend

The farewells over we boarded and left on the evening tide. We would lead and Karl would follow. Neither Erik nor I wanted the young man of twenty summers to be exposed alone to the wild seas around Ynys Môn. There would be time enough to see what his drekar could do when he and his crew had more experience. Besides his drekar had but thirty-five crew all told. Ours had twice that number. His had but one man on each oar. We had two on each of ours. If the wind was against us then the fine lines and speed of **'Odin's Breath'** would be negated.

The sun began to set in the west. It would be a long slow sunset and would act as a guiding light for us. We kept it to the steerboard side. It made it easier for Karl and his new ship's boys. I noticed that Olaf was standing by Erik. That showed how much my captain thought of the young man. Cnut Cnutson might have been put out but this was his last season sailing and, during the winter Haaken would begin his training as a warrior. His time at sea had been a way to show him what we warriors did.

Mann was passed before the sun set and then we hung a light from our stern so that Karl could follow. This was the riskiest time for an error would mean he would ram us and our voyage would be over in an instant. I deliberately kept my eyes from **'Odin's Breath'**. Had I shown I was nervous it might have made Karl worried too. Instead, I went over, with Aiden and Erik, our course.

"We will avoid Caer Gybi and Aberffraw. Unless they are fools they will have rebuilt and strengthened their defences. I plan on using the east coast of the island."

Aiden pointed to the chart, "The are many beaches here, Jarl but few coves. We would have to risk the drekar on the beaches."

"We will keep this drekar offshore and use the smaller **'Odin's Breath'** as our cargo ship. We can pull her off if we need to. She has new fresh timbers." I saw a worried look cross Erik's face. "If you have doubts about Karl then now is the time to tell me."

"I have no doubts. He has sailed with me these many years but even I have never deliberately grounded my drekar."

"Others have. It is not difficult."

He nodded remembering when Josephus his mentor had done so. "You are right. Olaf, go to the prow and keep a close watch to the land to the east. There are sandbanks there. Give me a shout if you see anything."

After he had gone I asked, "What is he like?"

"Already I can see that he is as good as Karl was. Sailing a small fishing boat in summer and winter gives a man skills. He has them. He knows the wind and he knows how to set a sail. He needs to learn about currents and hidden rocks but he has skills. You made a wise decision with that one, Jarl."

It was strange for Asbjorn had said much the same about Rolf. *Wyrd.*

Aiden used the hourglass we had captured from the Arab. He knew how long the night should be and, an hour before dawn he told Erik who shortened sail. They had estimated our speed and calculated when we would be near the

Viking Legend

Dee. They thought we would arrive an hour or so before dawn. There could be Saxon or Welsh ships using the Dee; it was a busy river. We wanted sea room in case there was danger.

When dawn broke I saw that we were less than ten miles from the Dee. I could see Wyddfa in the distance. I nodded my approval, "You have both done well. That hourglass was a good treasure to take."

Erik turned us to steerboard. We would head west. Now that it was daylight we could risk sailing out of sight of land although the island would always be visible, like a grey smudge on the horizon. We would sail slowly west and then head south to arrive shortly after dark. The night was our natural element. With our black cloaks and armour, we were hard to see. Aiden and Erik had identified a quiet beach not far from a large village. Aiden thought there was an even bigger settlement five miles inland. I hoped so for that meant we could take them both and then have a safe base from which to foray. That would be the true test of the new warriors. They would be fighting out of sight of their jarl and the Ulfheonar. I hoped that they would pass.

I took the opportunity to sleep. I was not needed nor were my rowers for we had a benevolent wind. If I watched it might make them think I did not trust them. I made a pillow of my wolf cloak and fell asleep with the easy motion of the drekar. My dream was of flashes and bright pictures; it was like the illustrations in a Holy Book. They made no sense but the blue stone and a warrior Queen kept appearing and then disappearing. We were close to the mountain and I knew that the spirit of my ancestor dwelt there. It was the power of the spirits that were making me dream. The fact that my people had loved and died so close to me was important. I would be under the scrutiny of the warrior who had wielded that sword which now lay on the wall of my hall.

I was woken by a gentle shake from Haaken. He handed me a horn of ale. "The island is close ahead. We can see no smoke but that means nothing."

"And have any ships been sighted?"

Erik said, "Not a one."

I went to the stern and made water. It was barely light and the sun was rising from the east but I could see that Karl's ship was still two lengths from us. He had kept station well. Aiden helped me to don my red cochineal around my eyes and I held my helmet. I would only don it when I was ashore.

I looked ahead and saw a bay which swept around in a wide arc. There were sand dunes behind a sandy beach. There were no cliffs, unlike the coast near St Cybi, and the ground sloped gently inland. It was a perfect place to land. I strapped my shield around my back. Aiden had a helmet and a sword. He would be coming ashore with us. I walked down the centre of the drekar to the prow. We were barely underway. Erik was taking us in on the tide. This time we would not have a ship's boy to tie us up to the shore but Cnut Cnutson was ready to jump into the sea to test the depth. He wore no armour. He jumped and I saw that the water came over his head. I waved my arm for Erik to take us closer to shore; our hull was safe. I saw Cnut wading next to the prow. He held up his hand. The ship's boys on the mast saw him and the sail was fully furled.

I jumped from the deck, splashing into the sea, smiling at Cnut as I did so. "Well done Cnut Cnutson and next time you come ashore, you will be a warrior." I donned my helmet and waded through the surf to the sandy shore. I had spent the last month or so building up my strength again. I would not lag behind my warriors this time! I raced to the top of the dunes. Even as I reached the top Snorri joined me. Normally I would have sent him off to scout ahead but with two crews we would do it differently this time.

I turned and looked at the beach. My men had disembarked and Erik had his crew sculling with the oars to back her into safer and deeper water. Karl brought his drekar in just as slowly but he ran his onto the sand. It leaned to one side as it grounded. Asbjorn and Eystein led the eager young crew towards us. It did not take long for me to be surrounded by them.

I gathered the Ulfheonar, Asbjorn and Eystein around me. "Asbjorn take your crew and ten of my warriors. Secure the village and capture what you can. Do not fire it and make sure no one escapes. Return here."

"Aye Jarl." Haaken had already identified the ten warriors they would take. They were the best warriors I had. The more inexperienced ones would come with me and the Ulfheonar.

I settled my helmet firmly on my head and pointed inland. Snorri and Beorn the Scout loped off in the direction of the large settlement we thought lay ahead of us. We began to march inland. Haaken gradually increased his pace so that the handful of Ulfheonar who remained formed a thin screen in front of me. They had senses my other warriors did not. Haaken waved us to the south and we found ourselves on a local trackway. It was not well used but it meant we would find the large settlement Aiden had identified. He was with the bulk of the warriors behind me. He could fight but he was no warrior. His skills were not to be wasted by exposing him to danger unnecessarily.

I smelled the wood smoke when were about an hour from the beach. We had moved swiftly for the land was flat. We had been lucky thus far and had not seen anyone. Haaken's hand waved us to the ground and we all dropped to a knee.

Olaf Leather Neck joined me. "There is a farm to the north of us and men are in the fields harvesting the wheat."

"They are up early. Taking advantage of the weather no doubt. Choose ten warriors and capture them and the grain. Take it back to the drekar."

He moved behind me and I heard him telling warriors to follow him. I turned and saw them moving in a wide sweep behind the farm which lay to the north. I gave him a few moments and then waved the rest of the warriors forward. There were still over forty of us and I was confident that we would be able to handle however many warriors we faced. Haaken and the others moved off when they saw us approach. We found Snorri and Beorn a short while later. They had reached the town and scouted it out already.

Viking Legend

"The town has no wall and it lies directly ahead. There is a church and I think it is market day. We saw carts and people approaching from the north and the south."

I wondered why none had come from the farm we had seen. I dismissed it immediately. If the farmer and his family were in the fields harvesting then that would be their priority.

"Snorri take ten men and go to the southern road. Beorn, take ten and go to the northern road. We will give you a start and then we will enter the town from this side."

Haaken asked, "And what of the far side? Will they not flee?"

"They might do but we will have to catch them will we not?"

He grinned, "Aye Jarl."

I waved my sword to the left and the right. My warriors spread out in a long thin line. We were the net and I hoped that few of these fishes would escape. My men at the northern and southern ends of the settlement would drive them back to the centre. If they did escape then there would be danger. The island was so small that the King, who had a castle at Aberffraw, could reach us within a couple of hours. We had to be quick.

The houses were all made of wattle and daub. There were few made of stone. It looked, as we approached as though there was little planning and houses had just erupted along the roads leading to the heart of the settlement, the church. However, what I did know was that if there was a market then there would be an open area and it was there that the people would be congregated.

We were seen when we were less than five hundred paces from the first house. A shepherd and his doges were driving nine or ten sheep towards the town. It was one of his dogs which alerted him. It turned and growled at us. I saw him run and shout.

"Vikings!"

"They have seen us. Run!"

We ran hard. The sheep scattered before us in panic. As the shepherd neared the town his shouts attracted attention and I saw faces appear and then disappear. They were men going for their weapons. Some of my younger warriors overtook me and I saw one make the first kill. A man emerged from his hut with a billhook. He swung it hopefully at Sven Gunnersson who blocked it with his shield and then rammed it into the man's middle. He glanced into the hut and then followed us, his sword dripping red.

I saw a column of smoke rising from the far side of the settlement. It was, no doubt, a signal. I had not expected that.

Even though the helmet made sounds dampened a little I could still hear the shouts and screams of alarm from ahead. I was almost taken by surprise when we emerged from the tangle of huts into the centre of the town and the market. A wall of men faced us. There were more than I had anticipated. There looked to be almost sixty armed men and at least ten were warriors. Behind them were boys and youths. I had no doubt that they would have

Viking Legend

slings and hunting bows. We could have stopped and formed but that might have allowed the ones with slings and bows to hit those of my men without armour. It was essential that we use the shock of our appearance and our weapons as quickly as possible.

"Charge!"

The first stone which struck me was a well-aimed one. It clanged off my helmet. If I had not had a leather inner then it might have stunned me. I saw one of my warriors pitch to the ground struck by another stone while a second fell clutching an arrow to his chest. It was a storm we had to endure. I ran at the warriors rather than the townspeople. My Ulfheonar were the ones to deal with shields and helmets. I ran directly at the wall of spears which surrounded the leader of the warriors. He was standing atop a cart and directing those around him. He was the only one wearing mail. It was an old byrnie and I saw flecks of rust and dirt.

We were not a solid line and I had to hit one spear with my shield while deflecting the second with my sword for there were more of them than us. A third spear came towards my head from the warrior on the cart but I shifted to the left and moved away from the spearhead. I brought my sword up, almost blindly, into the middle of the man to my right. I leaned into the one on my left as I did so. My sword bit flesh and I brought it back and then stabbed at the man who was falling to the ground on my left. Even as my sword sank into flesh I felt myself being punched in the shoulder by a spear from above. The mail links held but I dropped to my knees. As I turned my head and looked up I saw Haaken pull the spear and the man down from his cart. As he fell Vermund Thorirson hacked off his head.

I rose and looked for another enemy. There were none near me for my Ulfheonar had sent the warriors to their God. Before us were the boys and youths with slings and arrows. Even as I stared at one of them and raised my sword, they turned and fled. I yelled, "Stop them escaping!"

My Ulfheonar did not run after them; in our heavy mail, we would not catch them but the younger warriors we had brought set off like greyhounds after hares. I peered around the market. It was a scene of great chaos. Those families who had come to buy stood in fearful huddles. The sellers were trying to protect their animals. I saw Snorri approach. "None escaped my way."

"Good. Have your men begin to collect and drive the animals back to the drekar. You go with Aiden and search the church."

"Aye Jarl!"

I turned and saw Haaken, "Secure the villagers. Choose any that might make slaves and herd the rest into the church."

Beorn arrived, "None escaped north, Jarl Dragonheart, but I saw some heading west towards Aberffraw."

"It cannot be helped. Have your men join Snorri's and drive the animals to the drekar. You take charge. When you reach Olaf Leather Neck have him take his grain to the drekar." He nodded, "We may be pursued. We will try to hold them back. Have a line of spears ready eh?"

Viking Legend

"Aye Jarl."

The last of those resisting us had either been disarmed or killed. It was over but it had not gone as well as it might. I had no doubt that some of those who had fled would evade my pursuers. They would fetch help. I went to the church where the survivors of our attack, the old and very young, were being herded into the church. I saw that it had a stone tower but the walls were made of wood. It was, however, a large church. Aiden and Snorri emerged from the church with a chest. Aiden smiled, "A good haul, Jarl."

"Aiden find two captives to carry that chest. Get back to the drekar. There will be pursuit." Be prepared to leave in a hurry. I saw that there were two doors to the church. "Snorri, when the last prisoners are in the church bar the doors."

Haaken took off his helmet and wiped his brow as he approached. "A good raid, Jarl. We have carts and animals to carry the plunder and we lost but five men; three wounded and two dead."

"Aye, Haaken, but we will be pursued. Have everything taken back to the drekar. I want the Ulfheonar and ten warriors with us as the rear guard. Choose the best and find us spears from amongst the dead. As I recall the Welsh have horsemen."

"Perhaps their civil war still reigns and neither brother is in Aberffraw."

"The Norns and the gods are not that generous to us. One will have emerged as the victor. We will be pursued but, mayhap, we will escape before they reach us."

I took off my helmet to allow the air to get to my head. My scar was also itchy. I wondered about shaving off my beard for it seemed to aggravate the scar. I almost laughed that I could think of such a thing at that moment. I had more important things to do rather than worry about an itchy beard. The marketplace was now a scene of devastation. Bodies lay in untidy heaps. Some animals had died in the fighting. Anything of value had, however, been taken.

The men who had been pursuing those who had escaped returned. Siggi the Fleet was one of the last to reach me. He was breathing heavily. "Jarl I think they reached their warriors. When I reached yonder high piece of ground I saw standards fluttering in the distance and moving this way."

The signal from the fire had worked. It had alerted their King, whoever that was, and he was on his way. "You have done well and I will reward you. get to the drekar and tell all whom you pass to hurry." He ran east. "Haaken! They come. Tell the rest to go east and get to the drekar."

I donned my helmet again and took the spear which he gave me. There were just seven Ulfheonar and my ten warriors but I knew that we were the best that we had. The rest of my oathsworn would be preparing the defences at the beach. The huts which lay on the east side of the town were all made of wood, wattle and daub. The wind was blowing from the west. "Use the fires in the huts; spread them so that the huts themselves burn. We will make a pall of smoke which will hide us."

Viking Legend

My men went into the huts and used the cooking fire to set the huts alight. It did not take much to make them burn. The wind blew the flames and the smoke away from the church which lay on the western side. I hoped that the ones in the church would break down the doors and slow down the pursuit. If that did not work then the smoke drifting across the island would make pursuit more difficult.

As we moved quickly towards our boats Haaken began coughing with the smoke. "Was this wise, Jarl? It hampers us as much as the enemy."

"They cannot know where we landed. The smoke will stop them from seeing further than a hundred paces or so. It will not be comfortable running in the smoke but we will be hidden for longer."

We had made almost four miles before I heard the sound of hooves. This was where I missed Snorri and Beorn the Scout. The smoke had thinned somewhat and there was a chance that we would be seen. I wondered how long it would be before they were upon us. I needed somewhere to defend. The only place I spied was a small copse which rose, just a little, above the surrounding land.

"Make for the wood. We will fight with our backs to the trees." As we ran I asked, "How far do you estimate we are from the beach?"

Haaken sniffed, "It cannot be more than a mile. I can smell it."

One of the warriors from the rear, Harald Haraldsson shouted, "Horsemen!"

I glanced over my shoulder and saw them through the thinning smoke. They were less than five hundred paces from us. The copse was, thankfully, less than fifty paces ahead. "To the trees. Form a shield wall on me!"

The last few paces were uphill which reassured me. Their mounts would have to slow. I turned with Haaken on my right and Finni the Dreamer on my left. I swung my shield around and held my spear before me. There were forty horsemen and they rode beneath the Gwynedd standard. They rode large ponies rather than horses and they had no mail. We had a chance. I glanced behind me and saw that the trees would hamper a pony but not a man. "Be ready to retreat through the trees on my command."

"Aye Jarl Dragonheart!" They sounded confident. My Ulfheonar were always confident and the other ten had been chosen. That would make all the difference to the way they fought.

"Today we show these horsemen how Vikings fight. Make sure it is they who die!"

They all roared, "Dragonheart!"

I hoped that the shout would intimidate the approaching Welsh. This time we had a wall of spears before us. The horsemen had formed a loose line but, like those we had fought in the land of Alt Clut, they had no stirrups. If they tried to charge us they would be thrown from their horses. They did not try that. Instead, they wheeled when they were ten paces from us and hurled their spears. That tactic might have worked in their civil war against warriors with a small shield but ours were huge. They were heavy to wield but, as the spears either stuck in or banged off them, they proved their worth.

They continued their wheel to allow them to draw their swords. Some of my men laid down their own spears and threw the Welsh spears back at them. One pony was felled and two Welsh warriors were wounded. I saw that the spear which had hit mine had a broken haft. I left it there. I did not want to risk pulling it out.

They came again and this time they rode down our line slashing at us with their swords. They had to lean out to do so for their swords were not as long as mine. I jabbed forward with my spear as I deflected the sword aimed at my head. I saw it sink into the thigh of a warrior who was pitched from his pony. As they reformed I saw that there were five empty saddles. Glancing down my line I saw only one warrior sporting a wound. Perhaps we would drive them off.

"Jarl Dragonheart, look beyond the horsemen."

I saw, appearing through the mist like smoke, a column of men and the glinting told me that some were mailed. They would be able to close with us and would make short work of my men who had no mail.

"After the next attack, we turn and run to the beach!"

"Aye Jarl Dragonheart."

It may have been that the sight of the reinforcements heartened the horsemen for they pressed this attack home with more vigour and determination. They came straight at us. The ones near the three of us in the centre pulled back their ponies' heads to make them try to strike at us with their hooves. Had they been horses then they might have damaged us. As it was they were only large ponies and I struck first with my spear, to strike into the chest of the pony and then, as I withdrew it, punched the beast with the boss of my shield. The effect was to throw the wounded pony and rider to the ground. The falling beast and the other horsemen who were felled caused great confusion. The attack faltered. I shouted, "Fall back!"

While my newer warriors ran as ordered the Ulfheonar jabbed forward with their spears before retreating. My spear caught a Welsh horseman on the knee. I twisted as I withdrew it enlarging the wound. He wheeled away bleeding heavily.

I turned and followed my warriors. As I did so I slung my shield around my back. It afforded me some protection and was easier to carry that way. It left my left hand free. It was only a small copse and we emerged on the other side within a very short time. It would not take the horsemen to realise what we had done and we hurried. Ahead of me, I saw a line of warriors. Snorri and Beorn had organised a defence. I could only see twenty warriors and I wondered if they had had trouble. Where were Asbjorn and the new men? I did not glance over my shoulder. There was little point. I would hear the hooves if the horsemen were near and a glance behind might make me trip. Only inexperienced warriors did that.

Viking Legend

Snorri and his men opened their lines and we passed through. There I saw, to my great relief, the rest of my men formed up in the dunes. Asbjorn raised his sword in salute. Snorri had hidden our numbers. I saw that our two drekar were broadside to the shore and *'Odin's Breath'* was floating. My two captains had done well and when the threat from the shore was gone we would be able to sail safely away. I saw the decks crowded with animals and captives. The journey back would be interesting.

"Jarl!"

I turned and saw that the Welsh had indeed caught up with us. I wondered how they had done so. Perhaps they had been on the road already when the refugees had found them. There were three mailed warriors on horseback along with the lightly armed riders we had seen before. Behind them were about eighty warriors some of whom were mailed. Their leader lifted his helmet and rode forwards a few paces. His standard bearer accompanied him. I saw that he held the royal standard. All that he would see was a line of fewer than forty warriors standing on a sand dune. He would not know that we had as many again waiting to reinforce us.

He spoke in Saxon; he butchered the language. "Before I slay you, Norseman, know who brings death to you. I am King Hywel ap Rhodri Molwynog and you have dared to raid my realm."

I nodded. "So you have defeated your brother. Have you rebuilt the castle I destroyed? For know you that you face Jarl Dragonheart of Cyninges-tūn and I do not fear you. I raid where I choose and take what I wish. Your brother and his priestesses made the mistake of taking what was mine. You and your people will ever suffer my wrath! When we have defeated you and returned home beware for we will return."

I saw the anger on his face and he shouted, before jamming his helmet back upon his head, "Slaughter them! No mercy! No prisoners!"

I said, "Ready Asbjorn?"

"Aye, Jarl. We await your command."

The King waved his men forward. The two mailed warriors led the men on ponies. If they thought to frighten us they failed. Behind them, the two lines of warriors also raced after their comrades. We matched their line of horsemen and, as they approached, we held our spears behind us and then thrust them as the ponies and horses wheeled. My spear struck one of the horses in the neck and it screamed in pain and reared. With no stirrups, the rider fell. My spear was plucked from my hands by the dying beast and I stepped forward to despatch the rider who lay prone beneath his thrashing mount with my sword. I stepped back and shouted, "Now Asbjorn!"

Suddenly there was a second line of spears which appeared above us. The line of warriors was stopped by the dead and dying horses and warriors. Their king had placed them in a solid line but the human and equine barrier now broke that up. I knew that this was the moment for a decisive act which would break the will of the faltering warriors. Raising my sword, I stepped onto the body of the dead horse and shouted, "Ragnar's Spirit!"

Viking Legend

The effect was instantaneous. All my warriors stepped forward and slashed or stabbed at the men before us. I saw the Welsh King wave his sword back at me and then shout something to the archers who stood close by. A flurry of arrows flew at me. I was hit by one in the chest. It felt as though I had been struck by a punch but I felt no pain. I roared, "Kill them" and moved towards the four Welshmen who stood before me. They had open mouths as I swung my sword. It tore through the throat of one and caught a second a blow in the side of the head. The other two ran. It was like a small hole appearing in a dam. The trickle became a flood as my outnumbered warriors hacked and slashed the shocked Welshmen.

Their furious King had no alternative but to flee. I turned to face my men. As I raised my sword I saw the looks of shock and horror on their faces. Rolf Erikson, my new young warrior pointed at me. "Jarl, you should be dead!"

I took off my helmet and, as I did so I noticed the arrow sticking from my chest and yet there was no blood. Haaken joined me and pulled out the arrow. He had to tug hard. The shaft broke from the head. The arrowhead was embedded in the golden wolf I wore around my neck. He twisted the head free and held the arrow up for all to see. He turned and shouted at the departing Welshmen. "You cannot kill, Jarl Dragonheart! He is protected by the gods!"

My men all cheered. This was a rare opportunity. They had witnessed a miraculous occurrence and it added to my reputation. I too raised my sword. I had been lucky. Perhaps Haaken was right but, whatever the reason the story spread through the land of Gwynedd and then when we returned, our homeland. Jarl Dragonheart had been struck in the chest by an arrow and lived. It added to my already outrageous legend.

Viking Legend
Chapter 6

The voyage back was both crowded and smelly as my drekar was filled with many animals and people. However, it was a swift journey for the same wind which had blown the smoke now blew us home. Nor did we have an angry crowd of captives. They had seen the arrow strike and cowered when I walked by. I had survived certain death and yet I looked as hale and hearty as any man. To them, this was dark and arcane magic and I saw them clutching at crosses and making the sign of the cross as I passed.

Haaken loved it. "What a saga this will make! It might even exceed the success of the Sword Saga."

He spent the whole voyage coming up with the words to do justice to the event. Aiden was also impressed but for a different reason. "You were spared, Jarl but I think it was Wyddfa's power which did so. The spirits cannot be happy with two brothers fighting over their land. I spoke with some of the captives and the King's brother, Cynan, lives still close to the mountain and calls himself king there. I found no more treasures of Myrddyn but perhaps this is the sign I was seeking. His spirit watches over you still." He looked at the mountain, now on our right. "You know, Jarl, I believe we could conquer the island if we wished. The spirits would protect you."

"I believe you are right, Aiden, but I do not want it. I know that it was an ancestor who lived there and you would think that would be enough but it is not. I do not want the island. It is where Cnut died. It is where my ancestor was killed. Many men would try to take it from us. It is indefensible and besides the Norns have shown us an older thread. The thread which leads to the Queen and the sword I found. My ancestor ended up here but his journey began to the east of where we now live."

He nodded, "True. I should have seen that. I am too obsessed with this Myrddyn."

"And you forget one other thread, Aiden, I was taken from the river which runs close to the land the Queen ruled. It is a circle and I must complete that circle."

He could see that I was right and, for once, I had the last word. I took the wolf from around my neck and looked at the mark that the arrow had made. It had struck near the wolf's mouth and it appeared, now, to be laughing. I would not have it repaired. It was a symbol. I was the wolf. This was *wyrd*.

When we landed I went directly to Asbjorn and Eystein. I had not had time to speak with them before we left. I was anxious to know what had happened to them. "How did the new warriors do?"

"They did well, Jarl Dragonheart. A couple were too keen to impress us. They threw their lives away recklessly but the rest were solid. When they attacked the Welsh line they did not flinch even though they fought men with mail and helmets."

Viking Legend

Eystein laughed, "They showed that they had heeded our words and all now have a helmet and most have a better sword. That is thanks to the dead Welshmen"

Our rapid departure meant that the bodies could not be completely stripped of all treasure as was our practice. "That is good. And the raid on the settlement?"

"It was a poor place but we found animals and grain. It was Olaf Leather Neck who brought back the most grain."

"Do you think they will want another raid before winter comes?"

They both nodded, "For certain, Jarl. They have had their appetite whetted and they wish to do the same with their blades. They talk of the arrow in your neck and how the gods favour you. they believe we are invincible."

"Then I will speak with my son. I am sure he will wish to raid too."

Our quick journey meant there was no welcome party at Úlfarrston and we hurried back to Cyninges-tūn. Our young men were keen to tell their tales and who could blame them? It was dark when we reached the safety of our walls. Those younger warriors, like Rolf, who were keen to boast of their valour had reached the town before we did. They had run all the way. Brigid and Kara waited for us at the gates of my hall. Kara waited for Brigid to kiss me before she hugged me.

"It is good to see you home safe."

"Did you not know I would? Are your powers waning, daughter?"

She laughed, "No but the power of Wyddfa is such that it clouds my vision."

We told them all. Brigid tut-tutted when she heard of the arrow and the pendant. Kara admonished her. "You should be pleased, sister. It means the spirits protect the Jarl. And I agree with you father, there is something here in the north which ties us to the past."

"It is late in the year to venture east but when the snow has gone I will see what we can discover." I downed the last of the wine. "I used some of our treasure to have Coen's captain buy some more wine. Seguin I Lupo might be the Duke of Vasconia no longer but they will sell. We might have to pay more but it is always worth it." I smiled, "And if the price goes up then we can take it."

My daughter frowned, "You are not immortal, father. You survived an arrow to the chest but there are many enemies in this world who would see you dead."

"I do not court death. I just live my life the way I always have done. But I will not be leading the next raid. Perhaps I will travel to see Wolf Killer in the next few days. Asbjorn would raid again with the young warriors before winter. Perhaps my son would like to join him. If not then I will loan my ship to Sigtrygg. He has commissioned a drekar but it will not be ready this season."

"Elfrida is with child again, father. He may wish to stay at home."

Viking Legend

For some reason, I suddenly felt guilty about leaving Brigid. Erika had never minded my raids but Brigid might be different. I glanced at her and she laughed, "Do not worry about me. I feel safe here and I am certain that I will be looked after by Kara and her women when I birth. I cannot see you being much use. Not unless our son fights!"

The three of them laughed together as though it was a joke. I could not see it myself.

I left for Wolf Killer's alone. Aiden still needed time to study his parchments and my Ulfheonar were busy with their families. If I was not safe in my own land then it was a poor state of affairs. It would take me almost a day to ride to his stad. I could have ridden faster but there was no rush. I still ached and was bruised from the battle. I rode a horse rather than a pony; the gait was easier on my spine. The leisurely journey gave me the time to speak with some of the farmers I rarely saw. I did not go by Windar's Mere as I could have done. I went through the part of my land I rarely visited. I was gratified by the reception I received. I might not see them very often but they appreciated what I did for them and seemed remarkably well-informed about my activities. Part of that was down to Haaken and his sagas which recounted my life for all to hear.

The land close to Grize's Dale was a quiet and empty land. Empty that is, save for the insects which feasted upon my flesh and annoyed my horse. Its tale flicked angrily from side to side as it tried to rid his body of them. He tossed his mane too. I wondered if I should have worn mail but then I realised that they would have penetrated even Bjorn's finest work.

Once, years ago, there had been those who had lived close to this spindly tangle of trees but raids and the insects had driven them hence. It was, however, the shortest way between my home and that of my son. A more pleasant route would have taken me along to Windar's mere and then down the side of the mere. That would have taken a whole day. This was better.

I watered my horse at Esthwaite Water. The walls of the farm there had long since fallen into disrepair. The Water had been named by me for the farm had been, at that time, the most easterly of my farms. I could not even remember who had farmed it. The family was long gone. I washed my face too and, for a brief time I felt refreshed. It was when I tightened the saddle that I caught a hint of movement in the trees ahead of me. It was not the movement of an animal. It was that of a man. I forced myself to act as though nothing was wrong. If this had been a friend, one of my people, they would have spoken. Their silence meant danger.

There was no one until the farm of Gray. He lived between here and the southern end of Windar's Mere. Unless he was hunting he would not be in the forest. I mounted my horse. Badger was a sound horse and not given to panic. His jet-black colour had given him his name. I wished that I had worn my black wolf cloak for then I would have been harder to see too. I set off down the trail. Until a short time ago the greatest danger had been the insects. Now it was man, or was it, men? It had been a long time since I had travelled alone

Viking Legend

and used my own senses and not those of Snorri and my scouts. Time was I would have smelled enemies. I was getting old and lazy.

I surreptitiously slid my sword in and out of my scabbard. Ragnar's Spirit and my seax were both sharp. I had not grown that indolent. Now that I was aware of enemies I began to hear them. It was a 'them'. There were noises on both sides of the trail. They were slight but my pursuers could not keep totally silent. They brushed the branches of trees and twigs broke underfoot. I wondered why they did not attack. I cursed myself for being a fool. They were afoot and I was mounted. I kicked my heels into Badger's flank and he began to trot. "Come on Badger, I have had enough of these insects!"

As soon as I began to move quickly I heard louder noises behind me. I turned and saw three men running after me. Each held a spear. They did not look like our people. Their dress was that of Saxons. I kicked harder. If I could make it to the farm of Gary and his wife then the two of us might be able to hold off the three outlaws. The three had to be outlaws. They were too ragged to be warriors. I saw the trees thin and the spiral of smoke which rose from Graythwaite. I felt relief that I had made it. As my horse galloped into the clearing I reined him in. "Gray!"

A man came from the hut with a spear in his hand. It was not Gray. It was another outlaw. I kicked hard and drew my sword. The Saxon stood with his spear in two hands. I turned Badger's head away from the spear as I slashed with my sword. Although my blade bit into his neck and ended his worthless life my horse could not keep his feet and we slithered to the ground. I rolled as we hit the ground. When I stood I saw the three outlaws running towards me. Badger, too had risen. I saw a red wound on his neck and he ran off, east towards the Mere. He was frightened and I was alone.

I rose and drew my seax. I could see them clearly now. They were young men and had a spear and a seax each. They ran down the slope towards me, eager to finish me off. I could have run but I had no doubt that they would catch me. If they surrounded me then I was dead. I had two weapons and I knew that I was a better warrior but, without mail, I was vulnerable. As they closed with me I took my chance, slight though it was. I ran at them as fast as I could. They had been running hard following me and were a little out of breath. And my sudden attack was unexpected.

The danger of my attack was that I needed to be quick and I was not certain I was quick anymore. As soon as I ran at them they began to separate. I ran for the middle one. He held his spear in his right hand. That was a mistake for I knocked it aside with my seax and brought Ragnar's Spirit around in a wide sweep to bite into his side. It bit through to his ribs.

I spun around and was barely in time to knock aside the second spear which came at me. As I ripped across his throat with my seax I felt a savage pain in my shoulder as I was speared in the back. I whipped my arm around and felt it bite into soft flesh and heard a scream of pain. I looked down and saw that I had sliced through the upper arm of the last outlaw and into his chest. He lay on the ground bleeding to death. He opened his mouth to say something but death took him before he could speak.

Although my left shoulder was hurting I needed to know if there were others in the hut. I approached cautiously. I noticed that the first one I had killed was a much older man, almost my age. He must have been the leader of these outlaws. Were there more within? The wood which blocked the entrance at night had been moved. I saw that there was a fire glowing inside. I heard breathing. The darkness prevented me from discerning who was within. I was aware of blood trickling down my back. The longer I waited the less chance I had of defeating whoever waited for me. I ran in and braced myself for a blow. The blow never came. With my back against the wall, I peered into the dark. As my eyes became accustomed to the dark I saw Gray's wife, Thora in the corner. Her head was down and she was shaking.

As soon as I had satisfied myself that she was alone I sheathed my weapons and went to her. I held out my hand, "Thora, it is Jarl Dragonheart. You are safe now. I have slain them all."

She looked up and I saw the relief on her face. "Oh, Jarl! Thank the Allfather you have come. These nithings killed my husband and…" She shook her head. I will not speak of it."

I led her into the light. "Come, we will go to my son's home."

She shook her head, "We must bury my husband. They killed him and left his body in the woods. I would not have animals despoil him."

I needed my wound attended to but she was upset and I followed her. We went just a short way behind the farm and found his hacked and slashed body. They had used their seaxes on him. His body had been abused after death. I could see that the rats, foxes and birds had already made inroads into his flesh.

We dragged him into the open. I stumbled and when Thora put her hand out to help me it came away bloody." Jarl! You are wounded!"

I nodded, "They are all dead but one speared me in the shoulder."

She ran back into the hut and returned with a skin of water and some salve. Lifting my kyrtle she gasped. "This is a deep wound, my lord. It is bleeding heavily."

I nodded, "Then you must use a brand from the fire and staunch the bleeding." I smiled at her. She was young, a little younger than Brigid but she and Gray had been strong enough to survive in the wild. She would be able to manage. "Be strong, Thora; you can do this."

She went back into the hut and returned with a burning brand. She held it in two hands. "You had better kneel, Jarl." She smiled. "You are bigger than I am."

I did so and braced myself. "Hold it there for the count of five if you can, and if I can bear it."

I first felt warmth then heat, then excruciating pain. There was the smell of burning hair and flesh. I fought the darkness which threatened to overwhelm me and then the pain stopped. She began to dab the hot flesh with water. I was not certain that Aiden would have approved but it felt good. "The bleeding has stopped. I will put on this salve and then you must rest."

As she applied cool salve I shook my head. "No, we must bury your husband and then get to my son's."

"You are hurt."

"And I am a warrior. I have suffered worse. Thank you, Thora."

It was a crude burial that Gray was given. I laid his seax, which one of the outlaws had taken, across his body and we piled stones upon it. The animals would feast on outlaws' flesh and Gray would remain undisturbed. While Thora gathered her few belongings I went for Badger. He was just a short way into the forest. The blood had dried on the wound. It was a scratch only but I would put on some of Thora's salve. Badger would be our only hope until we found another farm.

Thora had few belongings. She had tied them in one of the outlaw's cloaks. After we had cleaned the wound on Badger and applied the salve I said, "Get on his back."

She shook her head, "You are wounded and you are Jarl Dragonheart. I will walk."

"True, I am Jarl and I order you to mount."

She shook her head and became tearful, "I cannot ride!"

I laughed, "You do not need to ride. Just sit on his back. Come he is a gentle horse." I cupped my hands and heaved her into the saddle. It was a mistake for the movement sent paroxysms of pain through my shoulder but I gritted my teeth and said nothing. I handed her bundle to her and led Badger towards the mere.

I knew that Finn had a farm at the southern end of the mere and I hoped we would find help there. To take my mind off the pain I asked Thora about the Saxons.

"They came six days since. The first I knew was when they burst into the hut with Gray's blood still upon them. I could not understand their words but they did not speak over much to me. They…," she hesitated, "they took me and abused me. I hope they suffered when you slew them."

I nodded. "So you have no idea where they came from?"

She shook her head. "Finn has sons and they hunt the woods to the south. I do not think the four of them would have passed his farm easily." She shivered as though to exorcise a demon. "They were cruel men. Are all Saxons like that?"

I remained silent. I was half Saxon. Sometimes I could be cruel too. Was that the Saxon side of me emerging?

When they heard my horse approaching Finn and his sons armed themselves and came towards us. When they recognised me, they relaxed. "Hail, Jarl Dragonheart what brings you this way?"

"I was on my way to Wolf Killer's when I was attacked by four Saxons who killed Thora's man."

Thora blurted out, "He is wounded!"

Viking Legend

Finn's wife rushed over to Thora while Finn and his sons crowded around me. "Is it a bad wound, Jarl?"

I shook my head, "A spear in the shoulder. I will be fine. Could I leave Thora here with you?" I lowered my voice. "She has suffered much. She needs care and the company of a woman."

Finn nodded, "I will do so but you cannot travel alone." He turned to his sons, "Sven, mount your pony and escort the Jarl."

"There is no need."

"Jarl, there is. The ones who attacked and killed Gray were not the only ones. Four days since we hunted three who had taken one of my sheep. One spoke before he died. They are from Mercia. There are many men who have been outlawed and they have moved further and further north. Who knows how many may be twixt here and Wolf Killer? I would sleep easier knowing that you were escorted. My son can return on the morrow."

His wife, who had taken Thora indoors, returned with a horn of ale, cheese and some rye bread, "Here Jarl it is little enough but it will keep you going." She shook her head, "It is good that Thora is young. She might get over this. She is hurting."

"Thank you. I know that you will care for her." I ate gratefully. As I handed the empty horn back to Finn I said. "I will have my son send warriors to scour the forest and rid us of this infestation and I will send a message to Sigtrygg Thrandson. You should be able to live safely within my lands."

"And we do."

I looked over to Thora who was being comforted by Finn's wife, "Not all live safely. I have let down my people and I will make amends."

Sven was pleasant company and it was easier for me to ride Badger rather than walk. He told me more about the hunting of the outlaws. He sounded like a handy warrior. "Have you no thoughts of a wife and a farm of your own?"

"There are few women hereabouts and it is too far to travel to Windar's mere or Cyninges-tūn."

"But there is good land aplenty."

"Aye."

I had a sudden thought, "And Thora will need a man. She would make a good wife. She has iron in her."

"Thora? She is comely. Perhaps I will give thought to it. Gray was our friend and I do not think he would mind."

I learned much about my people as I rode the last few miles to Wolf Killer's settlement. Their lives were hard enough without raids and attacks from outlaws. We arrived just before dark. My late arrival and my escort brought Wolf Killer and Elfrida to the gate. I would have remained silent about my wound but Sven blurted it out. I did not like fuss but I was forced to remove my kyrtle, once we were in the hall, and show Elfrida the injury. She nodded when she saw what Thora had done, "It has been sealed with a flame but you should not have ridden so far. You are pale, father. You will stay here until I am happy for you to leave."

Viking Legend

Wolf Killer smiled, his wife was a strong-willed woman and a force of nature. Sven joined the men in the warrior hall and I sat with my son, grandson and Elfrida. I had much to tell them. After I told Wolf Killer the reason for my visit I added, "But first I think we should scour the land for these Saxons."

He leaned forward, "I will scour the land and you will rest until my wife says otherwise and when you go to visit with Sigtrygg then I will have my men escort you. We cannot afford to lose Jarl Dragonheart."

I spoke before I thought, "There was a time not so long ago when you did not think so."

He coloured a little and I thought I had upset him but he laughed. "You are right and I apologise. Let us say I was not as grown up as I thought and I have learned since then. My wife is a good teacher. Perhaps I needed to have a son to learn what it is to be a father."

Ragnar was now old enough to be inquisitive and unafraid of upsetting his elders with his questions. I was quizzed about my sword, my battles, Brigid, the Scots, my voyages... everything! I was exhausted when he was hurried off to bed. Elfrida made sure I had some warmed honeyed ale to send me to sleep and I was put to bed like my grandson.

My bed was welcome and the ale had made me sleepy. As I lay down to sleep I realised how close I had come to death. The four men I had fought were not warriors but I had been at my most vulnerable. I could have died. I was not afraid of death for myself but I was beginning to understand the effect it would have on my land. I thought back to my grandsire, the Warlord. When he had fallen his world had ended as though it had never existed. Could I wish that upon my people? I remembered my mother who had been nobility and then reduced to life as a slave. That would not happen to my family. I would make sure that when I went to the Otherworld my land was in safe hands.

I woke in the middle of the night. The pain in my shoulder was amongst the worst that I had borne. Once awake I found it hard to sleep. The attack and the wound had been a warning. I was not immortal. I had a sword touched by the Gods but I was not touched by the Gods. I lifted my head. I did not wish to wake the others. I found Thora's salve and rubbed a little on my shoulder. It seemed to give some relief and I lay back down and stared at the wood above my head. I turned as Elfrida appeared next to me.

"You are in pain?"

"It is to be expected." I gave a wry, dry chuckle, "I should not be surprised. I am not Wolf Killer. I fell from my horse and I had a spear in my back. I should expect discomfort."

She nodded, "Here drink this draught." I cocked an eyebrow. "Do not fear, Kara taught me to make it."

I drank it down and it felt warm as it entered my body, "Thank you. You are kind and my son is a lucky man."

"We are all fortunate, Jarl, and that is largely due to you."

Viking Legend

I closed my eyes and she kissed my forehead. The pain was now a dull throb but the potion worked and I slept. I slept so deeply it felt as though I was dead. The sleep was so deep that I awoke long after the others. I rose and looked around the empty hall. Ragnar was sitting cross-legged by the fire staring at me. "I thought you were never going to wake grandfather."

I heard Elfrida's voice, "Let your grandfather wake before you bother him." She entered with two thralls who carried food and ale. "I see that you slept. How do you feel?"

"Stiff but that will pass. Kara's potion worked."

"It is magical and now that Aiden has the wizard's parchments we will be able to use many more such potions and elixirs."

I left to make water. Looking into the sky I saw that it was almost noon. I had slept a long time. When I returned, the food and the ale were on the table. "You let me sleep o'er long. Where are the others?"

"Sven led my husband and his men to search for the Saxons. He has sent a messenger back to Cyninges-tūn to tell them you are safe."

"But they did not know what happened. They would not have been worried."

She laughed, "Finni would have sent word, believe me. Your son also sent a messenger to Sigtrygg."

"Good." I was relieved. That would save a journey. I ate and every mouthful was watched by young Ragnar.

When the food was gone he said, "Is it true you were a thrall like Peter." He pointed to the old man who was sweeping the floor.

"Aye, I was taken as a thrall and I earned my freedom."

"How?"

I smiled, "You are named after Ragnar who was my master. I cared for him in the high mountains. One day a wolf attacked us and I killed the wolf. I was given my freedom."

"That is how you became the wolf warrior?" I nodded, "I would like to kill a wolf and be like you and my father. He is Wolf Killer you know."

I saw Elfrida smile. "I know. I was there when he killed his wolf but it is a dangerous task to kill a wolf. They are both cunning and brave. One of the warriors lost two fingers that day and another almost lost a hand. A wolf is a fierce creature and a clever hunter."

"Like you and the Ulf... Ulf..."

"Ulfheonar."

"Yes them." We laughed. I enjoyed the afternoon. My wound meant I could not practise with him as I normally did so walked around the river and the old Roman fort. I noticed that two of my son's guards kept a wary eye on us. It would not do to have the father and the son of the Jarl attacked. It was good to talk with a young inquisitive mind. Soon I would be able to do this with my new son.

Viking Legend

My son and his men did not return until after dark. I saw the worry on Elfrida's face. It was a hard job to wait at home. Ragnar ran up to him and greeted him warmly. "Did you slay the outlaws?"

He nodded. "We found five and they now hang in the forest as a reminder to others who would transgress in our land."

I nodded. My son was becoming ruthless. He would need that when I went to the Otherworld. "And Sven?"

"He is a good warrior. He returned home."

"I told him to take a wife and a farm."

"We need warriors like that."

He sat opposite me at his table and waved thrall over with ale. "I will take my drekar and voyage with your men but I would not leave my land undefended. Have you enough men to give me half a crew?"

I nodded, as I swallowed the fine ale, "And more. I have many young men who wish to go a-Viking."

He smiled and touched horns with me, "I am happy that things are well between us."

"For my part, son, you never stopped being part of me. I was just sad that you did not want to be that part."

He looked over to Ragnar who was practising with his wooden sword against one of Wolf Killer's oathsworn. "The more he grows the more I shudder at my behaviour. Why did you not lose your temper and strike me?"

"Because that was never my way and never your mother's. You choose your friends but your children are something different. You hope they will grow well and you do your best but, in the end, it is in the hands of the gods and the Norns. I am just happy that it has turned out well. Magnus the Foresworn is an example of someone who turned out bad."

"What will you do about him? He is still out there and he strikes me as a malevolent snake."

"I will send out my ships for news of him. He likes himself so much that he will surface and when he does I will follow him." I looked into Wolf Killer's eyes. "I fear he will wish to revenge himself upon me and he may strike here."

"Do not worry, father, I have some of my oathsworn who watch what I love as closely as I."

"Good. We have fought for what we have. We do not give it away to those who would steal and live on the endeavours of others."

Sigtrygg arrived the day after my son. He felt guilty that he had not stopped the Saxons travelling through his land. "Sigtrygg Thrandson, take it as a sign that your land is strong and our enemies will not risk your wrath."

He seemed satisfied with that. "My drekar will be ready soon. I will keep her along the Lune and then I can raid after the snows."

"Let Wolf Killer and I know when you do so. We will keep watch on your lands for you."

"You have done more than enough for me Jarl Dragonheart. I needs must stand on my own feet."

Viking Legend

I shook my head, "When a child learns to walk it needs a parent to be close by for he will fall. Until you and your people are strong enough let us be your parents. The stronger you are then the stronger we become as a people. I want our people to last beyond my death."

Both Wolf Killer and Sigtrygg looked concerned and I laughed, "I do not intend to die but I am no longer a young man and I won't make plans."

As I went out to play with Ragnar I saw them deep in conversation. I had made them think about a future without Jarl Dragonheart and that was no bad thing.

Viking Legend
Chapter 7

In the end, I spent four days with my son and then he allowed me to go home with an escort of ten warriors. I thought that was too many but both he and Elfrida insisted. I called in at Finn's farm. He smiled when I asked about Thora.

"She has iron in her that one. She and Sven have returned to Graythwaite. They have my blessing."

I nodded, "This is *wyrd*. I am happy."

"Thank you, Jarl. You are a good man. I knew it before but now I see it as clearly as a sunrise over Windar's Mere. You care about people and that is a rare thing in a great man."

When we reached Graythwaite there was no sign of the Saxons' bodies. I said nothing but I could see that Sven had taken charge. Thora looked happy and they both kissed my hand. "We thank you, Jarl Dragonheart. We have been of your people all of our lives but it was not until you rode through this valley that we realised what a thoughtful man you are." Sven nodded, "My sons will fight for you."

"Sons?"

Sven laughed, "Many sons and, perhaps a daughter or two."

I had a homecoming like no other. All of Cyninges-tūn, it seemed, turned out to greet me. I was touched. Kara, Brigid and Aiden looked particularly concerned. After the welcome, which went on for some time I was taken into my hall where Kara, Aiden and Brigid closely examined my wound. "I am not something to be poked and prodded."

"You could have died! Fighting four men! Without armour! What were you thinking?"

It was at that moment that I saw the difference between Brigid and Erika. Erika would not have shown me her feelings but Brigid lived with every emotion on display. I could not have chosen two such different women to be my partner. When the three were happy that my wound was healing I had to tell them all.

Aiden nodded. "It is good that your son takes more responsibility."

Kara smiled, "You should be able to take life easier."

"Why? Am I different now from the warrior who went to Hibernia to fetch you back or travelled to Ynys Môn to rescue you and Elfrida? The day I stop being Dragonheart is the day I will die. I am what I am and I cannot change my nature." I shrugged, "I do not think you would wish me to change that nature either, would you?"

They looked at each other and Brigid, laying her hand on mine said, "No. We would not change one hair on your head."

I was determined to regain my former strength and I worked each day with Snorri and Haaken. I did so without armour. I had been too slow when I had faced the Saxons. None of them had any skill and I had allowed one to get behind me. I could almost hear the scorn in Old Ragnar's voice. I would be ready when the snow which had yet to fall had melted. I knew what I had to do. I had to find Magnus the Foresworn and end his life. The Saxon outlaws were like the bites of the lice; they were annoying but they would not hurt us. Magnus had the power to tear my land apart for he was of our people. He was now my enemy.

As the winter drew close Asbjorn along with my son and their warriors returned from their raid. They had struck the lands of Mercia. With Wolf Killer's ship with them, they should have had great success but they had lost warriors and although they came back with treasure it was not the wealth we had brought back from Ynys Môn. Both Wolf Killer and Asbjorn were unhappy when they came to my hall.

I knew that they were comparing themselves to me. They had chosen a strong enemy to raid. "The Mercians have fought us many times. It is to be expected that they would prepare for an attack from us. You brought back grain and animals. We will eat and they will starve. Some of your warriors died but those who survived are stronger. We are wolves and not sheep. The sheepdog will take a wolf now and then but we will still succeed more than we fail."

The first snow came soon after the return of the drekar. We became an island surrounded by a wall of ice. We retreated into our halls. That winter we had plenty of food and wood and we prospered. I took solace from the fact that my decisions appeared to have been the right ones. It was, thankfully, not a wolf winter. We heard none howl. That was fortunate for there were no warriors who were ready to hunt the wolf and become Ulfheonar.

Brigid became larger as my son grew within her. I had no doubt that it was a son for the spirits never lied. Kara kept a close eye on her. Wolf Killer had been estranged when Ragnar was born and she would be able to see this nephew born. I knew there would be a close bond. It was unlikely that Kara would ever bear children and yet she yearned for one. Kara showed how much this meant to her for she encouraged Deidra and Macha to celebrate the White Christ feast with Brigid. When I asked her about it she shrugged and said, "We call it Yule. If they wish to celebrate the birth of a baby a thousand years ago then it is no bad thing is it?"

My son was born twenty-one days after the shortest day of the year. He was healthy and he was large. Kara had seen many babies born and she commented on his size. "He will grow to be a huge and mighty man." As Brigid nursed him my daughter asked, "What will you name him?"

I had not thought about it. I had no preferences and I looked helplessly at Brigid. She smiled, "Since I knew he was to be a boy I had but one name in my head. There were many at my father's court who were unkind to me but I had an uncle who always gave me affection and made me laugh. With your permission, I would name him Gryffydd in his honour. And, I hope, yours." I nodded. She kissed his head and then added, "I dare say you pagans will

Viking Legend

change it and call him Gryffydd the Mighty or, "she stroked his head, "the Bald but to me, he shall be Gryffydd son of Dragonheart."

I smiled, "Let it be so."

Brigid changed a little that day. She was a mother now and that became her life. It was not that I was ignored, I was not, but she spent each waking, and I dare say sleeping, thinking about our son. She doted on him. I suspect that was one of the reasons he grew so quickly and so well. Infants, especially those born in the winter, often did not see the end of the month in which they were born. Gryffydd was the exception. Another reason that she threw herself into motherhood was the fact that I was busy. We would be raiding once the weather improved. With Sigtrygg's new ship ready we would have four drekar. Nowhere would be safe from our wrath.

I woke each day to the sound of Bjorn's hammers as he and his smiths worked from dawn until dusk making the helmets and swords which my young men had ordered. A Viking does not feel dressed unless he can face an enemy with a helmet, shield and sword. A spear is a temporary weapon until he can afford better.

Before we could raid I had to visit Úlfarrston. We had need of trade with Thorfinn Blue Scar on Ljoðhús and we still had some of the treasures from the Welsh which Coen ap Pasgen could sell in Lundenwic. This time I went with Aiden and Haaken. My days of travelling alone were over. My shoulder which now ached when the air was damp was a constant reminder of the dangers of being alone. Now that I was a father again I spoke with Haaken about his children. He now had two girls and a boy. At first, he had not taken to fatherhood but, as he became older, he had grown into it. He saw his blood ensuring his line in the future.

"Aiden, why have you not taken a wife?"

"I do not know."

"You enjoy women do you not?" I knew there were some men who did not care for the company of women.

"I like women but none has touched me yet the way Lady Erika and Brigid have touched you. Perhaps I am meant to be alone as your daughter Kara is."

"Then that is sad for our world would be better for more children like Kara and Aiden."

It was not often that I could make Aiden keep silent and think but, that day I did. I was just making conversation but oft times such idle words are like a pebble being knocked from the top of a mountain. By the time it reached the bottom, it had caused an avalanche.

As I passed the shipyard Bolli was just completing the work on Sigtrygg's drekar. Bolli looked pleased. "Has he named it yet, Bolli?"

"No Jarl and I hope that he will do so soon. A ship does not like to be nameless. She needs love and she needs attention. A good drekar is like a wife she performs best when she knows she is needed."

"Fear not Bolli I know he is eager to sail and I would expect him any time soon. The other drekar are at Úlfarrston?"

Viking Legend

"Aye Jarl. Erik led them there when the last of the snow went. He prefers the sea to the river. He says it is better for his ship."

We left to ride the short way to the coast. There the three drekar bobbed up and down on the sea with four knarr close by. It seemed the ships were all keen to be away. Siggi and the other knarr captains had all been trading during the winter. They took advantage of the times when the weather was clement and made short journeys only. They went to Dyflin and to Ljoðhús as well as some of the other islands close to Ljoðhús for our good standing with Thorfinn helped make new trading partners. They all had news for me.

We gathered in Coen's hall for the news was of interest to us all. It was Siggi who spoke for them. "The Scots and the Picts are pushing west. The men of Ljoðhús and the Norse on the other islands have ever sent them back but they seem keen to retake the islands. Thorfinn Blue Scar want as many swords and helmets as we can take."

"I will speak with Bjorn but I am interested in why there is this pressure."

"It seems that the King of Northumbria, Eanred is pushing west too."

Haaken asked, "I thought they were a spent force."

"They were Haaken. When Eardwulf and Aelfwald fought for the throne they bled the warriors of Northumbria dry and the land appeared weak. Since Eanred has succeeded to the crown he has been building up his forces and hiring warriors. He cannot defeat Wessex and so he expands to the north and west."

"Then I must send a warning to both Ketil and Arne. Their land borders both the land of the Scots and Northumbria." I shook my head, "I had thought we were safe from any Northumbrian incursion. It has been many years since they attempted to take from us. How does he pay for his hired men? It was not a rich kingdom."

Coen's captain, Raibeart smiled, "The same way we make gold, Jarl. He has many monasteries and they sell the Holy Books that the monks make and sell them in Lundenwic and in Frankia. The warriors come from both Frankia and Lundenwic to serve this Saxon king in the north. He pays well. It is said he even has some warriors who fought against the Eastern Emperor."

As I headed back with Aiden and Haaken I pondered this development. Perhaps we might risk a long and hazardous voyage around the north of Britannia and raid the monasteries. If the monks were producing such numbers then we might profit from them. I sent riders to all of my jarls when I reached home and I had my Ulfheonar begin to recruit the warriors we would take on our raid.

Kara shook her head as she saw the young men all practising. "It is well that our womenfolk are so hardy and handy. They have to raise children and farm for the young men do not wish to soil their hands with earth. They wish to bathe in blood."

"It is the way of our people, Kara. You know that."

"Aye, and it is well that so many children survive here to replace the dead."

Viking Legend

It was fourteen days later and we had just gathered the men to begin the journey to Úlfarrston when a rider galloped in. "Jarl Dragonheart I come from Jarl Ketil. He is under attack. There are Saxons assailing his eastern farms." I nodded, "And there is more. Amongst them are Vikings. Magnus the Foresworn has returned. The Jarl managed to gather his people in the stronghold and I left before he was surrounded. I barely made it with my life. There are enemies all around. They are ravaging the land."

That treacherous snake had never been far from my mind and I had hoped to find him and end his life. Now, it seemed, he had come to me. "We march north to Ketil's stad." I turned to the rider. "Rest for a while and then follow us. I may have need of you. Kara, send a rider to Wolf Killer and ask him for some of his warriors. I will meet him at Ketil's fort."

It was thirty miles to the Roman fort Ketil used as his stronghold. He had repaired the stone walls and deepened the ditches. It was as strong as my fort. We would pass Windar's Mere and Ulf's Water. We could pick up more warriors. I hoped that we might reach Ketil with a hundred men but it would take a whole day and Gói was not long passed. The day would be a short one and the weather cold. I berated myself in my head. I was wasting time arguing with myself.

"We leave now!"

Cnut Cnutson ran up to me. "Jarl, you said I would fight this year."

"Aye, I did. Have you your father's sword and shield?"

"I have."

"Then join the other young men who go to war this day."

I saw that he had them nearby. He had not forgotten my promise and I would not be foresworn. He would go to war with his father's shield; I just hoped he would not come home on it.

Snorri and Beorn the Scout led the way and set the pace. They had us running the downhill sections and we marched up the hills. We only stopped when we reached streams where we drank. We ate on the move. Ketil's rider had passed Windar's Mere and there were a dozen warriors there awaiting us. We hurried on. Another ten warriors waited beneath the shadow of Úlfarrberg and swelled our ranks. Although we had only gained a few warriors all were well armed and half had mail byrnies of some description. More importantly, all had experience.

The sky was darkening as we began to ascend the Roman Road which led to Ketil's stronghold. Ketil's rider had joined us shortly before we had reached the Úlfarrberg. I waved him forward. Snorri and Beorn had stopped short of the deserted village of Penrhudd. "Is this a good place to camp?"

Ketil's rider, Leif nodded, "I would not risk going closer. The Saxons had surrounded the fort. In fact, I am surprised that they have not advanced this far already."

Snorri said, "Ketil may well be drawing them upon him. The Saxons do not have much skill in tackling forts but Magnus the Forsworn served with you Jarl. He knows how to do so."

Viking Legend

"Then we will camp here. Haaken, gather the Ulfheonar we will find where the enemy lines are." I turned to Ulla who led the men from Ulf's Water. "You command here until I return. Be watchful." We dropped our shields. They would get in the way and we drew our seaxes this would be close in killing.

We slipped along the road like wraiths. Asbjorn and Eystein rejoined us for we would need their skills. The wolves would hunt once more. The sky ahead of us was dark. There was no moon. Snorri led us to the north so that we could approach the Northumbrians from the north east. I did not want Magnus and the Saxons to know that we were close. I need not have worried for they had ringed the stronghold with fires. I saw arrows and spears sticking out of the wooden walls showing that they had attacked but they had not breached its defences yet. Ketil had been attacked before and he had cleaned out the deep Roman ditches. He had made them ankle breakers once more. The attackers would need to build a ram if they were to break in.

We needed to estimate numbers. I waved my men to the side of me and we moved slowly in a long thin line. When we were a hundred paces from what looked like the camp I came upon the first sentry. I saw his shadow against the firelight and I dropped to my knee. He was ten paces from me. I remained still as he turned for I knew he would not see me. I was encased in black. No flesh showed. I knew he had turned when I could no longer see his white face. I rose and walked towards him. In two steps I was upon him. I wrapped my left arm around his mouth as I drew the seax across his throat.

I lowered him to the ground and stood in his place. To anyone watching from the camp all that they would see would be a dark shape and they would assume it was the sentry. I looked along the line of the camp. It was a large force which had come to attack Ketil. They were mainly Saxons I could see but there were one or two warriors wearing exotic armour and helmets. They would be like Magnus, mercenaries. Before we had seen them I had wondered if this was just a raid. Their presence around the walls showed that they wanted this as their own stronghold. If they held it then they would have a toehold in my land. This was King Eanred spreading west. Perhaps he had made peace with the Scots.

Glancing to my left I saw Haaken and to my right, Snorri. I waved my arm forward. It was time to create terror. I half crouched as I moved towards the camp. I did not need to signal my men; we moved as one. Each one of my warriors would kill two or three sleeping Saxons and be gone before they even knew that they were dead.

Haaken and Snorri closed with me. We saw three warriors around a small fire. They were cooking something. They were facing the stronghold and their backs were to us. I chose the middle warrior and I pulled his head back and plunged my seax through his open mouth. The other two lay dead by the time I lowered the body to the ground. Snorri snatched the roasting meat and we slipped back. We waited at the road and, gradually, in ones and twos, the rest of my men rejoined me. We did not speak and Snorri led us back to our camp; he ate his stolen meat as we walked.

My men had not lit a fire. We would eat cold rations and drink but water. I gathered the Ulfheonar around me and the two leaders of the men from Windar's mere and Ulf's Water. "How many men do you think they have?"

Each warrior told the number they had seen and I counted them up. "Then there are seventy warriors and that is just on this side. We must assume they have the place surrounded so let us say two hundred."

Karl Word-Master laughed, "Less the fifteen or so that we slew this night."

They all smiled at that thought. "I hope that they think we came from the north but Magnus knows us. He will suspect that it is us. I want to draw him hence. He hates me more than anyone else. Tomorrow night we go in again and this time we use the sound of the wolf. It will tell him who attacks and it will tell Ketil that we are close."

"They might breach the walls tomorrow."

"True, Haaken but to do so they will need a ram. We will watch. If they have a ram then we change our plans. And now we move."

"Move!"

"Yes Vermund, there was another Roman fort just across the river. It is ruined and it is small but it will afford us better protection should we be attacked and it cannot be seen by our enemies. We remain hidden until I choose to reveal myself."

We did not have far to go and, with sentries set, we all fell into an exhausted sleep. My men let me sleep until noon. Haaken brought me some water from the stream and some dried venison. "Snorri and Beorn have gone to scout. He pointed to the south. "Wolf Killer and his men are two miles away. One of our sentries saw them."

"Good for we will need his steel alongside us."

Wolf Killer reached us within a short time. He had brought twenty of his best warriors. I had not expected him to leave his stad undefended. After we had apprised him of the situation he nodded and said. "I told Sigtrygg what we were about and asked him to watch our lands."

"I fear that I will not be raiding this summer. That will have to be you and Sigtrygg."

"What will you do?"

"I will end this and teach King Eanred a lesson."

Wolf Killer smiled, "And yet here we are outnumbered by our enemies. It is no wonder your name is feared. I would not have you as my enemy. You are relentless."

"As you will be, my son, when you lead our people."

Snorri and Beorn reached us during the afternoon. "Your plan worked. The Saxons have parties to the north searching for our trail."

"Good then we will rest and as soon as it is dark we will put my plan into operation." I spent an hour going over the details of it with my jarls and

Viking Legend

leaders. There were risks but if it succeeded then the pressure on Ketil might be lessened.

After a frugal meal, my Ulfheonar prepared their night faces. We would not need our shields for we would use our swords and seaxes. It would not be as easy this night for they would be prepared for a night attack. It would be a real test of my men's skill. We moved in a tighter line that night. I wanted a deeper penetration so that when we howled it would come from the heart of their camp. It would be in the place they felt the most secure.

This time the white faces of the sentries were looking out. It seemed there was one every twenty paces. We had alarmed them. As we were close together that meant that each sentry would have two of us attacking him. We moved slowly as only the Ulfheonar or a wolf can. It is almost imperceptible. The closer we came to the sentries the harder we were to spot for their eyes were fixed in the distance. My men rose as one. I put my hands across the mouth of the sentry and Haaken thrust his sword up between his legs and into his body. He slumped dead. I glanced to my left and right. We had not been seen.

Moving towards the fires we pounced, silently on the small groups of resting and sleeping men. It was not honourable work for they died without resistance. As we went we picked up their short axes and seaxes. I saw a group of what looked like leaders standing around the fire arguing. I recognised Magnus. He had grown somewhat but he still had the wild mane of hair I remembered. I knew we could not remain where we were for long. I took one of the small throwing axes we had taken and held it up. The others nodded and each one held either an axe or a seax in his hand. I held up three fingers then two and finally one. I hurled my axe at the group of leaders. The others did so. Even while they were in the air we all began to howl like wolves. The faces at the fire turned at the noise. Warriors stood and stared.

The screams and shouts of the five men hit by our weapons seemed to be the signal for them to get their arms. By then we had turned and with weapons drawn were running from the slaughterhouse we had created. There were few warriors between us and safety. Those who tried to stop us were slain where they stood.

Behind me, I heard the roar as we were pursued. We slowed down so that they could see where we fled. That was part of the plan. We needed them to follow us. Wolf Killer and the rest of my men were waiting by the river to ambush them. It was easier going for we were running downhill towards the stream. When I heard Snorri splashing in the water I knew we had reached it. We waded fifty paces down and then turned, each with two weapons to face our enemies.

I saw that they had run hard and the first warriors were less than thirty paces behind us. Two of them foolishly ran at us and Haaken and Karl slew them easily. The rest waited. They were all Saxons. I had hoped that Magnus would be close so that I could kill him. Perhaps he was already dead. We had hit some of their leaders by their fire. I saw a mailed leader organise his men into a wedge and they came at us purposefully.

Viking Legend

I shouted at them to focus their attention on me, "I am Jarl Dragonheart and you have strayed into my land. Leave now and you shall live. If you remain then all of you will die!" I spoke in Saxon so that they would all know my words.

Their leader, who had continued to lead his men towards us laughed, "I am not afraid of a dozen men who wear the cloaks of dead animals and howl like women."

As he raised his sword to signal the charge the trap was sprung. Those on either side of the wedge hurled spears and loosed arrows. The leader stared around him in shock. Then he roared a challenge and hurled himself at me. I deflected his spear and ripped my seax across his throat. He gurgled his life away. "I warned you!"

Then my men fell upon the survivors of the wedge and slaughtered them. The Saxons at the back, who were a little slower, saw the slaughter and fled back to their camp. "Wolf Killer, set guards. The rest of you take whatever you can from the dead."

Some of those we had killed had mail and we would need as many mailed warriors as we could get when Magnus attacked us the next day. We made our way back to our new camp and prepared for what I knew would be a hard day. We cleared as many of the stones from the old ditch as we could and we piled them up on the wall. There was no gate; as a fort, it was not particularly good but it gave us somewhere we could retreat. It gave us walls behind which some could fight. And it was at the top of a hill which would sap energy from legs. It would also afford protection to those young warriors who had no mail.

I had the men use the poor-quality spears the Saxons had carried to make traps in the ditch. The haft was rammed into the soil with the spearhead pointing up so that it formed a rough hedgehog. I intended to put a half circle of warriors, three lines deep before the gateway. I wanted to draw our enemies upon us and break themselves on my Ulfheonar and Wolf Killer's warriors. We would fight as a single body.

Snorri had organised scouts and they came running towards us at noon. "Jarl, they come!" They pointed behind them.

I had my wolf standard sticking from the remains of the tower. It fluttered bravely in the breeze from the east. The black wolf on the blue background stood out. Kara had sewn a yellow eye on the wolf and given it a long red dragon tongue. It inspired my men. This day I wanted it to draw Magnus on. He would recognise both it and me.

I saw them in the distance. The Norse who followed Magnus were in the centre and they were flanked by the other mercenaries. These other warriors were an unknown. How did they fight? What weapons did they favour? I knew how to fight both Saxons and Vikings but the men from the east and Frankia fought in different ways. The Saxons formed the bulk of the army but I guessed that the Northumbrian Eorl who led them would want the hired men to die first. I had been roughly correct with my estimate. There appeared to be about a hundred and fifty warriors who came towards us. We had slain some and they would have some maintaining a watch on the walls. If Ketil could sally forth then we might be able to end this threat here before the walls of his stronghold. I could neither count on nor expect Ketil to bring aid. He had his people in his walls and they were his first priority.

The ground which led to the low hill was not smooth but had hollows and dips. Had I had time I would have dug traps. I had not had the time and nature would have to be our ally. The enemy halted at the bottom and I saw one of the mercenaries issue orders. He was encased in armour but it was not mail which was made of links. It looked like overlapping pieces of metal. I had seen similar armour in Miklagård. His shield confirmed it. He carried an oval one and his helmet looked eastern for it had an aventail. As I scrutinised those around him I saw that there were six who had similar armour. This mercenary had travelled a long way. A half dozen others did have mail but their helmets were unusual. I had seen ones just like them in the land of Vasconia. I took them to be from the Empire. King Eanred had spent much of his riches on hired warriors. How would they fight?

The Norse were placed in one wedge and, next to it, like a boar's head were the other fifteen mercenaries. Their leader filled the gap with Saxon.

"Magnus will come for me. Wolf Killer the mercenaries from Miklagård and Frankia will come for you. They will be skilled."

"Fear not, Father. I have watched you and learned."

"Those behind the wall, release your arrows as soon as you can and then throw your javelins when they are about to charge."

I heard young Rolf shout, somewhat cheekily, "We will, Jarl!"

Olaf Leather Neck chuckled, "Young cockerel. He has fought one battle and he thinks he is a Viking hero already."

Snorri said, "It is good that they are confident Olaf. I was not when I was his age."

"Aye, my friend, and you have survived! Think about that."

I did not ask for silence. The banter helped to calm nerves. The wedges were two hundred paces away and moving steadily.

Haaken had a good voice and he began to sing the rowing chant whilst banging the hilt of his sword on his shield. Soon everyone joined in. it sounded as though the gods themselves were singing.

The storm was wild and the Gods did roam
The enemy closed on the Prince's home
Two warriors stood on a lonely tower
Watching, waiting for hour on hour.
The storm came hard and Odin spoke
With a lightning bolt the sword he smote
Ragnar's Spirit burned hot that night
It glowed, a beacon shiny and bright
The two they stood against the foe
They were alone, nowhere to go
They fought in blood on a darkened hill

Viking Legend

Dragon Heart and Cnut will save us still
Dragon Heart, Cnut and the Ulfheonar
Dragon Heart, Cnut and the Ulfheonar

I knew that Cnut Cnutson would be particularly proud as he stood behind the wall with the other young warriors. This would be his first battle and his father's name was being sung.

The song and the chanting seemed to enrage Magnus and his men. I suppose it was because they knew the song. To the others, it was just a Viking chant. Whatever the reason Magnus and his wedge surged ahead of the rest. I heard the eastern mercenary leader shout something but Magnus ignored it and came directly at me. The sudden movement exposed more of his men to the arrows and the javelins which rained upon them. The two warriors next to Magnus fell with javelins sticking from their chests. Magnus seemed to bear a charmed life.

He roared at me as he thrust his spear towards my head. I turned my shield slightly and it slid down the side. I swung my sword not at his shield as he expected but at the shaft of the spear. I severed it and he was weaponless. I punched him in the face with the boss of my shield and he tumbled backwards. To my left, I heard screams as some of the Saxons fell into the spear-filled ditch. The second wedge struck but as we had already held and thrown back our wedge the effect of the double attack was wasted.

Three warriors stepped forward to face me. They had to be Magnus' oathsworn. I could no longer see Magnus. Two spears and a sword came at me. Haaken's sword hacked through one spear and I took the blow of the sword on my shield. The last spear found my helmet but Bjorn had not only repaired it, but he had also improved the design and the spearhead slid harmlessly down the highly polished side. I jabbed forward with my sword. The three men were so close together that their shields were jammed and they could not move them easily. My sword found a gap and I felt it slide into soft and yielding flesh. I turned the blade as I punched with my shield. I saw the warrior grimace as it found vital organs. He began to slide down. Haaken too scythed his sword into the neck of one of them and the third stumbled. I stunned him with the edge of my shield and Haaken despatched him.

Asbjorn shouted, "Jarl! They are climbing over the wall." He pointed and I could see that they had filled the ditch with dead and dying and the Saxons were using the dead as a bridge to get into the walls. The ones within were the least experienced of all of my warriors and the ones with the least armour.

"Wolf Killer, withdraw into the fort."

"Aye Jarl!"

I could not see him but I heard him. He was less than five warriors from me but he and his oathsworn were surrounded by eastern and Frankish mercenaries.

"Back!"

My Ulfheonar had practised this move and we punched with our shields as we stepped back through the gap. I saw a Frankish warrior raise his two-

Viking Legend

handed axe to bring it down on the head of one of my son's oathsworn. I lunged with my sword and it went through his side. I tore the sword sideways and he fell screaming at my feet. Another had his back to me and as I pulled my sword free I hacked into his neck. The pressure on my son's flank disappeared and they began to edge towards the gateway. I stepped back and saw that my Ulfheonar had bolstered the line of warriors who bravely faced the Saxons without mail.

I hurled myself into the mass of men who had just tumbled over the wall. I caught them by surprise. The weight of my armour, my shield and myself bowled three of them over and they were like fish stranded on the beach. I hacked and slashed at them. With three of the fastest strokes, I had ever made I finished them off. I felt the blood rush through my veins. I yelled, "Ragnar's Spirit!" and, using the dead men as a bridge, I ran and launched myself into the air. I did not rise very far but I must have terrified the Saxons who saw the black, red-eyed wolf with a sword leap amongst them. I landed, luckily, on my feet and I used both my shield and my sword offensively. I whirled around with my shield and my blade. The Saxons tried to strike back but I was too quick and my armour too strong. I felt their blows hit mail and leather but they did not break.

I heard a collective shout and Cnut, Rolf and the other young warriors also ran at the weakening Saxon line. They had no mail but they had energy and courage. It proved too much for the Saxons close by us and they fled. There are some, only a few, but some battles which are decided by one crucial moment. It was the charge of the young warriors which did it. With the Saxons on the right fleeing the Ulfheonar, the men of Windar's Mere and Ulf's Water fell upon the unguarded flank of the Eastern and Frankish mercenaries. They were brave but they stood no chance against our wild assault.

I watched with pride as Wolf Killer faced the leader of the mercenaries. The easterner had a sword which was longer than that of my son. Wolf Killer did what I would have done. He stepped in close and tried to stab the warrior in the side. His blade slid along the overlapping armour. Unable to swing his sword the Byzantine brought the hilt around to smash into the side of my son's head. Wolf Killer went with the blow and, as he fell hacked across the back of the warrior's legs. There was no armour behind the leg and blood spurted as the tendons were cut and the warrior fell to his other knee. Wolf Killer was fast. He leapt to his feet and, using his sword two handed, swept it through the back of the warrior's neck. His head flew into his dying men.

It was the moment we had waited for and the handful of mercenaries who survived were slaughtered to a man. I went to the body-filled gateway and saw the Saxons, most of whom still survived, racing back to the stronghold of Ketil. Amongst them were Magnus and his Norse survivors. We could not let them escape.

"Every man who can fight, follow me! We end this today!"

Viking Legend

I saw that only Karl Word-Master was not with me as I led the Ulfheonar and the others down the slope. I hoped he had survived for I could ill afford to lose more of my oathsworn. I did not lead a huge number of warriors. There were, perhaps thirty and the Saxons outnumbered us but the Saxons had been beaten. If they could be rallied it would take twice as long to defeat them. The uphill section towards the fort was hard. I saw Magnus at the Saxon camp exhorting his men to turn and form a shield wall. If they did then they could fall upon us.

"Ulfheonar, shield wall. The rest form a second rank." We locked shields and the spears of my young warriors appeared through the gaps. "Advance!"

We moved up the slope steadily. We were too tired to rush and it would have availed us little anyway. Magnus' lines awaited us and then I heard a roar from our right as the gates of the fort were opened and Ketil and his men erupted to attack the enemy's left flank. This time there was not even an attempt to fight. The Saxons just ran. Magnus pointed his sword at me and shouted, before he ran off, "This is not over, Dragonheart!"

"After them!"

Magnus was a slippery customer. He and his Vikings had horses and ponies waiting. They grabbed their mounts and galloped through their fleeing allies. I stopped. There was little point in chasing horses but we had won anyway. The siege had been lifted and we had won a mighty battle.

Viking Legend

Chapter 8

Battles might be glorious but the aftermath is not. We had lost friends and we had lost both young and old. Karl was not amongst the dead but he was badly wounded. He had lost his left hand. Five of Wolf Killer's oathsworn had fallen defending their Jarl. It had been a costly battle but not as costly as it might have been.

Ketil, who had pursued the Saxons for a short way, came to me with his hand held out. As I clasped it he dropped to a knee. "I knew you would come, Jarl Dragonheart. My people owe all to you."

Lifting him to his feet I said, "They owe as much to you. Had you not made your defences stronger then this would have fallen. You have justified my faith in you."

We were in no condition to pursue and we spent seven days repairing the damage to the walls of the fort, burning the enemy dead and burying our own. We shared the treasures we had taken and then Wolf Killer, the men of Windar's mere and Ulf's Water left for home. I spoke with my son before he left. "I would that you lead the raid this summer. I will not be sailing. My young men can take '**Odin's Breath**'. I will take my warriors and hunt this Magnus. Now I know where he hides."

"We will come with you. You have not enough men."

"For what I intend I do not need a large number. I cannot think that King Eanred will be happy at losing his mercenaries and so many men."

"Magnus is the only one left to report the events. He will blame others."

"True but enough Northumbrians will return to their King for the rumours to undermine his position. Fear not, my son I will not throw my life away. I now have a second son. I would watch him and Ragnar grow up together."

We clasped hands and they left. I sent a rider to Arne asking if there were any of his warriors who wished to come with me on a vengeance raid. I then took Asbjorn and Eystein to one side. I told them what I planned. "We should be with you for we are Ulfheonar."

"You are and today you showed me that you have lost none of your skills but I have seen other skills. The boys you trained fought like men today. They are the future and I would have you make them even better. Follow my son and Sigtrygg and raid. Bring back great treasure and, more importantly, warriors who are stronger."

"Aye Jarl. What shall we say to Kara and your lady."

"Tell them I go to end this feud. They will understand."

The two of them gathered their young warriors together with the booty they had taken from the dead. I saw that Rolf Erikson now had a leather byrnie as well as an axe and seax. I had no doubt that he had some coins and jewels too. He was becoming a warrior. Had he forgotten Hlif already?

As they formed up I heard a voice behind me. It was Cnut Cnutson. "Jarl, do I go with the other young men or follow you?"

Viking Legend

Cnut was not like the others. There was a bond between us because of his father. "What would you do?"

"I would follow you."

"Then you shall but I have to tell you that it will be dangerous. There will be more safety on the drekar."

"I have sailed enough. It is time to get soil beneath my feet."

"Good." I gave all the warriors who remained the chance to go home but all eighteen chose to stay with me. It took another three days to gather the supplies and ponies for the journey east. By that time four warriors had come from Arne and six of Ketil's men begged for the chance to come with me. I found out that they had all lost family to the raid of Magnus and the Northumbrians. I could not gainsay them. They deserved their revenge too.

We headed east across the high part of the land. We followed, as our defeated enemies had, the Roman Road. We found their bodies as we made our way to my enemy. They must have feared pursuit for none had been buried. They lay, with their hands folded across their bodies but all weapons had been taken. They must have had no healer with them. It was sad to see the waste of warriors who had died only because there was no one to heal them. We reached the high point before noon on the first day of our journey. Still, they headed east. There would come a point where they could head north east or continue east.

I sent Beorn and Snorri, on ponies, to scout well ahead. One took the north eastern route and the other the one directly east. They had not returned when darkness fell. We had crossed the highest part of the land. There had been few farms and homes on our route. In fact, the only sign that man had ever been here was the Roman Road on which we marched. There was a dell off to the side of the road and a small stream bubbled east. With a few scrubby trees for shelter, it was a good place to camp.

Beorn returned first. He pointed to the north east. "I spied the main Saxon band. They were heading north east. I found one of their stragglers and asked him where they were heading. Before he died he told me, Din Guardi. It is the castle of their King."

"And what of Magnus?"

He shook his head, "I saw no sign of them. The band is led by an Eorl called Aethelfrith. He is no friend to Magnus."

Where had Magnus gone? "You have done well." As he hungrily wolfed down some of the food we had brought I said, "This is where we need Aiden and his maps. He would know where this Din Guardi is."

Between mouthfuls, Beorn said, "It is on the coast but not near a river. It is close to the island where the monks make their holy books. The Saxon was quite talkative. It is many leagues to the north."

Snorri rode in well after Beorn had finished eating. He looked exhausted. He almost fell from the back of his pony. "I have found them. They are heading east along the twisting river."

Viking Legend

I felt the hairs on the back of my neck prickle. That was the river where I had lived until I had been taken as a slave. I had lived on the northern bank amongst the woods which rose from its bluffs. It was indeed a twisting river but it made sense for Magnus to use it. He would need a river for his drekar and, from what Beorn had said, there was no river at Din Guardi.

"How far ahead of us is he?"

"A day at least. I rode hard. I saw no sign of the Saxons."

Beorn shook his head, "They have split."

"Then we must hurry tomorrow. I would not have him slip away again and escape. We found him once but I am not certain we could do so a second time."

Our second day's march was much easier for we were going downhill and we had a purpose. We were closing in on Magnus the Foresworn. There were few bridges over the river but it was narrow enough to cross without difficulty. Snorri had told us that the trail led along the northern bank. If he crossed the river by one of the bridges then it would mean he was heading for the town called Jorvik. There, I knew, would be many Danes. There I was a wanted man. I hoped he was not heading for that walled town. I would still follow him there but it would mean more danger for us all. We came to the first Roman Bridge. We spied it from the hills above. I saw a big Roman Road crossing it and heading north. There were people living there and there was an old Roman fort.

Snorri took off his armour and headed down to the village. We kept a close watch on him. He spoke Saxon well. We concocted a story of how he had become separated from Magnus and his men. It was s risk. Vikings were treated with suspicion in this land.

He returned, safely, a short time later. "They did not cross the bridge and they headed east yestereve." He shook his head and laughed, "Magnus was not popular for his men took some of the food from those in the town without paying. I told them that I did not like him either for he had deserted me."

"Do we have to pass through the village?"

Snorri shook his head, "We can head north and then swing back south after the road. It is flat land and there are woods to the north. We will remain hidden."

I did not want word reaching Magnus that a band of Vikings was loose close by him. He was slippery and it might make him flee. I wanted him to spend some time licking his wounds before we pounced. As we headed through the woods to the north of the river I calculated that he would probably have reached his lair by now. We would struggle to reach it by morning. And we did not know exactly where it was save that it was on the river. It would be the drekar which would identify where he and his men waited.

The further east we went the more we stayed close to the river. Here there were no roads. There were tracks and greenways used by the people who lived here. That made tracking easier. Beorn could tell that we were following Magnus from the tracks and droppings which we saw. He laughed at one point. "I could follow these by smell alone." He pointed to a tree. "One of them made water here and in yonder bush one of them had the shits. I can smell them."

That boded well for once Beorn had the scent in his nostrils he would not lose them. We slowed down for night was falling. And now we had another problem for there were many settlements dotted around this river. We managed to avoid most of them for we could smell their wood smoke but we needed to find somewhere to hide for the night while Beorn and Snorri found them.

There were a series of large loops in the river. There were many houses close to the water and I knew that they would use the loops to net fish. Snorri led us away from the river to a wooded area. A stream ran through it and, in the middle, there was a small clearing. We camped there but I kept a good watch while Snorri and Beorn headed back to the river and our quarry.

Now that we were closing in my men prepared themselves for war. Whetstones were used to sharpen swords, seaxes and spears. I sat with Cnut Cnutson and Haaken. Haaken was helping our youngest warrior. "Spit on the blade before you sharpen it. You get a better edge."

I picked up Cnut's shield. It had been an old one of his father's. His best shield lay buried with him and his sword. Cnut had been a rich warrior. Cnut Cnutson had a good shield and a good sword. "When we get back home have the smiths put a strip of metal around the edge of this shield. This can be a weapon too."

He nodded, "I saw some of those warriors from the east who fought at Ketil's Stad. Some of them had small shields with a spike in the middle."

Haaken shook his head, "They look good but they are not for us. You need a shield which covers most of your body and the spike can hurt your own warriors just as much as an enemy. It is a shield for a horseman and we fight with the good earth beneath our boots!"

I saw Cnut taking in Haaken's words. He was learning.

We were lying down to prepare for sleep when the scouts came back. "They are not far away. There is a cliff above the river. The river is just wide enough for a drekar to turn around and they have theirs moored beneath their camp."

"How many men do they have?"

"There are twenty oars on each side but I do not think they have enough crew to double oar them. We counted no more than fifty men and some of those look to have been wounded."

I asked the most important question, "Did you see Magnus?"

Snorri nodded, "Aye and he was storming around the camp like a bear woken from winter too early. We heard some of the words but not all. It seems he has lost the trust of the King. The Eorl who split from him refused to pay him. The men with Magnus are not happy either."

Viking Legend

Haaken said, "That is the trouble with being a mercenary. Without the pay, you expect what is there to fight for? We fight for Jarl Dragonheart. That is reward enough."

"Can we get there by morning?"

"We could but the men had travelled a long way in a short time, Jarl."

"Without a paymaster, there is no reason for him to stay. He may leave." I was desperate not to lose him again but my scouts knew the problems I was creating.

"He will not leave until daylight for the river is very narrow and it twists."

"All the more reason to get to his drekar, at least, before dawn. If we can disable his ship then we have him." I stood and walked around the edge of the camp. It gave me time to think and evaluate what they had said. I realised I was acting too hastily. The hot blood was racing around my head. I came to a decision. Snorri was right, the men were tired and they were not Ulfheonar. I would give them the night. "The Ulfheonar will go tonight and make sure the drekar cannot leave in the morning. Beorn, you bring the rest of the warriors. Be there when dawn breaks. We will wait on the eastern side."

Beorn nodded, "Aye Jarl."

There were just nine of us who loped off along the trail towards the camp of Magnus the Foresworn. If we could damage his drekar then it might dishearten his already demoralised men. I saw what my scouts had meant when we reached the river once more. The earth cliffs rose as high as eight men above a narrow and twisting river. A drekar could sail along it but not unless it was daylight. Snorri led us down to the river where there was a narrow trail. It looked to be a trail used by those fishing and hunting along the river. The brambles and other thorny bushes plucked at our cloaks and our mail. Although annoying it meant that our enemies would not be looking for us this way.

Snorri held up his hand and I went forward. He pointed to the stern of Magnus' drekar, **'Red Snake'**, which was moored to a tree some hundred or so paces from us. We moved slowly from then on. We moved aside the twisting and clinging bushes. We watched where we placed our feet. And all the time we kept an eye on the deck of the drekar. Unless Magnus was a complete fool there would be a deck watch. We had to kill them silently. With mail on our backs, we could not risk an attack from the river. We would need to slip over the side close to the tree to which it was moored.

Each of us had our shields across our backs so that we could use both hands. I drew my seax. When we were less than twenty paces from the drekar we stopped. I spied a warrior at the prow and one at the stern. The two appeared to be the only guards. Snorri was the silent killer. I pointed to the guard at the prow and Snorri nodded. He slithered along the path which was next to the drekar. I knew where he had gone and even I could not see him. I waved Vermund and Erik Ulfsson. I pointed to the stern watch. I gestured for the others to follow me and we took up a position halfway between the drekar

Viking Legend

and the camp which, from the noise, was just two hundred paces to the north of us in the woods.

If any relief came then we would have to eliminate them. We stared up the slope and then Erik tapped me on the shoulder. They had succeeded. We slipped down the slope and boarded the drekar. The two sentries had been silently slain. I went to the steering board while Haaken and Ulf cut the ropes which tied us to the shore. It was not a strong current but it still took us slowly into the middle of the narrow river. Snorri stood at the prow. He signalled when it was time to turn. We took the drekar through three loops. Snorri miscalculated or perhaps I was not as good as I thought I was for the drekar grounded. It was on the north bank. I took off the steering board and handed it to Haaken, "Hide this where we can find it later." The drekar was disabled and was going nowhere. We made our way back to wait for dawn and our men. We had Magnus now.

It took some time to make our way upstream for I had wanted the drekar well out of sight. I knew that the drekar would be missed. There would be a change of guards at some point. I needed to be as close to the camp then as I could. When we were a little way to the east of the camp I sent Snorri and Vermund to wait for Beorn and my warriors on the western side. I needed to cover both up and downstream.

They scurried along the river bank while we climbed through the trees to get a better view. Magnus had no guards out. He was confident. The camp was largely asleep but I saw small huddles of warriors sitting around fires and talking. I briefly contemplated taking my handful of me to slit a few throats but the risk of awakening the camp was too great. Haaken suddenly pointed and I saw that three warriors who had been talking stood and, gathering their goods, headed surreptitiously through the silent camp to the horse lines. They untied three horses and led them away to the north. They were deserting. Within moments they were gone from sight. There was disunity in the camp. When I looked I saw that the other two who had been talking saw the three leave. After a moment or two, they too rose and followed them. They chose two good horses and they left. Magnus was losing his men and his horses. It suddenly occurred to me that this might work to our advantage. He might see the loss of his drekar as the work of deserters rather than us.

The rest of the camp remained asleep. We waited in the cold dark forest. We were well hidden and remained unseen. Warriors rose to make water and returned to lie by their fires. The first hint of dawn had appeared in the east when I saw Magnus rise. He had the place closest to the dying embers of the fire. It had died down to a faint glow. He stood and stretched. He walked over to one of his men and kicked him. He spoke to him but the words were indistinct. The warrior walked down towards the river. I knew then that there would soon be a commotion. I did not need to wake the Ulfheonar. They were alert.

Magnus woke his other men and the camp came to life. A number of things happened at once. One of his men went to the horse lines and saw that there

Viking Legend

were gaps and the warrior who had gone to the river came back shouting, "The drekar has gone!"

. The warrior shouted from the horse lines. "Harold and his men are not here. There are horses missing!"

Magnus gave an animal-like roar "I will give him the blood eagle when I catch up with him. To arms! We go to find this traitor and my ship."

Men raced around gathering arms and helmets. I kept my eye on Magnus. I had to trust to Beorn and my younger warriors. I had said to be there when dawn broke and, as I watched the warband prepare to move, I felt its warmth on my back. I said, quietly, "Ready?"

"Aye Jarl." I only had six men with me but the seven of us were a force to be reckoned with. When we stood every eye would be upon us and it would allow the rest of my men to fall upon them.

I stood and shouted, "Magnus the Foresworn. Now is your day of reckoning. Prepare to die!"

Seven Ulfheonar standing up less than thirty paces from where you have slept must have terrified some of the warriors with Magnus. Our sudden appearance in their midst would have appeared as almost magical. Their hands went to their amulets for protection. Before anyone spoke Haaken gave a wolf howl and the others took it up. It would tell Beorn that we attacked.

Magnus laughed, "We are not children to be frightened by such a noise. There are only seven of you! Kill them!"

They hesitated and that gave me heart. I stepped forward and my men came with me. The warriors with Magnus took a step back. Were we wraiths? Were we sent from Hel to punish them? "Are you afraid? Shall we come to you?"

That appeared to enrage Magnus' oathsworn. There were ten of them all dressed in mail. They looked to be young warriors. Few had warrior bands. They had the mail but would they have the skill? They ran at us. As usual, they came directly for me. They wanted the honour of killing the Jarl with the magical sword. I did not mind for it allowed my warriors to attack freely. As one swung an axe at my head a second stabbed at me with his sword. I stepped forward and deflected the axe with my shield while fending off the sword. I pulled my head back and head-butted the axe man who fell at my feet. I brought the edge of my shield around to strike the man with the sword in the neck as he stumbled. I stabbed him in his middle and then hacked down across the neck of the axe man. My blow was so powerful that I severed his head and his helmet fell away.

I reached down and, picking it up by the hair, threw the head towards Magnus. The men around him recoiled as it bounced towards him. "One of your oathsworn has gone before you, Magnus! You will be next!"

Then I heard a roar as Snorri, Beorn and Vermund charged the rear of the enemy lines with my young warriors. There was a collective wail from Magnus' men. They were surrounded. I felt a blow coming towards me and I instinctively brought around Ragnar's Spirit. It blocked the blow from the

Viking Legend

side. I saw the young Viking's sword bend a little. "Spend gold on a better sword before you buy cheap mail!"

I punched at him with my shield. He was not expecting the blow and I winded him. He tried to swing his sword across my face but it was unbalanced. I dodged my head out of the way and then ran him through with my sword.

Magnus stared around him in horror at the change in his fortunes. He had been facing seven and now there was a warband. He was slippery and he was a coward. He and the last of his oathsworn abandoned his men and ran towards the last of the horses. The ones who had attacked us died to a man but they bought enough time for my prey to evade me. I watched as he galloped from my sight and I was helpless to do anything about it. The men we fought saw their leader flee. Many of them fled after them and others threw down their weapons. Some were slow to do so and were slain.

Haaken shook his head in disgust. "These are not Vikings! A Viking would fight until he died."

"They were badly led. They leave us with a problem."

"There is no problem. They deserve but one punishment; they die!"

"Perhaps not. I am inclined to show mercy."

The six Ulfheonar who stood around me could not believe my words. "Mercy!"

I took off my helmet to allow the cool morning air to clear my head, "We could kill them but if we disarm them, take their weapons and their treasure then what will they do?"

My men looked confused. "There is nothing for them to do. A man without a weapon will soon die."

"These men are warriors. They surrendered because they have been defeated by us twice. Some may even wish to join us."

"I would sooner fight alongside a snake!"

"I did not say I would take them on, Olaf. These men will survive and to do so they will have to take. When we go home King Eanred will reap his poor choice of leader for he will have outlaws and bandits here in the heart of his kingdom. His land will be cut in two and he will have to send his Eorls to rid his land of them. And others will hear of my mercy and may surrender rather than fight." In explaining what I would do I had convinced myself. "It is my decision but I also hope that by showing them mercy I can discover where he, Magnus the Foresworn will go. They may even wish to hunt their faithless leader."

Snorri, Beorn and Vermund joined me. "Take some of the men downstream and secure the drekar. We will sail her home."

"It is too small to accommodate all of our men and horses."

"I intend to ride home. It will be quicker. The voyage around the north of the island will take some time. Riding we can be home in three."

"Who will captain her?"

Viking Legend

I pointed to Snorri, "Snorri was a ship's boy for many years and Cnut Cnutson has some skill. They can take the drekar and the Ulfheonar will travel west."

Everyone nodded and when my men had gone to collect the drekar, Haaken took me to one side. "There is more to this than avoiding an arduous sea voyage. Tell me what is on your mind."

I pointed west. "I have been drawn eastwards by Magnus and the Norns have allowed him to escape again. There must be a reason for that. Why have they brought me back to the land from whence I was taken? I know that this is the land where the Queen whose torc we have lived. Aiden told me that she had a castle not far from here. We must have passed it when we came east. I would go back and see her home."

Haaken nodded his approval, "It is *wyrd*."

"But before we leave I will speak with the prisoners."

There were twenty-two of them. Some had wounds and most were young. There were two older warriors. One had a grey beard. "I am Jarl Dragonheart. Your fate lies in my hands. I could have you all executed where you stand."

I saw a resigned look from the young warriors but the older ones began to show signs of interest. "However, I may be disposed to mercy if you answer my questions and swear never to raid my lands again."

This time even the young warriors looked interested. "Firstly, I want to know where Magnus the Foresworn will go."

One of the young warriors shouted, "How can we know that, Jarl?"

The greybeard spat, "We know! And I will not die to protect him. We swore to fight for him and he abandoned us. An oath works two ways." His eyes stared into mine, "You swear we can have our lives?"

"You can have your lives. I so swear. I am Jarl Dragonheart and I am never foresworn."

"Then he will have ridden to Din Guardi, the King's home in the far north."

"Will he not risk punishment for losing so many warriors?"

"He and Eorl Aethelfrith argued about the attack on the hill. Magnus is rightly named Foresworn. He will blame the Eorl and the dead Count of Miklagård. The King likes Magnus; I know not why. He will believe his silken words."

I nodded and held my sword by the blade. "This is the sword which was touched by the gods, Ragnar's Spirit. Swear now that you will never attack my lands again and you can go free."

The greybeard said, "I would follow you Jarl Dragonheart. You are a real Viking."

I shook my head, "My men would not fight alongside you. Find a better life for yourselves. Do you now swear?"

They nodded and placed their hands on their seaxes and swore.

"Then leave this place and next time choose a better leader."

Viking Legend

One or two of the younger warriors tried to retrieve their shields but my men stood firm. They followed the greybeard. Within the time it took to sheathe a sword they had disappeared into the trees. I never saw them again. The land was empty and there were many places to hide.

Viking Legend
Chapter 9

The drekar, '***Red Snake***', was not in the best condition but Snorri was happy that it was seaworthy. He refitted the steering board while the young men and warriors boarded. It accommodated my men but only just. It did mean that they would be safe from attack for they were well crewed and there were two men on each oar. We watched them row down the twisting river. Snorri would be a cautious sailor but the voyage would bond the men. Next time they fought they would have more in common than just a leader. They would have faced the sea together.

We headed west. "We will cross the river downstream from the Roman Bridge. I would remain hidden from the Eorls who live hereabouts. By now the King will know that we are abroad and when Magnus arrives at his castle I have no doubt that he will direct the King's attention to us."

Haaken smiled, "It is why you wanted just the Ulfheonar."

I nodded, "We can hide if we have to. My young warriors did well. I would not have their lives thrown away because of me."

"Where is this place of the Queen?"

"It was called Stanwyck but Aiden seemed to think it was close to the Saxon village of Aldeborough. The fort is supposed to be within a short journey from the Roman Bridge and the river."

"Then we can be there by dark."

"I hope so."

I was silent as we rode east. There was just a handful of us but I trusted these warriors like no other men. They were like brothers to me. We were comfortable in our silence. I was thinking of the spirits and the way they worked. Since the day I had been born, they had gradually pulled the curtain back on my ancestors. I had learned more and more. I had travelled back in time. Yet I was now certain that it was the Norns who were making me what I was, a legend. My ancestor had been a warlord and his name still resonated. The more I discovered the more I wanted to know. In discovery lay adventure. I would now be trying to find someone who had lived before the Romans had first stepped onto this island. That was so long ago it made my head spin.

We used the trail which ran along the river. I scanned the water, as did Beorn, for the place where we could cross. The sun was dipping towards the west and Beorn raised his arm. "There Jarl; it looks shallow."

I nodded and he nudged his horse into the water. It came up to its withers but no higher and we all followed. Towards the middle of the river the current tugged a little but I dug my heels in and my horse surged up the other side and shook himself when we reached dry land. The bank looked flat and there were trees. I thought that we would be hidden from sight. "We will camp here and search for the fort tomorrow."

Viking Legend

We risked a fire for the cold river had chilled us. If there was to be a pursuit of us it would take some time to organise. We might be in danger during the coming days but this first night we would be safe.

Olaf Leather Neck sighed, "I could do with some beer."

Vermund snorted, "There you go. Always wanting something we don't have. Why not wish for a comfortable bed and two wenches to share it?"

Olaf sat up, "You have them?"

Vermund picked up a handful of grass and threw it at his friend, "Fool!"

The banter was a good sign. They were not worried about the dangers of roaming deep in the heart of enemy land. We had never yet met a Northumbrian we could not best.

Haaken lay down and stared up at the stars, "Like you, Jarl, I am intrigued but I know not what we seek or why."

"You accept that it will be better and quicker for us to ride home rather than sailing home."

"Aye."

"And the route we have chosen is the shortest."

"It seems that way."

"Then as there are few enemies between us and home I believe the Norns wish us to travel this way and who am I to go against their will? As for what we seek; that is a different question. I do not know but there will be something. When I was trapped deep in the Welsh hillside I could not have imagined that I would discover a sword. When we found the cave I could not have expected it to be a tomb. There will be something at this fort."

"You are right. And besides this is another great opportunity for a song from me. I have nearly finished the one about you with an arrow sticking from your throat."

"But that is not how it was!"

"I am the song teller. I write what I know will make people listen."

"But you write the stuff of legends and not what really happened."

"I was there, Jarl. I know what happened and you were saved by the gods!"

There was no arguing with him. I did not sleep well for my mind was beset by Magnus. He seemed destined to ever escape me. Perhaps I could let him go. He would die from someone else's hand, I knew that but at the back of my mind was the fear that he could hurt my family. I could not risk that.

We headed west until we came to the Roman Road. From Aiden's description, I knew that the fort lay somewhere alongside the road. I wondered how I would know it. I almost laughed, when an hour later I saw its ramparts rising like rolls of earth before me. I could not have mistaken it for anything other than what it was; an ancient monument to the ones who ruled this land before the Romans.

We reined in and Haaken shook his head, "Did men truly build this? It must have taken them lifetimes!"

There were concentric lines of ditches and mounds. A stream meandered along the lowest one. As we let our horses drink in the stream I saw that it had been cunningly made so that there was no one way in. Beorn pointed, "There is a gap, Jarl. I think there must have been a gate to enter at one time. I can see the holes in the ground where the posts stood."

Dismounting we led our horses through the gateway and along the ditch. The entrance to the next ring was further along. We kept climbing as we entered this cleverly designed fort. We found two other gates before we reached the top level. There we saw the deserted and ruined huts. People had lived here. There was a palisade which ran around the top. It looked as though it needed repair and the gates at either end had been thrown down. I saw a number of mounds. We went over to them.

"Think you one of these is the grave of the Queen?"

"I know not, Haaken. I doubt it, they are too small and mean. But I am not about to despoil the grave of a Queen." I turned, "Beorn, you and Erik hunt. We will explore this today and stay here."

As they went off Haaken said, "There is nothing here, Jarl."

I swept my arm around the huge interior. "You call this nothing? Have you seen anything as impressive in this land? Even the castle on the cliffs in On Walum was a hut compared to this. I would sleep within the rings and dream."

I knew I had not convinced him but I was Jarl and my heart told me to stay. In my heart, I agreed with Haaken. There would be nothing here for me to find. It was not until dusk came and the sun set that I finally finished my exploration. As dark storm clouds had been gathering during the day my men had repaired two of the huts by putting branches over the half-wrecked roofs. We ate well for Beorn and Erik had managed to hunt some game. Olaf still complained about the lack of beer but it was a fine meal, nonetheless. We had barely finished when the rain began. It didn't just fall, it cascaded like a waterfall. The temporary repairs did not hold it back and rivers ran along the floors of the huts but at least we were saved from the worst.

When the thunder began and the horses became frightened Beorn and Erik went to calm them. The storm increased in intensity and the lightning lit up the skies outside as though it was daylight. The thunder crashed so much that even Haaken became worried, "Jarl, we have offended Odin by coming here."

A bolt of lightning illuminated the interior of the hut and I smiled, "I have stood closer to the god's anger before now, Haaken. Should I draw my sword for Odin to strike it again?"

That made all of my oathsworn drop to their knees, "We beg you not, Jarl! We are not you! We would be burned to a cinder."

"Then fear not. We will not be hurt."

I was proved right but I knew not how. The storm abated but not for a long time and the rain eventually stopped. We managed to find dry patches inside the hut and we lay down. I slept well but I was not certain that my men did.

I dreamed.

I was an eagle flying high above the land and there were Roman horsemen below me. They were advancing to fight a mighty horde of wild half-naked warriors. They were outnumbered yet they advanced bravely. I

Viking Legend

saw that they had the standard of a dragon and it wailed as it moved. Their red horsehair plumes and cloaks over their metal byrnies made them look like a long snake. The sun reflected from their armour and their swords. When they struck the line of the barbarians it was like an axe striking a tree. They broke the line asunder. I saw a Roman chief fighting a barbarian. They fought long and hard. The barbarian fell dead but the Roman had been mortally wounded. When he handed his sword to another red-cloaked horseman I knew that he was dead. I watched as the Roman's oathsworn carried his body. They went to a secret entrance to a long barrow and removed stones. I saw them enter with his body and then emerge without it. They replaced the stone and covered the stones with soil. It was only then I saw that there were two women standing weeping with the warriors. The sky became black and I lost sight of them. I flew higher hoping to get above the darkness but it became blacker and blacker and then I felt a pain in my chest and when I looked I was no longer an eagle and I was falling. I was hurtling back to earth.

I opened my eyes and saw light coming through the holes in the roof. I was awake and it was daylight.

When I stepped from the hut I was struck by the devastation. The only two huts which remained upright were the two we had repaired. There were blackened marks on broken parts of the palisade showing where it had been struck by bolts from the gods. I stood at the broken gateway and saw that we were now in the middle of what looked like a collection of tarns or rivers. Had we slept where we had the previous night then we would have drowned. *Wyrd*!

My men joined me as they woke and they too were stuck by the devastation. Vermund shook his head, "It is dangerous to be with you, Jarl. The gods toy with you. We are mere mortals and we have no magic sword to protect us."

Haaken shook his head, "That is where you are wrong, Vermund. Last night I too was afeard and I should not have been Cnut was with Dragonheart when the sword was struck and he survived. When the Jarl fought to rescue Aiden, it was his enemies who were struck by the anger of the gods. Aiden and the Jarl were unharmed. So long as we are true to our jarl then we will be safe."

I laughed, "Haaken, do not make this into a saga I beg of you!"

He spread his arms, "I merely record what it is that happens to you, Jarl. I do not command their appearance."

We spent the morning packing and waiting for the waters to abate somewhat. It was noon when we attempted to leave. Our horses had to swim the stream we had walked across. The land was like our home. It was covered in tarns, meres and waters. Were it not for Beorn's skill we would have become lost but he led us unerringly out of the confusing muddle of puddles, water and mud. I was silent and distracted and I did not pay much attention to our surroundings. I trusted in Beorn's skill. My horse suddenly whinnied and

Viking Legend

it arrested my attention. I looked up and I recognised the land from my dream. "Hold!"

My men stopped and their hands went to their weapons. I pulled my horse's head around and rode up the slope to the jumble of rocks I saw on the skyline.

"Jarl! Where do you go? That is not the way home."

Haaken's voice sounded excited, "Peace, Beorn, do you not see. It is the work of the Norns!"

I knew where we were. We had found the place where the warrior had been buried. I recognised the entrance for the rain had washed away the covering of soil. Two huge stones stood like sentries guarding the entrance. The barrow had been like an upturned boat with rocks forming the side. I dismounted and dropped the reins of my horse. I took off my helmet out of respect as I walked into the tomb of the dead. I had not despoiled this tomb; that had been the work of the gods. I was intended to walk amongst them.

I recognised the bones of the warrior. They were close to the door. His armour had long rusted but I knew what it was. The horsehair had long disappeared as had his cloak but his skull looked to his left and there I saw the bones of someone smaller. Around the head was a small circle of gold studded with blue stones. I picked it from the skull and felt power race through me. A voice in my head told me what I already knew, this was the Queen I had sought. This was a Queen who lay with a dead Roman warrior.

I know not how long I stood there. I heard Haaken's voice, as though from a long distance, "Jarl, is this the Queen you sought?" I nodded dumbly. "How did you know it would be here?"

I turned and saw my awestruck oathsworn. "I dreamed it last night. This warrior led warriors and defeated a mighty host. He died and was laid here next to the Queen." I pointed to the jumble of bones which lay deeper in the barrow. "This is an ancient tomb. See there are many ancient dead. Take what you will for the gods have given this to us. Odin himself stripped back the top. We were meant to find it." They hesitated. "You know I am not foresworn and I tell you that we were meant to come here. I will take this circle of gold to Kara for it belongs with the torc."

They entered the long narrow tomb and began picking up the pieces of gold and jewelled stones which littered the floor. I held the golden crown. It had dirt upon it and the dust of the dead but its quality was unmistakable. I could almost feel the presence of the woman who had been dead for such a long time. Perhaps that was the power of the women in my family.

When the tomb had been cleared of all valuables Haaken asked. "Should we rebury the bones, Jarl?"

I shook my head, "The gods wanted them exposed and we will leave them. Soon nature will reclaim this barrow and it will be as though they never existed." I held up the crown, "Save for this and the sword and now they will be reunited."

Viking Legend

Haaken's mouth opened and closed as he took in the import of my words, "You mean the sword you found under the mountain?"

"I dreamt in the storm last night and I saw the sword in that warrior's hand." I pointed to the rotting armour. "He is here with the Queen. When we return to Cyninges-tūn I will ask Kara and Aiden if I have unravelled this riddle. In my heart, I believe I have."

We mounted our horses. Rain clouds rushed in once more and we fixed our cloaks over our shields. They needed protection as much as we did. We now left the line of the river and headed south and west. This was not a familiar country to us but the journey home would be easier for we would pass through shallow valleys which were not as exposed as the high moors. There would be woods and streams. If we rode hard we could reach Ulf's Water by dark but we had tarried too long at the tomb and we would make a more leisurely journey.

Each of my Ulfheonar had become much richer as a result of the gods exposing the tomb but I doubted that they would part with them. We all knew the power of objects which had lain in Mother Earth for so long. She imbued them with her power. Allied to that was the fact that the gods had given them to us. We had experienced something few mortals would ever know. We had almost come face to face with the gods. The storm, the lightning, the rain and the tomb all pointed in one direction; we had been directed thence and we had been chosen. We had been a special band before that day but after we were bound by more than an oath, by more than blood, we were bound by the threads of the Norns.

We left the road at dusk and headed down to a clearing by the river. It was the same river which passed Arne's Fort. It was comforting to know we were within a day of friends. Ketil's fort lay less than twenty miles away. We would be there by noon the next day easily. The rain had not ceased all day. I regretted that we had no shelter for the night. We used our riding cloaks to make a rough roof between the trees. It protected the fire and stopped the worst of the rain from falling on us. Despite the conditions none of us was downhearted. We had been when Magnus had escaped but, since that time, we had had luck on our side.

We still had some of the meat which Beorn had hunted and we used some of the river water, herbs from the banks and berries to make a stew. Hot food was always more satisfying. We had just finished it when one of the horses whinnied. Most warriors would have ignored it but not us. We all looked at each other and, without a word being spoken we prepared for danger.

Beorn stretched and said, loudly, "I will go and make water."

Haaken rose to head to the horse lines, "The horses have yet to be watered come with me, Erik."

I walked over to the fire to put another dried log upon it. As I bent down I used my sword to poke around the fire. I did not know where the attackers were but I knew that they would be watching. The other Ulfheonar all slipped a weapon into their hands as they eased themselves into the shadows. I reached down, ostensibly to move a branch to a better position but I was preparing a missile. The attack when it came was sudden but we were ready. I sensed a shadow from my left and I hurled the burning brand blindly in the direction of the shadow. I turned and saw the warrior clutch at his face which had been burned by the brand. I stabbed him in the stomach with my sword.

There were more than a dozen of them. I saw that the man I had slain had warrior bands and the hammer of Thor; he was Norse but the one who had been felled by Vermund was a Saxon. These were bandits. I drew my seax as two men rushed at me. One held an axe while the other had a long seax. I fended both weapons off with mine and then twisted both my wrists at the same time. The seax and the axe were knocked to the side and I swung my seax and sword horizontally at the two men. They ripped through the throats of the men. Erik was being assailed by three men. I brought my sword down on the back of the skull of the largest of the three. The shattered pieces of bone splattered the two warriors on either side. Erik slew one and I rammed my seax into the side of the third.

And then it was over. We had killed the bandits. Olaf Leather Neck had suffered a bad cut to his left arm. I watched as he bound a rag around his elbow to slow down the bleeding. When all danger had gone we would stitch it.

"Beorn search for any others." I kicked over the bodies of the three Erik and I had just killed. There was a Frank, a Dane and a Saxon. "Bandits and brigands."

Haaken nodded, "It is not to be wondered at. So many have been slain by our forces that some must have stayed hereabouts to prey on the weak. It is like those who attacked you close to Wolf Killer's home."

I nodded. I had had enough of this, "Then we put a bounty on them. We would do so if we were plagued by wolves. It is no different with dogs such as this. When we reach Cyninges-tūn I will announce that we pay five silver coins for the head of any bandit they find and bring to me."

Beorn came back an hour later. He was shaking his head, "There was a village yonder. They have been using it. None who lived there are alive but I found their bodies. They had used infants for sport and inflicted cruel wounds on all."

"Then tomorrow we bury them and we mark the place with the heads of these… these nithings!"

We kept a pair of us on watch all night in case any of the vermin had survived. We took the heads and their spears with us when Beorn led us to the village by the river. It was as he said. Some of the dead had been dead for a week. We made a communal barrow for them and adorned it with the heads of the bandits. We headed west with a sour taste in our mouths. All of our good feelings had evaporated with the discovery of the village of the dead.

Olaf's wound was stitched. It would heal well and it would not affect his ability to fight. Having lost Karl as a warrior I could ill afford to lose a second Ulfheonar.

Viking Legend

Ketil was still improving his defences when we rode in. He was surprised to see us. When we told him of Magnus' escape he shook his head angrily, "Why do the gods allow such men without honour to live and yet good warriors die."

"The gods always have a purpose but he will not escape justice for long. I know where he hides and he is running out of bolt holes."

Ketil was surprised, "You would risk Din Guardi?"

"If that is what it takes then aye."

"You are a determined man, Jarl."

"I am," I told him of the slain villagers.

Shaking his head, he said, "I wondered why they did not come to the safety of the fort when I sent out my messengers. I will keep a closer watch now."

"And there is a bounty on every head. We will rid the land of these vermin."

"We need no bounty."

Ketil had pride. I needed results. "Your young men need to be richer and this will encourage them."

The delay meant that we did not reach home for another day. Brigid and Kara had been worried when the young men had passed through on their way to Úlfarrston. I could not contain my excitement and I waved away their concern. "See what I have found!"

I put the small bejewelled crown on the table. Aiden picked it up. "Where did you find this?"

I told them of the hill fort and the storm. I told of my dream and then of how we had found the tomb. Kara nodded approvingly, "I believe you are right, father. The torc, the crown and the sword should be together. The three of them have a magical unity for none is superior to the other. This is most marvellous for our people. The spirits of the dead have moved from the tomb and reside here. I can feel them can you not too, Aiden?"

His eyes were wide with excitement, "Aye, I can. The power makes my fingers and flesh tingle." He looked at me, Jarl Dragonheart, I pray you to fetch the sword."

I went to the wall and brought down the rusted sword which was too badly corroded and decayed to be used as a weapon. I had wondered why I had been sent to find it. Now I knew. It was not as a sword that we needed it but as a link to the torc and the crown. I placed it carefully on the table. Aiden laid down the crown at the pommel end. Kara had fetched the torc and she laid it at the tip of the sword. I was no galdramenn but even I could feel the glow from the room.

Kara's eyes were bright. I thought she might burst into tears. She and Aiden held hands and closed their eyes. They both began to chant. I neither heard clearly nor understood the words they used. I put my arm around Brigid and my nursing son. We were both mesmerised as the two of them spoke to the spirit world. In my heart, I knew that this was a good thing but I could not help worrying a little. Should I have taken it from the tomb? Perhaps the

Viking Legend

attack in the woods had been a punishment. Even as I thought it I dismissed the idea. Had it been a punishment then we would have suffered and we had not.

They opened their eyes and turned to me. Kara spoke, "We have spoken with Mother and with your mother. This is a good omen. The spirit of the Queen was restless and all of nature was out of balance. The sword which was lost had been found and it cried out to be with the Queen once more. This will bring harmony to our land and the which the Queen formerly ruled."

"The Queen?"

"The Queen of this land which was once the home of the Brigante, Jarl."

Kara pointed at the sword which now looked different to me. "Aye, father and the sword were hers but it came from a land far away. The sword had a journey to reach this land. It is ancient. The blade is over a thousand years old."

Aiden nodded excitedly, "We saw the ones who held it and they stretched back in time."

I went to the three objects and placed my hands on them. They felt almost hot. "What do we do with them now?"

"They have come here for this is a holy place. The Water and the mountain protect us. They will also protect these three. We will have a chest made and it will be guarded, here in this hall. They will protect us for as long as we protect them." She looked at me seriously, "If our line fails then the last of our people should throw the chest into the deepest part of the Water and there Old Olaf and the spirit of our mother will guard it for eternity."

The import of her words was not lost on me. I had a responsibility now which was greater than that of a jarl to his people and his family. I had a responsibility for all those who had wielded the sword and ruled this land. I wondered if I was up to the challenge.

"When Wolf Killer returns then we must tell him of this momentous event."

"Aye father and the Ulfheonar, when they are all returned, must swear to protect them. They are the guardians of the sword and the treasures. The spirits spoke to us. Now we know why the numbers have diminished. The ones who follow you now are the only ones there will ever be. These are the last of the Ulfheonar and it is their destiny and yours to guard these treasures with your lives."

I saw Brigid's face it was a mixture of pride and horror. I had a greater responsibility now. She hugged our son tighter. I nodded, "Aye Brigid, our son is part of this too. Our world has changed this day and there is no going back."

Viking Legend
Chapter 10

It did not take long for my Ulfheonar to hear of my daughter's words. Poor Karl was distraught. The loss of his hand meant that he would not be a guardian of the treasures. He would no longer be an Ulfheonar. He might still be able to fight but he could never be that most special of warriors. It must have seemed like a death sentence to him. For the rest of the Ulfheonar, after the storm and the wrath of the gods, it was a further sign that they were special. I noticed that each of them went to Bjorn and had him make them each a smaller copy of the sword. Haaken told me that they had decided that amongst themselves. They would wear the miniature sword around their necks with the wolf pendant. I had given them the golden wolf but the gods had chosen them this time and they would be the guardians of the box as well as my oathsworn.

Bolli, the shipwright, carved the chest which would hold the magical objects from oak. He carved the bottom and the sides from a single piece. It came from the bole of a tree. He had used the tree to make the masts for our drekar. It had been very straight. He had retained the bottom part to carve a figurehead. This was as important a task as a figurehead. It took him and his apprentices many hours but they, like the rest of my people, felt honoured that we had been chosen by the gods for such an honour. While his apprentices hollowed out the middle he carved the lid. In honour of me, he carved a wolf on its top and then he added details which told the story of our people. The lightning touching the sword, and the sword itself were all incorporated. In the centre was a heart which also represented me. When his apprentices had hollowed out the middle he carved a dragon which would itself around the outside to add its protection. It was the dragon protecting the heart.

The completion of the chest coincided with the return of the drekar. It had been a successful raid and the Mercians who live south of Sigtrygg had filled our granaries and our treasure chests. The slaves were put to work in the mines. Bolli told my son and the others of the treasure as they returned up the greenway to Cyninges-tūn. They almost ran the last half mile to see the treasure. My son did not disappoint me. He too felt the weight of our ancestors on his shoulders and he faced up to the responsibility. He heard what my Ulfheonar had done and he swore to be as one with them.

The chest was handed over to Bjorn Bagsecgson. He used gold to make the lock and he forged strong iron plates for the corners. We held a feast on the day it was completed. Wolf Killer brought his men over too and we gathered in the centre of Cyninges-tūn. I had a table placed in the centre. Bjorn reverentially placed the magnificent chest on it. It had been made to accommodate the three objects and no more.

Kara placed the torc within and then Aiden the crown finally I took the sword and laid it upon them. There was total silence until the lid was closed. Bjorn locked it and handed one key to me and a second to Kara. They were

Viking Legend

both on leather thongs and everyone waited while we hung them around our necks. As soon as that was done everyone cheered and we began to celebrate. I cannot ever remember a more joyful feast. It was but a wooden box but it was a symbol that the gods and the spirits of the past had chosen our people for this honour.

While everyone else celebrated outside I retired to my hall with my family and my Ulfheonar. My men had drunk great quantities of ale but were not yet drunk. They were replete and out of deference to Brigid, Elfrida and Kara behaved impeccably. Ragnar was allowed to sit with us and he remained silent in the presence of so many great warriors.

I listened more than I spoke. I heard how my young warriors who were led perfectly by Asbjorn and Eystein had withstood a charge of the Mercian horse. They had used the same tactic we had done and stood their ground. Wolf Killer was impressed and determined to employ his own young warriors in the same way. I had to listen, again, while Haaken told the tale of the storm and the tomb. I could hear him developing the story to make it into a saga. It was at the end when Vermund let slip my decision to go to Din Guardi. As soon as the words were out I saw his face as it fell. It had been the ale. I smiled. I could not blame him. I had intended to tell them of my decision when the time was right.

"You would go into the heart of the enemy's lands and try to enter the impregnable castle of Din Guardi? Father, have you taken leave of your senses? Magnus is nothing! He is less than nothing. Let him rot far from here. Some other will end his worthless life."

I ignored his tone for he too had drunk a great deal and I smiled. I stood and went to the precious chest which stood on the table. I spoke quietly. "I have to go and it is because of this. Magnus knows our land. He was one of us. It will not take long for news of this to spread beyond our world. Even now I expect that it will be creeping ever east and south and north. It is in the nature of such things. And the tale will grow. It will not just be an old sword, a torc and a crown which reside within this oaken chest. It will be a chest filled with treasure. It will become two chests, three chests. It will be a treasure so big that it takes the crew of a drekar to carry it." I shook my head, "I am honoured that the gods have put this in my charge but I know the dangers it brings. Remember my sword? Remember how warriors came from all over the island to take it? They will come for this too. Wolf Killer you will need to make sure your borders are well protected. Ketil has the northern border secure but the centre of our land is empty. By going into Din Guardi and killing Magnus I send a message that my reach is long and that no one escapes my justice. Hakon the bald and Thorfinn Blue Scar respect us enough to steer clear of our land and they are our friends. They have told me that they would not want me as an enemy. Can you not see that I have to be ruthless and single-minded? The day I am not is the day that our enemies flood into this land."

Viking Legend

There was silence and Brigid squeezed my arm. Aiden said very quietly, "This is *wyrd*. I was reading some of the old parchments and one of your ancestors did as you did. He went to Din Guardi. He went with Myrddyn and they managed to kill a king, Morcant Bulc. It was said that Myrddyn flew into the castle. They escaped without being discovered."

Everyone in the hall was amazed save Kara who merely smiled as though she knew it all along. I said, quietly, "But of course, he did not fly in did he, Aiden? You have already told me that his magic lay in healing and speaking with the spirits."

Aiden nodded, "He found a secret way in."

My warriors leaned forward. They were all totally mesmerized by this revelation. "And does that way still exist?"

There was a pause. Aiden was as good a storyteller as Haaken. "No one knows precisely. I know where the entrance was but I know not if it still exists. It lay at the foot of the walls and was a cave which led to a tunnel. The tunnel ended at a door in the castle."

"Then we have a way in."

Beorn the Scout said, "Of course, there is another way. Magnus cannot stay inside the walls of Din Guardi forever. When he comes out we can kill him."

"That might take time."

"It would be worth it to take him without risk."

"We shall see but, in my experience, taking risks pleases the gods and brings results. Sitting on your backside invites danger."

I emptied my horn of beer. Brigid asked, quietly, "When do you go?"

"Before the land freezes over. I will be gone within ten days."

Haaken said firmly, "And the Ulfheonar will be with you."

In the end, it was longer than ten days for I wanted to be certain that Snorri and my warriors had managed to sail the '***Red Snake***' safely around the treacherous northern coasts. When they reached Cyninges-tūn I saw pride in their stride and on their faces. Most were young and were unused to a drekar and yet they had returned. I clasped Snorri's arm, "You have done well, my friend."

He waved his arm proudly around the young men. "They are good warriors, Jarl. A man could not ask for better."

"And the journey?"

"It was fine weather and that was good for the drekar is not the best. I have left it with Bolli for repairs although I would not like to go to sea in it."

"We do not need it. When I return I will discuss its future with Bolli."

Snorri was animated. "I spoke with him and he told me of this treasure. Is it true that you and the Ulfheonar seek Magnus yet?"

"I waited only for your return. I would have you stay and guard my family."

He shook his head, "No, Jarl. I have missed out on the visit of the gods. If you take the Ulfheonar then you will need Snorri. I will come whether you allow it or not! Kara has said the Ulfheonar are the guardians of the treasure and I am Ulfheonar."

I smiled. I could not imagine such a journey without my best scout. "Very well Snorri."

We made brief farewells and left before dawn for I wanted little fuss and a swift journey. As we rode Snorri told us of the news he had gathered. He had called in at the islands of Orkneyjar as well as Ljoðhús. He had heard that Alpín mac Echdach was expanding his land over the minor chiefs whose lands bordered his. He called himself a king now although his kingdom was smaller than the land I ruled. Our bloodying of his forces on Ljoðhús had stopped his seaward expansion.

"Thorfinn Blue Scar said that we ought to watch our northern borders. He has heard that this Scottish leader now wishes to punish us for aiding Thorfinn. He needs no ships to attack us. And it seems he has made peace with Eanred."

"So we have another new enemy. And I thought it would be the chest of treasure which would draw our enemies on."

Aiden had been listening. "Your name is so well known, Jarl as are your exploits, that it is hardly surprising that you draw enemies to us like moths to a flame."

I pondered those words as we headed for Ketil's fort. My rousing speech at the feast seemed hollow now. Was this vanity and pride which made me want to do something impossible? We reached there just after noon and we stopped for a meal and to speak with him. He and his were practising. More had helmets not than hitherto and some had mail. They looked more like warriors than armed farmers. Ketil had learned his lesson.

I drew him to one side. "I have heard that Alpín mac Echdach intends to come south and fight with us. I know not when but I suspect it will be next year. However, send a messenger to Arne and warn him. Keep a close watch on our northern borders and use riders to fetch help from the jarls to the south. You two are the ones who watch and protect our northern borders. Be vigilant."

"I will, Jarl Dragonheart. You go for Magnus?"!

"I do but keep that news close to your chest. It will be hard enough to do what we intend without every Northumbrian keeping watch for us. Let him think that I stay at home."

We left after resting the horses and pushed on north east. We crossed the old Roman Wall through one of the many gaps and camped, exhausted, after dark, in a valley in the huge forest that stretched for many miles across Northumbria. We had seen no one thus far and when the biting insects began to leave a mass of red welts and lumps we knew why. Aiden came to our aid. He had with him some of the herb which smelled of lemons. He used it to make a balm. When he put the leaves on the fire the insects shunned us and disappeared.

Viking Legend

Olaf Leather Neck nodded, "Now that is magic, Aiden. Did you learn that from the parchments of the wizard?"

"No, it was my own accidental discovery."

Haaken cocked his head to one side, "You of all people should know that there are no such things as accidents. You were meant to discover that."

The look on Aiden's face told me that he had not thought of that. He was becoming wiser each day and his skills seemed to be growing. We practised with swords and Aiden with his mind.

The next morning, we left for the last part of our journey. Although we were halfway to Din Guardi the next march would take two days. We had to negotiate the seemingly impenetrable forest which covered most of the land of Northumbria. Here there were no tracks and no greenways. There was no sign of a Roman Road. The only paths were those made by animals and they were of little use to us. Here we were reliant on Snorri and Beorn. Like Aiden, they had learned by experience and they knew that the moss on the trees grew on the side which faced north. They kept us going steadily north eastwards. It took some time but we saw neither man nor animals. We saw signs of deer and wild pigs but the only sound we heard was the buzzing of the insects which teemed in the forests. There were so many that they were almost like a cloud hanging over each warrior and horse. It was a relief to leave the insect-infested forest. Our faces needed no red cochineal to make them terrify people; we were all covered in red bites.

There was a new danger once we left the forest; people. The Roman Road lay ahead and we saw the smoke from the houses of those who farmed the land. There were also small settlements; many of them. Snorri and Beorn took to ranging far ahead and then returning to keep us hidden. In that way, we avoided any contact. We made a serpentine journey through the land. Sometimes we had to hide when parties of merchants and their guards headed north or travelled south. We could easily have taken them but our purpose was to be invisible, to remain hidden. We had to reach our destination unseen.

"Jarl there is a large settlement ahead and it has a palisade. It rises above the river in this valley."

Aiden looked at his map and pointed to a river. "The river was known to the Romans but not the fort."

"Is there a way around it?"

Snorri pointed to the north. "There is a wooded hill above it. We would need to cross it at night to avoid observation."

Vermund said, "That all adds time, Jarl."

"But it keeps us hidden."

Haaken snorted, "Have you a woman waiting for you back in Cyninges-tūn that you wish to hurry home?"

The others laughed, "Snorri, find us somewhere safe to lie up until dark."

"There is somewhere just this side of the town. It will mean we cannot have a fire and we will have to be silent but it will shorten our journey this night."

Viking Legend

The first mile was fraught with danger as we skirted the road and twisted and turned to avoid farms. When we saw the trees, we knew that we would be safer. Once again there was no trail and we disappeared into the wood which lined the lower slopes of this rocky outcrop. We climbed until we came to a bare area. We could not be seen from below for we were hidden by the trees and it was unlikely we would be discovered. Even so, we set sentries.

I sat with Aiden as he used charcoal and a piece of sheepskin. "What is it that you do?"

"The charts I have at home are largely of the sea. We need to know what the land is like too. I have marked the castle and the forest through which we travelled. When I return I will make a new chart with the places we have passed. When you and I are long dust then Ragnar's and Gryffydd's children will rule the land and they will use these charts to keep the land safe from our enemies. It is my legacy to them."

As I lay down to rest I reflected on his words. He was speaking of our mortality. I did not want to leave this world just yet. I wanted to see both my new son and grandson grow. I wanted to avoid the mistakes I had made with Wolf Killer so that Gryffydd would be an even greater leader than his brother. I wondered about my decision to make this quest. Perhaps everyone had been right and it was a mistake. I fell asleep dreaming of my son and grandson grown. I woke feeling troubled for when my new son and grandson were grown I did not see myself. I just saw Wolf Killer and Brigid. Where was I?

I had no time to ponder my dream for we had to leave and travel through the night. The journey in the dark was on foot and we led our mounts. The bare hillside was covered with treacherously placed stones which could have skittered down the hillside to alert the farmers and we could have fallen to a rocky death. It was safer to walk than to ride. It was a slow journey but it was safe for we remained hidden.

When dawn came I saw that we had descended closer to the coast. The early morning light showed a brief flash in the distance. It was the sea. We were closing with our quarry. We mounted and our scouts left us. When they rode back in it was with more bad news, "There is an even larger town and fort. It nestles in the loop of a river. We will have to turn north to avoid it. Luckily there is another wood and we can hide within it."

Aiden said, "This river has a name, the Aln. We are not far from the sea and our destination. King Eanred must have built these forts and castles recently for they are not on the ancient maps."

It was as we moved through the trees that I realised we would not have enough supplies to get home. The delays meant we had taken a day longer to reach Din Guardi than I had planned. That would mean we would have to spend an extra day scouting out the castle and finding the secret entrance. We would run out of food within a day of killing Magnus. I would have to deal with that in due course. I learned that you dealt with one problem at a time. First, we had to get to the castle. Then find the entrance. And all of that was before we could even think about killing Magnus.

Viking Legend

It was dark by the time we were close enough to the coast to smell the sea. We halted while Snorri and Beorn rode to find this citadel. Now that we were close we looked to our weapons and armour. We would not be fighting yet but we needed to be ready to do so instantly. We had not used our swords and they were sharp but we slid them in and out of scabbards and tightened the straps on our shields. It was pitch black when the two scouts rode in.

"It is four miles or so away. It is a formidable stronghold, Jarl. I have seen nothing like it save Alt Clut."

"Is there somewhere closer to camp?"

Beorn nodded, "There are two possible hiding places. One is a small rise about five hundred paces from the castle and the other is by the sea. It is two hundred paces from the castle."

Haaken asked, "Is that not too close?"

"It is in a wood and it is bordered on one side by dunes and by a trackway on the other. The trackway does not go through the woods which look to be thick."

They all looked at me. It was my decision. I wanted to be as close to the castle as we could be. "We use the wood."

We led our horses the last mile or so. They were well-trained and silent animals. The most dangerous part was crossing the trackway although it was unlikely we would be seen for it was dark. As we crossed the road I saw the castle looming up to the left of us. It was inspiringly high. Snorri and Beorn scouted the woods while we selected somewhere to camp. There was no water but our skins were full. We would have to husband our supplies. We took off our shields and used them to make a small barrier down the side facing the sea. It stopped sand from being blown into our camp and protected us from the wind. Asbjorn, Eystein and Olaf Leather Neck went to the roadside of the woods to make traps and trips. We would be warned of any intruder. Snorri and Beorn returned. "There is no one close by. The beach is on the other side of the woods less than fifty paces from us."

"How long until dawn?"

"We have two hours, no more, Jarl."

"Vermund and Erik, finish the camp while we inspect the castle."

Aiden had told us that he believed there had been an entrance from the beach which had allowed the wizard to enter. That had been almost two hundred years earlier. Was it still there? There was just one way to find out. We headed along the beach. To my dismay, I saw that the tide was only just on its way out. Would the base of the castle be underwater? I had taken the tide into my plans. The Norns had!

There was no moon and we waded through the surf to the rocks at the base of the castle walls. Snorri and Beorn had strung bows in case a sentry saw us. If they did then all would be lost. We had to remain hidden. Thankfully the noise of the surf on the rocks hid any noise we might have made. I could not see anything which looked like an entrance. The castle walls rose high and smooth before us. Weed clung to parts and I could see no entrance. Aiden climbed to the castle walls and began to move rocks from the top of what looked like a slide of stones. I thought that it was a forlorn hope but we all went to help him. We made a human chain and moved them down to the lower rocks. I saw patches of sand appear. The sea was receding. Asbjorn and Eystein placed them randomly at the bottom of the stones closer to the sea. It would not do to have an eagle-eyed sentry see order amidst nature's confusion. Suddenly Aiden stopped and lay down. A rogue wave broke upon our backs and soaked us but Aiden kept his position even though he was inundated. As the wave receded he kept staring and reaching down.

He rose and waved us down. He said nothing as he led us back to the camp. I was desperate to find out what he had learned but I knew him well enough to wait. I saw that his decision was a wise one as the first light of dawn appeared over the sea. We reached the camp and stood around our galdramenn. All of us were chilled and wet from our soaking but each of us was desperate to know his news.

"Well?"

"I think I have found a cave of some description. The water which surged over me went down and did not return. I think I have found the cave. We will need to continue our work tomorrow and, possibly the day after."

"But the tide."

"It will be later tomorrow. We will have most of the night to complete our task. We just have to be prepared to get wet."

I nodded. "We will pair up to watch. Aiden and I will take the first watch for I would speak more with him."

When we were the only ones awake I asked him more about what he had read. "I think there is a cave beneath the castle, a tunnel and a door at the far end. The fact that the stones have covered it makes me think it might still be a secret from those within the walls."

"And if not?"

"Then you and your warriors will have to fight your way in."

"And Magnus may well escape. He has done so before." I thought about this. "I will have to have three of my men watching the front gate. Snorri, Beorn and Erik are the best horsemen. If he tries to flee then they will need to follow him."

I saw a curiously self-satisfied expression on Aiden's face. "What do you know?"

"Know? Nothing? Believe, ah that is a different question. It is good that you make a plan in case things go awry but I believe that we will gain access to the castle. I am not certain if we will manage to kill Magnus. After all King Eanred will have his oathsworn in the castle. If the gods wish us to find Magnus and punish him then the King and his guards will not be a problem."

"And where will the King be? Where will Magnus be?"

"Tomorrow I will put on plain clothes and be an Irish healer looking for work in the village by the castle. It will give me the opportunity to wander the huts and speak to the people. I can also inspect the castle without attracting attention. I am certain that there will be no work for me and I will head south once more. They will think nothing of it."

"It seems a huge risk. Is it warranted?"

"I do not think it is a risk. I am too slight for a warrior." He smiled, "And too pretty! Unlike you warriors, I have neither a beard nor scars. No one would take me for a Viking. I can play the part of an Irishman for I am one. I speak Saxon with an Irish lilt. This is a remote part of the land and I doubt that they have many healers hereabouts. Those they do have will serve the King."

What he said made sense, "Take no risks. You are precious to all of our family."

"As you are to me. I would give my life for any one of you. I am honoured to be part of your family." The way he said the words suggested a deeper meaning. I thought nothing of it at the time for I was preoccupied. My mind went back to Din Guardi. The castle was far bigger than I could have expected. How many were in the garrison? Was I about to sacrifice my men for nothing? Aiden's peaceful face, which studied me still, made me relax. If he was not worried then I was not.

We woke our reliefs and snuggled down to sleep. I was awakened at noon. "Aiden left a while ago. He said you knew where he was going."

Haaken's statement sounded remarkably like a question to me. "He knows what he is about. Trust the galdramenn. He has never let us down yet. Have we seen any danger?"

"No. The trackway is heavily used but the ones who are heading north seem keen to get into the castle while those going south move swiftly too. They pass by this wood without a glance." I nodded, I was satisfied. "It is a formidable castle. I have never seen one with so much stone; at least not since Miklagård."

"It is impressive and explains why Eanred hides away here. Even King Egbert would struggle to winkle him out of this hole."

"Have you thought beyond breaking into this castle then?"

"We find Magnus and kill him and then we leave."

Haaken laughed and then shook his head. "And that sounds so simple. Where will he be? How many guards will Eanred have? How many men remain with Magnus?"

I gave him the knowing smile Aiden gave me, "Have a little faith, Haaken. The spirits and the gods are on our side. Do you think they wish Magnus to live?"

"I know not but they keep allowing him to escape us."

"And each time he does we find something of greater import. The torc we received from Thorfinn. The treasure for the tomb. Are you not curious about what we may find here if he escapes us again? We are being set puzzles and riddles. The Norns are testing us. We could refuse the tests and then we would spend the rest of our lives wondering, what if. We are meant to be on this journey. Do you wish for a dull life?"

He shook his head and laughed, "That is unlikely so long as I follow you."

Viking Legend

I had set my oldest friend a riddle and he spent the rest of the afternoon pondering my words. I became restless as the sun dipped in the west. I went to the woods which fringed the trackway. The last people from the road south were hurrying to reach the safety of the town walls before dark. Where was Aiden? I had almost given up when I heard his distinctive whistle as he strolled down the road. There was something wrong I could tell from his gait.

I hissed, "Snorri, Beorn." They appeared at my side as though by magic. Aiden approaches and I fear trouble. Have your blades ready."

I knew not what danger came our way but we would be ready. Aiden had warned us by whistling. If there was no danger he would have approached silently and entered the woods already. Aiden passed me and dropped to one knee as though he had something wrong with his boot. "Three men follow me."

He stood, almost without a pause. I turned to my two scouts; held up three fingers and then drew my hand across my throat. The sun dipped behind the hills opposite and the trackway became much darker. I saw, however, the three men who followed Aiden. None were warriors and they looked like cutthroats. As they passed us I waved my arm for my two men to follow. I glanced to my right along the trackway and was relieved that I could not see the castle. I moved silently behind them. I needed them to be killed without a sound. I spoke to them, quietly, in Saxon. "Friend, did you drop this?"

I held out my right hand as though something was in it. My seax was behind my back. The proffered right hand would allay their fears. They all turned and their hands went to their own weapons. Behind them, I saw Aiden slip into the woods.

I shook my head and stepped back as though I was affronted, "If it is not your coin then I will keep it but there is no need for knives."

"Where did you come from?" The leader spoke suspiciously. In the dark, my black cloak and armour disguised what I was.

I used my right hand to point to the castle but looked at them all the time. "From the town."

They moved purposefully towards me. "You lie for we did not see you."

"You watch everyone in the town?"

They were now close enough to see my mail. The leader said, "You are a warrior, where is your weapon."

I saw, out of the corner of my eye Beorn and Snorri move like cats and I jabbed forward with my seax and ripped it across his throat. "Here!" Before the other two could do anything Beorn and Snorri had slain them. I grabbed the body of the man I had killed and dragged him into the woods. We pulled them as close to the camp as we could. "Snorri, clear away any traces."

Haaken and the rest of my men appeared as did Aiden. He shook his head, "I am sorry, Jarl Dragonheart. It seems I am too good a healer or an actor. I was paid in silver for my work and these three, who had been watching me all day, followed me. When they said nothing to the sentries at the gate then I knew they were robbers. They would have taken my silver."

"They are dead now."

Snorri reappeared, "I have cleared all signs that there was a struggle. The blood must have gone on their clothes for I saw no sign on the track."

"Come and tell us all."

He sat down and took, from his bag, a cheese and some smoked fish. "I thought this would improve your mood!"

Olaf said, "Some ale would make me wish to marry you."

"You are too ugly and, besides, I could not carry any." He handed around his purchases. "There is a garrison of twenty men. Magnus has but five warriors with him. I know not what happened to the rest. It seems he is not popular in the town either. They all know of him. He rarely leaves the castle but when he does he has his oathsworn with him. They strut around the town as though they own it. The King has a hall on the first floor of the castle. Below that it is his guard room and the kitchens are next to them. There is a cellar but they rarely use it because they have had much damage from the sea. I could not discover where Magnus stays but I would guess the north tower."

Haaken shook his head. I could see he thought this had been too easy. "How did you discover all this? Did you not make them suspicious?"

"I was healing and I never asked a question, at least not directly. When I said it was a magnificent castle they could not wait to tell me about it. They volunteered all of the information. I confirmed some by saying things like, '*I expect the King has many fine visitors*'. that was when they told me about Magnus. They could not wait to give me the details of his behaviour. They were disappointed when I said I could not stay the night. I said that I had to replenish my stocks of medicines and that was best done under moonlight. They believed me. They expect me to return in the morning."

I, too, was relieved. "When we do break-in we can expect most of the garrison to be asleep. That will make our task easier. We just have to get by the guard room and find this north tower."

Aiden looked up at the sky. "We had best search for this entrance. I do not think we will need to watch for Magnus to make an escape. The gate is barred from dusk until dawn. He would have to fight his way out."

We left Olaf to guard the horses. He was not happy about the task. We found it easier to make our way to the rocks even though the water was higher. We knew where we were going this time. The tide was on the way out but we had much work to do. Aiden and Snorri clambered to the top of the pile of fallen stones. The receding waters had brought more stones down and aided our efforts. The gods were on our side. Asbjorn and Eystein were up to their chests in the swirling black water. It would get easier but until the tide receded further they would have to suffer a soaking. I braced myself against the slippery rocks as Vermund passed the stones to me. Soon we got into a rhythm. My back began to ache as the monotonous regular action sapped my energy. The cold sea did not help either. I was reassured that it was working when I glanced to the beach and saw that my two men of iron were only

Viking Legend

ankle-deep in water and there was a large pile of stones gathered around their feet.

A huge wave struck and suddenly Aiden and Snorri disappeared as the waves sucked the stones from where they were working. Beorn, Vermund and I were swept from our feet and I found myself flailing in the sea. A huge hand hoisted me up and I looked into Asbjorn's grinning face.

Aiden! I scrambled up the slippery rocks. I could see a large hole at the top. Beorn beat me to the top and he pushed half of his body through the hole. I began passing stones down to Vermund once more. There was an entrance but it was too small yet. Beorn turned grinning and held up two thumbs; it was our sign that all was well. He passed two more stones down to me and then he too disappeared into the hole. I crawled up and wriggled through the gap. I turned to Vermund who had followed me. "Keep clearing the hole. We need it to be big enough for our bigger warriors too."

I found myself in the dark cave. I could see nothing. I heard Aiden's voice close by. "Snorri has gone ahead. Come. Keep a hand on the side wall and watch for your head on the roof."

The wall had weed upon it and it felt slimy. The sand beneath our feet seemed to suck us down but we moved down the dark, Stygian tunnel. My eyes actually became accustomed to the dark. I could see the white of Aiden's hand on the wall. Once I discerned that then I could make out his body. The cave turned a little and then rose. The sand no longer sucked at our feet and the walls became less slimy. When I felt rock beneath my feet I knew we were close to the end of the tunnel. Was there an entrance ahead or was this just another legend of Myrddyn? I almost bumped into Snorri and Aiden.

Snorri stepped towards me. He put his mouth to my ear and spoke quietly. "There is a door. It is made of wood but it seems rotten." He held up a splinter of rotting wood. Had this been the hull of a ship then it would have sunk.

My eyes grew accustomed to the dark and I saw shapes. Aiden ran his hands all over the wooden door. Seemingly satisfied he turned and waved us outside. It was easier going back for there it was now lighter towards the entrance as my men worked to widen the cave mouth. We stayed just inside the entrance. I thought we could risk speaking there.

"There is a keyhole in the door but it is so corroded and rusted that I do not think the lock works anymore. The gate is so rotten that it will not take much to break in."

"We will go back to the camp and dry off. The tide will be going out for some time. We will return before dawn and wait inside the tunnel. That way we can take kindling and make a fire. We will see if we can break in."

We made our way back to the camp and I explained my plan to them all. Haaken said, "But when the tide comes in we will drown."

I shook my head. "The cave near the door felt dry, or drier anyway. The cave rises. I think it may flood but only with a spring tide. It is a risk but we have come this far and I would risk all. If you want to wait with the horses...."

Haaken laughed, "I will be there, fear not."

Viking Legend

"Asbjorn you and Eystein will stay with the horses. If you hear the alarm then bring them to the beach."

"And if the tide is in?"

"Then bring them to the main gate. We will have to force that if the cave is underwater. Once we are in I will send Aiden back to you so that you know we have not perished."

We hurriedly ate and then prepared for war. Aiden carried the kindling and the flint. We made our way back to the cave. The entrance was quite clear now that the tide had gone further out. "We will have to disguise this. Pile stones up so that the entrance is hidden."

It took a short time and we left just the gap which Aiden had fallen through. As we put the last stone in place I realised that this could be our tomb. If had miscalculated and the tide came up to the door the Jarl Dragonheart and the Ulfheonar would drown in a cave beneath Din Guardi.

Viking Legend
Chapter 11

It was easier walking down the cave the second time for the water was almost gone and we now knew the height of the tunnel. When we found the door we took our cloaks off and placed them at the bottom and sides of the opening so that no light would be seen. This time we would light a fire and see what we needed to do. Aiden made the fire and after a few abortive attempts, he managed to light the dry kindling we had so carefully carried. We had brought plenty. When the cave was illuminated it felt as though we had gone to Hel. The green slime shone bizarrely brightly in the light from the fire. The black stones looked like precious jet but it was the red seaweed which looked the most terrifying. It looked like a man's intestines hanging from the rocks. I did not like the place.

Shaking my head, I went to the door. We had come here for a purpose. I examined, along with Aiden, the door. I pointed to the hinges. They were the weak point. He nodded. I pointed to the entrance. Reluctantly he took his leave of us. I wanted him safe when we assaulted the castle. I could not afford to worry about him. I pointed to the hinges and Haaken began to work at the rotten wood. I went to the lock and did the same. The wood was rotten but it still took time for we did it silently. I used my seax to tease the rotten shards away. I could have made a quicker job had I hacked but I was not certain what lay on the other side. The only sounds we made would have been mistaken for rats or mice. Haaken was relieved by Erik who soon removed the wood from around one rotten hinge. He had finished with the second one before I had managed to cut away the wood from around the lock. There was nothing holding the door in place now save the dust, dirt and weed.

Beorn tapped me on the shoulder and pointed. I looked around and I could both hear and see the sea. We had been working for hours and the tide was coming in. We stopped work on the door. Everything we could do we had done. We needed night to fall before we entered the citadel. If the tide was coming in then it was close to dawn or perhaps even morning already. The fact that we could not see light from the entrance was a worry. How would we escape our self-made tomb?

All of us faced the entrance to the cave. We could hear the sea coming closer and closer. With no sun and stars, we had no sense of time. The white-foamed water would surge and then recede. It would splash and splatter the roof. Then it would come in again. We had all day to wait. When we had endured the horror of being beneath the sea the tide would go out and we would be safe for a while. By that time it would be night and we could risk going into the castle. We had a long wait ahead of us. We could have slept but no one was going to lie down when the tide was rising.

A huge wave rushed in and threatened to engulf us. I realised the fire was dying and so I put another piece of wood on it. I did not want to be here in the dark. I wanted to be able to see the water and not feel it slowly rise to choke

Viking Legend

and drown me. I found it hard to breathe and it seemed to me that the roof and the walls were closer to me than they had been before. Beorn was at the end and when he shuffled closer to Snorri who had a higher perch then I knew the water had reached him. I pointed to the rocks and we climbed. It was only a pace higher than where we had been but it felt safer. We were not tightly packed around the fire and the wooden door. Suppose the water doused the fire? That would be a nightmare to end all nightmares. We were, for the moment, safe from the waters but how much higher would it come? I looked at the door and saw a mark halfway up. At some time it had almost filled the cave.

The sea reached far higher than I had anticipated. Haaken said, quietly, "We are beneath the sea." He looked up, "Above us are the waves crashing on the shore. It is as though we are dead and yet we live and we breathe. Have any other men done as we have done? Have they lived beneath the sea without drowning?" He nodded to me, "You are right, Jarl Dragonheart, we were meant to come here. This has been another test and we shall pass."

Erik said, "We will drown."

Haaken said, "No we will not. I feel it in my bones. We have to be strong and endure."

Beorn and Snorri had their feet underwater for what seemed an age but then the sea slowly started to recede. We could not cheer but the relief on all of our faces was evident for all to see. When we descended to our original positions I smiled for the first time in a long time. To celebrate we ate our rations and drank half of our precious water. We took it in turns to doze. We knew not what hour it was or how long we were there. I slept fitfully. When I awoke I walked to the end of the tunnel to peer out to the cave entrance. The sand was damp, and the rocks were slippery but the tide was well on its way out. I saw the light at the end of the tunnel. I had no way of seeing the height of the sun but I knew we were on the shorter end of our vigil. I returned to the others and I waited. And then the fire began to die. We had used all the wood. It was like watching the end of the world as the flames died and then the embers glowed. The glow became bluer and bluer until finally there was just a warm patch of ash which we could feel.

I whispered to Beorn, "See if it is dusk yet."

He appeared to be away an age but when he returned he put his mouth to my ear and said. "It is coming on to dark. The tide is on its way in."

I put on my helmet. I felt the others doing the same. It was so dark that we could only see shadows moving in the Stygian black. It was time. Soon we would be leaving this place which was neither land nor sea and re-entering the world of man. It was as though we had been to Hel and were now returning to the land of the living. Hoping my words would not be heard I said, as quietly as I could. "It is time. Let us move the door and find Magnus. We have to be out of here before the tide returns."

I put the blade of my seax in the hole close to the corroded lock. I gave Haaken and Olaf time to do the same at the hinges and then I began to lever out the rotten door. It sprang open so quickly that it took us all by surprise. Beyond the door appeared empty but there was a faint glow which showed us that this was a corridor. Snorri handed me my shield and I stepped through the door. I held my seax for the corridor was narrow.

I moved cautiously down listening all the time for sounds and sniffing for any smells which would alert me to guards. Snorri would have been better suited to the task but I was Jarl and this was my idea. I would shoulder the risks. We passed through a large chamber. The walls were covered in slime and I guessed that this had been the cellar they had abandoned. The floor began to rise and I saw a step. I turned a corner after ten paces and spied a door. There was a glow around which showed that there was a light behind it. I waited until my men bunched up behind me and then put my left hand on the metal ring that would allow us entry. I pushed and nothing happened. I turned it and, reluctantly, it turned. I heard a slight creak which told me that it had not been turned for some time. I pushed again and nothing happened. Was it locked? Then I pulled and there was a movement. This time the creak seemed as loud as a crack of thunder. I swung open the door quickly and stepped into the kitchen.

Two thralls were asleep before the fire which they used for cooking. One of them began to stretch. I waved Haaken and Snorri. With two blows from their hands, the men were laid unconscious. I saw a door at the far end. That could be the guard's quarters. When my men were all within I detailed Erik to remain in the kitchen. We needed an escape route. Erik would ensure that we would have a warning if the guards emerged before we had finished. Aiden's information said that we needed to be in the North tower. I opened the kitchen door. It looked to be the corridor used by the servants to serve the King. There were two rush brands burning in holders along the corridor. I took one. After four paces I found a stair to the right and I began to ascend. It was well-worn and confirmed this was the route the servants took. It had a faint smell of decaying food. If Aiden's information was correct then there would be the King's hall and quarters on the floor above. I sheathed my seax and drew Ragnar's Spirit as I climbed. I place the rush brand in a holder on the wall of the stairs.

There was no doorway at the top but I saw the glow of rush brands again. Ahead of me was a large door. It was a grand door and I deduced it was the entrance to the King's Hall and his quarters which would be beyond. I peered around and saw a guard whose back was to me. He appeared to be alone. My shield was around my back and I advanced silently with my left hand out. I should have kept my seax but it was too late to change hands now. He must have heard something, for he half-turned. I pushed my hand into his mouth as I forced my sword up through his ribs and into his heart. Snorri was with me in an instant and he helped me to lower the body to the floor.

I pointed to Asbjorn, Eystein and Vermund and indicated that they should keep watch. I was now disorientated. Which way was north? Snorri pointed to my right. I headed down the corridor and found another door. It was on the side opposite the King's quarters. I guessed it would lead either to the battlements or a tower. I opened it and found myself on the castle walls. Ten paces to my left was a tower; it had to be the North Tower. I stepped back inside and waved Snorri and Beorn forward. They would have to deal with any sentries. I gave them a few moments and then stepped out into the cold night air. From the skies, I guessed that dawn was not far away and we needed to move swiftly. Leaving my two scouts to deal with any sentries I led Finni, Ulf and Haaken towards the door of the tower. Even as I approached I could hear words being spoken within. They were harsh words too. That meant they were awake. If Aiden's information was correct then soon I would be face-to-face with my enemy.

I reached the door and listened. The words sounded muffled which indicated to me that there was another door within. Even though I had but four men behind me I took the chance and, after swinging my shield around, I pulled open the door. I was relieved to see a second door and a stair leading up to the battlements. The voices were still muffled but I could hear occasional words. 'Honour…. wolf…. hiding…women.' Then there was a blow and the sound of something falling.

I nodded to my men and, opening the door entered the chamber. It was a large guard room with pallets along the side. Magnus stood facing one of his men and he had his sword drawn. We must have terrified them for they just stared. There were six of them and three had weapons drawn. Ignoring the others, I swung my sword at Magnus. He rolled out of the way and, as he rose grabbed his shield.

"Now I will have that fine sword, Old Man!" He hissed. I could see the hatred in his eyes.

As I brought my shield tighter around me I knew I had to keep a cool head for Magnus had shown that he had improved his skills since he had sailed with me. He swung his sword at me. We both restricted because the ceiling was low and we had to use horizontal rather than vertical strokes. In the confined space you were as likely to be struck by a friend as a foe. I caught the blow on my shield and stabbed forward. It was not a favourite stroke of mine for the edge was better than the tip. He tried to move away from the blow but I scored a hit against his side.

"The gods do not like a faithless warrior who is foresworn. You have no honour Magnus the Foresworn and you have nowhere else to go. You cannot run from here!"

He had grown somewhat since he had followed me and he ran at me with his shield. As I went back I found myself falling over the dead body of one of his warriors. Magnus saw his chance and stabbed down with his sword. Even though I was falling I brought my shield around and, at the same time swung my sword. The shield stopped the blow and my sword bit into his calf. He stabbed at Finni's back and, pushing him out of his way, ran from the room. I was on my feet instantly. He would not escape again. I opened the door expecting a sudden sword strike but there was none. I saw a puddle of blood on the stairs leading to the top of the tower and I ran up.

Here he would have the advantage for the maker of the castle had ensured that the stairs favoured the defender. I almost slipped on the blood at one point but Magnus did not wait for me. I saw the door at the top was open and I sprang through it. A seax was hurled at me, striking me on the side of the helmet. It made my ears and head ring. I swung my sword blindly and was rewarded when I heard it strike his shield.

I turned and saw him. The glow in the sky behind him told me that it would soon be dawn. He rushed at me and swung his sword hard at me. I pivoted on one leg so that he spun around. I now had my back to the sea and the breaking day. I hacked at his head and he blocked it with his shield. He tried to stab me in the middle but my shield was too fast. I could see more blood oozing from his wounds and his left leg was trailing behind. I could see his face as he calculated what he needed to do to defeat me. He put his shield before him and ran at me. With the battlements less than a pace behind me he intended to knock me over the top of the tower. I dropped to my knee and as he hit me I rammed my sword into his groin and pushed up with my shield. His momentum and my left arm forced him over the tower. I rose and looked over. There, on the rocks, lay his spread-eagled body. The surf broke over it even as I watched.

I saw the white line which was growing on the horizon. Dawn! Glancing down I saw that the tide was well on its way in.

I ran down the stairs to find my men waiting on the battlements. I did not say a word but ran towards the door leading down. My three men looked relieved to see me. I pointed to the stairs leading to the kitchen and they headed down. We had done it. I was just about to follow them when the door of the King's chamber opened and a warrior stood there. He gave a sudden shout and although he was slain by Haaken the damage was done and the alarm had been sounded.

I followed my three warriors down the stairs and along the corridor. As I reached the kitchen I saw the door to the guard room begin to open and two warriors stepped out. They were quickly slain but I could hear the commotion behind.

"Snorri, Beorn, throw the tables onto the fire, Ulf and Finni get down the cave to the horses."

I joined my four warriors who were standing at the doorway stopping numbers from coming through. Haaken was the last one down from the upper floors.

"Hurry, Jarl they are following."

"Fire the door."

The three of them began to use the burning wood from the kitchen fire to set the door alight. Snorri must have found some pig fat for he threw a liquid on the door and it flared up. The room was well alight and there was thick black smoke. I yelled, "All of you leave!" I stepped through the door into the guard room. There were three dead warriors and the rest were hurriedly arming. I smashed my shield into the mouth of one warrior while I hacked across the thigh of a second. A third tried to spear me but I moved my head out of the way and brought my shield up into his mouth. He fell too and I stepped back. The door was partially blocked and it would take time for them to clear it.

I made my way through the smoke to the cave and felt the cool air hit me as soon as I clambered through. The water was already up to my knees. Ulf and Finni had enlarged the entrance which made it easier for me to get through. Olaf and Aiden were on the horses. Olaf suddenly shouted, "Down Jarl!"

I threw myself onto the slippery, weed-covered rocks into the sea as Olaf hurled a spear. I turned and saw the warrior who had been about to skewer me with the spear in his chest. Smoke was now billowing from the tunnel. I clambered to my feet and made my way to the horses. They were up to their withers in the sea but they were clear of the rocks. I ran as arrows began to fall from the battlements.

Aiden held my reins for me, "It seems we have outstayed our welcome, Jarl. Is the traitor dead?"

I pointed to the rocks just behind me. The light was now enough to see his crumpled body. "He fell from the battlements. He is dead."

I turned to Finni. "Magnus stabbed you. Are your hurt?"

He spat. "It broke the mail but not the leather. It will repair."

Snorri and Beorn were already putting their heels to their horses and we galloped south along the beach. We would rejoin the trackway south once we had passed the woods in which we had sheltered. I turned and saw that Asbjorn and Eystein were behind me. Looking ahead I saw that all of my men had survived. The gods approved of what we had done. Behind us, I saw smoke coming from the castle. Pursuit would be delayed. They had a fire to extinguish. I doubted that the hidden entrance would remain. It had served its purpose. The past had come to our aid once more.

The sun rose but it was hard to tell for the sky was filled with dark, threatening skies. Snorri led us towards the trackway. We had already decided to head south until we found a road or track west. I hoped that the fire would mean we would escape before the King could send horsemen for us. He would be loath to do so for he had only twenty men to guard him and some had died. There would, however, be riders sent to warn his people of the wolves from the north loose in his fold. It would take at least two days to escape his land and three to reach safety. The foreboding-looking clouds suggested wet weather and that would slow us down.

It was a wet and soggy journey. We had to travel away from the roads using tracks and greenways. We even used animal trails to avoid being seen. We did not stop and yet we had covered but a short distance. It was lucky that our horses had had three days of grass and rest. They were refreshed and kept going. The rain was relentless and we were soaked. We reached the large

Viking Legend

walled town by the small river in the late afternoon. We had passed it during the night the last time. We could not risk that this time. If the King sent riders then we might be trapped between two sets of warriors.

"Snorri, find a route around this place."

"Aye Jarl, but it will not be easy. The sun, if we could see it, will soon be setting and we will be seen against the light. When the forest ends we will be in open country."

"We have to risk it."

We rode as low in the saddle as we could. There was no way of avoiding the skyline for the slopes were dangerously steep in places. Unfortunately, there was no way for us to remain hidden the whole way. Each time I saw the town walls appear to our left then I knew that we, too, could be seen. We pushed as hard as we could but eventually, Snorri reined in. "Jarl, we must rest these beasts or we shall be walking home and not riding."

"You are right. Let us find somewhere secluded."

We had to settle for the river banks as we had emptied our water skins. It was like the whole venture, a huge risk for it was hard to find somewhere which could not be observed. The valley sides peered down on the small bubbling river and movement would be easily seen. We settled for dried food and we did not move beyond the trees which surrounded us. If we were seen then so be it but my men were right. We had to stop.

Olaf Leather Neck held up a piece of his mail. It was beginning to rust. "This will take much work from Bjorn. And we did not profit from our journey."

Haaken shook his head, "Not gained? Our names will become known far and wide. A handful of us entered the mightiest castle in Northumbria unseen; we killed a traitor and escaped unscathed! We have gained more than any warriors before us. We have lived beneath the sea and survived! The last two moons have given me more stories, sagas and songs than I can ever recall. We have riches which cannot be measured."

He put a smile on the faces of my warriors. He was right. Our names would live forever. This would not just be the story of Jarl Dragonheart but all of the others: Haaken One Eye, Snorri the Silent, Beorn the Scout, Finni the Dreamer, Erik Ulfsson, Asbjorn the Strong, Eystein the Rock, Olaf Leather Neck, Ulf Olafson and Vermund Thorirson.

We slept but took it in turn to keep watch. I do not think any warrior other than my Ulfheonar could have endured what they had done and survived so well. It felt as though they thrived on hardship. It was as well that we did use sentries. Just before dawn, Erik came to wake me. He said nothing but pointed to the road and made the sign for danger. I rose and we quickly woke the others. Snorri and Beorn slipped silently away. We still had the saddles on our horses and we donned our helmets and strapped our shields onto our backs. If someone was seeking us they would not smell smoke and they would not find where we had left the road. Then I heard the bark of a dog. That was how they had found us. They were hunting us with hounds.

Viking Legend

Snorri appeared first. He held up his two hands twice. He made the sign for horsemen. Beorn came from the other direction and held up his two hands once and made the sign for men on foot. I pointed to the river and they nodded their agreement. We led our horses to the water to avoid being seen. The water was icy but after the sea, it was not as bad as it might have been. The bubbling, shallow river was not wide and we had the choice of using either bank or continuing along our wet road. The noise of the water hid the sounds of our horses' hooves. Then I heard the dogs and they were much closer.

Beorn was at the rear. We had travelled another thirty paces when he gave a low whistle. I turned and saw that he was mounted. We all climbed into our saddles. Beorn had seen that they were close enough now that walking did not help. I dug my heels into the flanks of my horse and he trotted. I felt a blow in my back and, when I turned I saw archers standing in the river. I had been hit by an arrow but my shield and wolf skin had saved me. The river would aid us no longer. "Make for the road!"

The banks were not high but they were slippery. I imagined that in winter this area would flood easily. Once our horse's hooves reached the grass beyond the bank we went a little faster but it was muddy. That was why I had chosen the road. We could make much better time. As we mounted the road I saw shadows appearing from the first light of dawn. I kicked on and saw, ahead, that the road rose. I had an idea. I overtook my men and shouted instructions to each of them as I passed. When I reached the brow of the hill I reined in and turned. I wanted my horse to get his breath back. The others joined me.

"When I give the word then we charge in two lines."

"But Jarl, we do not fight on horses."

"I know Finni and that will surprise them. Remember those Welsh warriors we fought. Do not try to thrust but use a sweeping blow and grip your horse with your knees. It would be embarrassing if we fell on our arses as the Welshmen did. I want to frighten them by doing the unexpected." Vikings never fought on the back of a horse. I did not intend to fight as such but a charge down the hill would scatter them.

"Aye."

"Aiden string your bow and wait here. Aim at any who gets close to us. We charge. Disperse them and then return hither."

It was a risk. With no stirrups and no cantle on our saddles, there was nothing to keep us on our horses' backs. I gambled that the horsemen who followed us would have spears and they would suffer the same fate as the men of Gwynedd.

When they were just fifty paces from us I shouted, "Charge!"

Even as we charged I could see the archers, men with dogs and warriors on foot struggling to move up the slippery river banks and across the muddy grass our horses' hooves had churned up. We needed a decisive strike or we would be surrounded and outnumbered. In the last moments before we met I saw that they wore no mail and carried no shields. They had spears only. I also gambled that our armour would hold.

The first horseman I met was on my right and his spear came for my middle. I was holding my reins in my left hand but I punched the wood of the spear as it touched my mail. At the same time, I swung my sword horizontally towards his face. He was terrified. I could see it in his eyes and he leaned back. He tumbled from his horse and his fall made the next two horsemen swerve. I wheeled to my right and coming up behind the two men who had swerved I rode between them. I hacked into the side of the one to my right and then pulled my horse to the left. My mount was a bigger horse than that of the Saxon and the rider lost his balance and crashed into a tree where he lay still.

"Fall back!"

I turned and pulled my horse up. All of my men had disengaged save Erik who was fighting two men. He was using his hand to hold one spear whilst fending off the second with his sword. The men on foot were less than forty paces from him. I galloped towards them. I did not pull my horse up but barged into the side of the man whose spear was held by Erik. I brought my sword over and it bit into his arm. He jerked his reins around and fled as Erik leaned over and punched the other rider in the side of the head with the pommel of his sword. We both headed up the hill. I heard and felt the arrows as they thudded into our backs. Once again our shields protected us. My men had waited for me. "Do not wait! Ride!"

I counted them all again and they were still together but Finni and Ulf looked to be nursing wounds. When time allowed Aiden would have to tend to them. I glanced over my shoulder. We could see further now for dawn had broken and there was a thin grey light. We had broken their will to fight. We rode until I could see that the horses were lathered. We stopped at a stream and let them drink.

"Aiden see to Finni and Ulf. Any other wounds?"

"No Jarl, but I will have more respect for horsemen from now on. I know not how they fight. I was afraid to make a full swing in case I fell."

"Aye Haaken, and I will have mail mittens next time." Erik held up his hand. His palm was scored bloody by the spearhead he had grasped.

"There is another here, Aiden."

I took off my helmet and my cloak. When I removed my shield I saw that there were four arrows lodged in it. I like to think my mail would have stopped them but with arrows, you could never be too sure. Snorri came over. "We were lucky there, Jarl."

"I know. We will give thanks to the Allfather when we reach our home."

He pointed to the left. "There is a Roman Bridge yonder, as I recall and a deserted Roman Fort. It is the Tinea. The Roman Wall runs past it."

"When our horses are rested we will walk them and cross the bridge by the river. As soon as you and Beorn are able, scout it out for us. We could fight our way over but I would prefer not to."

Viking Legend

He nodded, "The threads of the Norns were as thin as gossamer this time, Jarl. Our close encounter with death has made me think about the future and my sons."

I laughed, "You have no sons. You need a woman first."

He smiled, "That is what I was thinking too."

Ulf and Finni both had wounds to their legs. They had been unlucky. The spears which had caught them had struck below their byrnies. The men who had struck the blows had been thrown from their horses. Had we not been on horses then Ulf and Finni would have struggled.

There were just four huts at the bridge but the people ran into them when we appeared. We left them in peace and crossed to the south of the river. The road rose a little and we camped on the ridge which ran east to west. I did not want to risk the men in the hut becoming brave.

As I lay down beneath the canopy of trees I realised that we had not managed a night of sleep since we had left our home. Although I fell asleep quickly I was thinking that I was too old for nights spent sleeping on hard ground and riding all day. Perhaps the discomfort made me dream or the place where we camped; we were close to a Roman Horse fort and the dead warrior was ever in my thoughts.

I was in a high tower. As I looked out to sea I saw that it was the same tower from which Magnus had fallen. I leaned out to look for his body and I fell. I tumbled down but I did not reach the ground. I found myself astride a jet-black steed. He turned his head away from the sea and began galloping through the air. I spied the hill fort close to the dead Queen's tomb and I saw a ring of Roman soldiers standing around. The horse was gone and I was with them. I heard drumming and thundering. I looked and saw wild barbarians riding towards us. They had chariots and fierce horses. I tried to run but it felt as though I was caught in the sand in the cave. I could not move. I heard Kara's urgent voice, 'Run!'

I woke.

Something had startled me. I stood and listened. I could hear, across the valley, horses.

"Wake! There are horsemen!"

I wondered why Finni had not heard them. I would discover that later. I donned my shield and helmet and sprang on the back of my mount. Although it was dark I could see lights in the huts by the river and horsemen were galloping across the bridge. I now knew why I had chosen the ridge. The spirits had guided us to a safer place. Snorri led us west. We had a lead and our enemies would tire their horses climbing the ridge but they had numbers on their side and our horses had been pushed to the limit. Aiden began dropping back.

"Do you have a problem, Aiden?"

"No Jarl, but I had Bjorn make me some of these." He held out his hand. There were iron nails twisted together. I had seen them before. Aiden had read of them in Miklagård. Whichever way they landed a prong stuck up. Horses hated them. They were not as effective when used on soft ground but we were on the Roman Road. In addition, it was night which would make them hard to see.

I nodded and we slowed down, allowing the others to overtake us. Asbjorn opened his mouth to speak. "There is no problem. Keep riding."

With no one behind us, I allowed Aiden to drop back. He began to sow the metal spikes on the Roman Road as though they were seeds. He emptied his bag and then caught up with me. We could not see the effect but we heard it a short while later. Horses whinnied and screamed. We heard riders shouting. It would slow them up and, more importantly, it would make them wary. Once dawn came it would be a different story for they would be able to see that the road was clear.

As we hurried to catch the others I asked. "How far do we have to ride?"

He pointed to the Roman mile markers, "Almost forty Roman miles."

"That is too far."

He nodded, "We will have to stop. The question is, will they?"

I did not know the numbers who followed us but I assumed that they knew ours and knew whom they chased. They were not fools. If they thought they could not defeat us then they would not pursue us. There was little point in speculating. Dawn would bring the answer.

Daylight brought us close to the small deserted settlement of Alston high on the east moors. It had been Saxon but the people there had long fled. It was the point at which we would begin to descend towards our own land. I called, "Hold. We must rest the horses. They need water." I turned to Aiden. "You are the lightest, ride back a ways and count them."

I dismounted and, taking off my helmet poured water in it for my horse to drink. Asbjorn asked, "What magic did Aiden employ?"

"No magic. Just twisted nails that spiked the horses who followed."

He shook his head, "It is magic that he knows such things."

Aiden rode up. "They are a mile and a half away."

Erik went to mount his horse. "Hold Erik. They have the hill to climb. I want them to hurry thinking that we are done. They will hurt their horses. The longer we rest the further we can go. If they fail to water their horses then they will be creating problems for them later." I turned to Aiden. "Are they together or strung out?"

"They are strung out. The ones without mail lead and they stretch for half a mile. There are thirty of them."

"Then we are outnumbered."

"Aye, Finni, but not by many. The next time we stop it will be to ambush the leading riders and whittle down their numbers." I remembered that it had been Finni on watch. "Why did you not hear the riders?"

He shook his head, "Sorry Jarl, I had the shits and I had gone into the woods. I heard them but I could not risk shouting. Sorry."

I laughed. It could have been any of us, "Do not worry. The spirits watched over us. Now mount. We ride."

Viking Legend

We could see them just half a mile away and they were hurrying to reach us. We cantered down the slope. Our horses had had water and a little rest. They were sweating but their gait was regular. They were good for some miles yet. As we rode down the road which crossed the open bare moors I tried to picture the land ahead. Soon, within ten miles or so we would enter woodland. No one had maintained the road and there were places to ambush them. Finni and Ulf would have a problem because of their wounds but they had bows as did Aiden. We could now hear the hooves thundering behind us. Perhaps it was my imagination but they seemed to be gaining. I glanced around and saw that they were now in a single file. The first ten had outrun their comrades. It was not by much. It gave me a glimmer of hope. It was little enough but it would have to do. Warriors used whatever advantage they could get.

I saw, in the distance, the ruined and deserted Saxon church at Melmerby. That would be the place. "Turn at the church and wait. I will drop back and they will follow me. Use your bows and kill the riders who follow me."

It was a risk for I intended to drop back as though my horse was failing. I leaned forward and spoke to Badger. "You shall have a short rest but when I command, then obey!" I rubbed his ear and his mane. He whinnied as though he understood. I knew that, behind me, the riders would take heart thinking I was trying to get the last few steps from my horse.

I glanced repeatedly over my shoulder. It would add to the illusion that I was panicking. The others had disappeared down the road and I saw the church just four hundred paces from me. As I turned around I saw that the leading two riders were now less than thirty paces from me. The next ten were bunched up together. I passed the church and I resisted the temptation to look to the right. My men would be there, in position. I could hear the Saxon horses labouring behind me. They had not been rested. I turned and saw the sweat and their lathered mouths. They were dead on their feet. I saw the others were almost at the church.

I drew my sword and wheeled my horse around. The two men were taken aback. Their spears were still lowered as I rode towards them. I had no need for speed. They were going at full tilt. I ignored the one on my left. His spear was nowhere near me. I brought my sword at head height and the rider to my right decapitated himself by riding into it. I wheeled my horse around, taking in the fact that the next band had been ambushed already. The first rider tried to turn but his horse could not manage it. He slipped on the cobbles and the rider was thrown. His helmet fell from his head and his spear shattered. I wheeled around and, as he stood, brought my sword down across his unprotected skull.

I kept riding west and soon my men joined me. Haaken laughed, "That will slow them up."

"Aye, but will it stop them?"

They did close with us but more slowly now. They would catch us and this time we had no tricks left up our sleeves. When I saw the standard fluttering from Ketil's fort I began to believe that we had a chance. Eystein shouted,

Viking Legend

"They are gaining, Jarl and my horse is becoming lame! I will turn and try to slow them down."

"No! You need not make the sacrifice. We all slow down. Ride at Eystein's pace."

"But they will catch us!"

"Aye Finni. Either we all live or we all die. We did not live beneath the sea for us to desert a brother when danger threatens. If it is meant to be that we have our last stand here then we will do so together and we will take as many of them with us as we can."

We dropped down the valley to the small bridge over the river. It would be on the other side where we would struggle as we tried to climb the hill to the gate. They would cut us down within sight of safety. I would halt there and we would fight on foot. That way we would give a good account of ourselves.

As we crossed the bridge I heard them close behind. They must have realised that they had us. The last two hundred paces would be too far. "On my command turn, dismount and fight them."

"Aye Jarl!"

"Turn!"

I had my sword out as we turned. We would not charge them we would stand and fight. I dismounted and watched as they formed two lines to charge across the bridge between the stands of trees which grew close to the river. Aiden held the horses and we made a shield wall with me in the centre. We would sell our lives dearly. They were just forty paces from us when Ketil's men suddenly attacked from the two Saxon flanks. Their bows and slingshots rained death and then his warriors rushed up to hack and slaughter the Saxon horsemen. None reached us. We were spectators as my eastern jarl and his men ended the threat. The ten horsemen at the back turned and fled. The rest were butchered. We had made it. We had reached safety.

Viking Legend
Chapter 12

We stayed with Ketil for more than a day. Our horses needed resting and, although we had only been away for a few days I was keen to know if there was danger from the north. We also needed time for Aiden to see to the wounds suffered by Ulf and Finni.

"Have you seen anything of this Scottish warlord?"

"Not yet Jarl but Arne has told me that he has seen a ship of the Scots sailing down his river. Perhaps it was a scout."

My Ulfheonar were with me when I spoke with Ketil and Haaken said, "When Bolli has repaired '**Red Snake**' we could give it to him. We need her not and it would be fitting for Magnus, after all of his treachery, to help us protect our northern border."

"That is a good idea. But there is no sign of an army yet?"

Ketil hesitated and then said, "Those who live to the north have been more vigilant. They say that they have seen signs of men but seen none. There are the remains of fire and footprints but no army. Perhaps they are scouts too. I know not if it is Scots or Northumbrians."

I smiled. Ketil was still young and had much to learn. "Snorri here will tell you how scouts can ghost unseen through the land. Keep a good watch as you did when you spied us in trouble."

"I will. The trouble is, Jarl, that soon we will be gathering in the crops for the winter and culling the animals we do not need."

I pointed beyond his walls to the valley below. "We no longer get rid of healthy animals during the harsh winters. We kill only the old and the ones who are sickly. Have your people bring their spare animals there. You and your warriors can watch over them and if you are attacked you can take them within your walls and laugh off a siege. If the Scots come do not try to fight them. You do not have enough warriors. You hole up here and send riders to me. It worked the last time and we now have more horses than we did."

"I will. That is a good suggestion Jarl. Preserved meat is never as good as fresh."

"And send a rider to Arne and tell him to be vigilant. I will visit him before the month is out."

"But you have spent the year outside your home!"

I nodded, "You are now a Jarl and you, too, will have to make sacrifices for your people. There are responsibilities as well as rights to your title."

"I am learning that. It is not all glory is it Jarl Dragonheart?"

When we left we rode hard. Pausing only to speak with those at Ulf's Water to warn them of the danger of the Scots we reached our home in one day.

This time there was no welcome for us. We arrived unexpectedly from the north. Our gates were open. The only time we now closed them was at night and the ones who watched the gates were the old men who played with dice or

Viking Legend

nine men's morris. We had had peace around my home for many years now. As we emerged from the forest they jumped to their feet to grab weapons. Had we been an enemy then they would have been skewered by arrows before they could have reached for anything. I would need to address that. This was not the time.

"Welcome, Jarl Dragonheart. Is the traitor gone?"

"He is dead."

Haaken leaned forward, "And when we next feast, listen to the tale of how Jarl Dragonheart and his Ulfheonar hid beneath the sea, crept unseen in the King's castle, passed his guards, slew the traitor and escaped with barely a scratch!"

Erik shook his head and looked ruefully at his hand, "He gives away the tale and yet does not do it justice!"

As we rode through the gates Haaken sniffed, "I give them a taste to interest them."

Brigid was rocking my son to sleep as I dismounted. Kara came over and kissed me and then Aiden. She smiled, "I told Brigid that you would return and return quickly."

Suddenly the dream returned to me, "You saw the dream. You were there."

She nodded, "My mind had been troubled and I used some of the potion Aiden discovered in Myrddyn's writings. I dreamed and I saw the horsemen coming. I have followed you through your mind," she smiled coyly, "and Aiden's."

I looked at him, "You did not tell me you had dreamed."

He looked to be irritated with Kara for some reason, "I dream all the time Jarl, you know that. I too saw the danger when we were close to the Tinea but you alerted the men and my words were unnecessary."

"The spirits protect us. I would have you tell me all, Aiden. There should be no secrets between us. Had I not awoken we might all have been captured or slain."

He and Kara looked shamefaced, "You are right Jarl."

Brigid had laid my sleeping son down and now she ran to me and threw her arms around me. "You are home." She kissed me and then stepped back with a furrowed brow. "And you stink! What is that smell?"

Kara laughed as did Aiden and the awkward moment was gone. I smiled, "We spent a night beneath the sea!"

I saw Haaken nod, "That is a good line, Jarl. I shall use it."

Brigid's eyes widened, "Beneath the sea? And yet you walk as though alive."

"I will tell you all when I am cleansed." I waved Uhtric over, "Have Einar Long Thumb take you to the sweat hut. I would have you light it for me and tell Einar to wait to take Brigid and me over."

"Aye Jarl."

I looked at Brigid, "And you can have a thrall watch our son."

Viking Legend

Kara said, "No, father, I will look after my little brother and Aiden can tell me your adventures. The dream world is like looking through a fog. He can give me clarity."

Brigid and I sat in the sweat hut and I could see the blood, sweat, dirt and salt run from my body. I had to immerse myself in the Water twice before I felt clean enough to be able to speak. Brigid used a beautiful bone comb she had made to untangle my matted mane and beard. She had placed rosemary and thyme branches on the fire and it was a pleasant aroma which filled the hut. Her combing was soothing. When her naked breasts touched my back I felt aroused. I had to force myself to think of other things.

"Our son prospers? He sleeps well and he grows?"

"He eats as though he is twins! But he is a good child. He sleeps all night and he does not cry over much. Your daughter has been a treasure. She helps me to care for him. She is much taken with him. She has a maternal look about her." She leaned around and said, "Not that I ask for help. I can look after our child!"

"I know and it is good for Kara will never have children."

It was silent save for the sound of the teeth of the comb in my hair. "Why do you say that? She is young enough to bear and her hips show that she would not find it hard as some women do. She has that rosy glow which shows she yearns to be a mother."

I shook my head, "She is dedicated to her magic. She is a volva and she believes that she will lose her power if she conceives." I laughed, "A child could never happen. It is sad I know but there it is. *Wyrd*."

She leaned close to me and spoke in my ear. The smell of aromatic herbs drifted into my nose as her soft skin touched my naked back. "You of all people know that you can never know what is possible. Even the priests in our church father children. It is natural for they are men too. It does not take away their power."

I pulled her round to my lap and kissed her, "They are priests and have no power. However, I do so leave your combing and come here."

She giggled, "Jarl!"

I could no longer keep my thoughts from her.

Kara had not been idle and when we returned she had food ready. While Brigid fed our son, I spoke with Kara. "There is danger, my daughter. The Scots are planning something. I fear it will be in the next month or so."

She nodded, "I have sensed danger but I was distracted for my thoughts were on you, Aiden and the Ulfheonar. I will dream again. Perhaps Aiden and I will use the sweat hut as it is still lit. We can use the potion I used. With two of us together then the power is increased."

"Good. But I will send for men from Sigtrygg, my son and my other jarls. I want an army gathering here."

"But it is harvest time."

"I will leave enough to harvest but this is a time for the women to bear the brunt of the work. We will bring the thralls from the mines and they can help.

Viking Legend

They can mine in the winter. Now we need the gathering of the crop. I intend to move north within ten days. Even that may be too long a time." I emptied the horn of ale. I had missed beer whilst on the road. "In fact, I will send Asbjorn and Eystein with the crew of *'Odin's Breath'*. They can march tomorrow and reinforce Arne. I will send a rider to Windar's Mere and tell Windar to send men to aid his son."

"Windar has been ill."

"So long as he lives he is Jarl. He will aid his son."

Kara and Aiden seemed keen to leave for the sweat hut as soon as the meal was finished. In fact, Brigid and I were still eating when they left. Aiden said, "We need to dream, Jarl. You prepare the warriors and we prepare the magic. These Scots are barbarians and have forgotten the old ways. They follow the White Christ now. We will use the power of the land against them."

When they had gone Brigid admonished me, "You people should know that there is but one God. I fear for your soul. I hope to be in heaven but you will be in hell."

I shook my head. It had been Aiden who had upset her and yet I bore the brunt of her tongue. "I will be in Valhalla with the warriors who have gone before me. You are a good woman and the Allfather will welcome you there. I am not afraid. He will forgive your whim."

Her nostrils flared and her eyes widened, "It is not a whim! I believe!"

I remained calm, "And yet you have seen much magic since you have come here."

"I have seen God at work."

I laughed, "God uses Vikings? Your holy men fear and despise us. I would not say that to them."

She smiled, "I am sorry. There is much here I do not understand. Deidre and Macha have told me that I can still be a Christian and live here because, at heart, all those who live in this valley are good."

"More than that, my love, all of the people who live in my land from Sigtrygg in the south to Arne in the north are good people. We are kind, in our own ways but we are independent."

"You could be king you know."

"And what would that gain me? A title that someone would wish to take. I do not wish for power." I smiled, "Did not your White Christ refuse to become all-powerful when your devil tempted him?"

Her mouth opened, "You know the words of the Holy Book?"

"I know the stories. Some of them are good tales. When we voyage Aiden sometimes tells them to us. Your White Christ sounds like he would have been a good leader but for his placid nature. A warrior does not turn the other cheek. He fights for what he has." I pointed to Gryffydd asleep in the corner. "Would you not kill to protect our son?"

I knew I had a victory when she remained silent. It was rare that I had the last word in any argument. I was so pleased that I broached the jug of wine which had come from Coen's latest trade with Vasconia.

Viking Legend

I rose early the next day. My first night home had been a joy and yet even as I rose I knew I would not enjoy it for long. I went to the warrior hall and I noticed that those who lived there were already up. My armour had been cleaned and oiled by Uhtric. Some of the others were cleaning their own. I saw that Bjorn the smith was busy repairing mail already. Before I spoke with Asbjorn and Eystein I took Karl One Hand to one side. He was a forlorn figure these days and had the hangdog look of someone who loves not life. "I needs must speak with Asbjorn but I have something I wish you to do for me. Do not go far."

His eyes lit up although he self-consciously hid his stump with his right hand. "Aye Jarl and can I say that I am happy that you have slain the snake."

"He is not worth a thought, Karl Word Master."

As I went to speak with my Ulfheonar I reflected that the snake had caused Karl's wound. To Karl, he would always haunt his dreams. He would imagine a life with two hands. "Asbjorn, Snorri, Eystein, Beorn, a word if you please." Leaving what they were doing they joined me. "You have done much for me already but I would have you do more. If you do not wish to then I will understand."

Snorri shook his head, "Jarl Dragonheart, we are your oathsworn. We have endured the wrath of the gods, we have been beneath the sea. Whatever you ask we will do."

"That is well. Asbjorn I would have you and Eystein take the crew of **'Odin's Breath'** and join Arne. Use the valley of the Grassy Mere. I fear the Scots will come sooner rather than later. I want you to be on hand and give support to Arne and Ketil. Take ponies for I would have you there swiftly."

They both nodded, "And when should we leave?"

I smiled, "Yesterday might be too late."

"We will go now."

"Snorri, ride to Sigtrygg. I need warriors from him. I would not have him leave his land undefended but there is danger from the north. Beorn got to my son and tell him the same."

"Aye Jarl."

I waved over Erik, "Ride to Windar and say that I ask him to send as many of his warriors as he can spare to his son. Ketil will have need of them."

That done I walked over to Karl who was waiting patiently on the steps to the warrior hall.

"How is the arm?"

"Sometimes I can still feel the hand. I think I can wiggle my fingers but there is nothing there. And it itches."

I nodded, "Haaken was the same when he lost his eye. For months afterwards, he swore that he could feel it. It will pass. But you now feel lost too do you not? You feel as though you have lost your purpose. There seems little point in life."

He clutched his wolf pendant and stared at me, "Jarl Dragonheart, have you the second sight that you can read my mind?"

Viking Legend

"Let us say I know my warriors and I remember old Ragnar and his withered arm. Your dark thoughts are not a surprise."

"I know I can never fight in a shield wall again. Even if I had a shield strapped to my arm I would not have the strength. I can still use my sword. I practise every day but what good am I now? I am a one-armed swordsman."

"You need not feel sorry for yourself. You are alive! Here is what you do. Firstly, take a wife and sire children. I would have warriors like you to follow my sons and grandson." He nodded, "And then I would like you to command my town."

He looked puzzled, "I do not understand, Jarl Dragonheart. Scanlan does that does he not?"

"Scanlan is not a warrior. He makes sure that the ditches are kept clean and that we have food. He manages the animals and he listens to the people. He is a clerk. He does a good job but I need a defender for Cyninges-tūn. I need a leader who can command my walls and fight danger. I need someone who can make sure that old men watch the gate and do not play dice all day."

He nodded, "And I am the man for that? Even with one hand?"

"I will be gone again soon. That is my destiny. I will always travel. When I leave I want my home and my family to be protected. I have a son, a wife and a sister. They need a warrior's eye and hand. Rolf did that but he is gone. He was not Ulfheonar but he was a good warrior. You are Ulfheonar you can do it even better. I want you to train every man in the village to become a warrior. I want you to train every boy from the moment he can hold a piece of wood. We need every boy and man to be able to defend the walls when I am gone. I would have you look at the defences of our town and make them stronger." I saw him nodding and smiling. "And you will be paid."

He stood proudly, "I need no gold to serve you."

"No, but you need coin to feed yourself and your wife and the many Karls whom you will sire. You will take the coin or you will not be the defender of Cyninges-tūn."

"You drive a hard bargain, Jarl Dragonheart. When do I begin?"

"Now. Come with me and we will visit with Bjorn."

My smith was hard at work, "I know not what you did at Din Guardi but I have never seen mail so damaged!"

"It was worth it. Magnus is dead."

"Aye, *wyrd*."

"Karl One Hand is to command the town when I am absent. He will train and organise every man and boy. We will need weapons. I will send Scanlan over later with coin to pay for them."

"It will be done."

By noon I was more than happy and I sought Aiden. He looked different somehow. I think that he had gained power from somewhere. Perhaps the dark cave beneath the sea had affected him. "Did you and Kara dream?"

Viking Legend

"We did Jarl. The potion and the sweat hut worked. We saw a sea of Scots and they flooded from the north. There were also men of Northumbria with them."

"Then the news we had was right. But you know not when?"

"No, but Kara and I felt that it would be soon. They would not come in winter. We have had a bountiful summer. That is because of you, Jarl. The spirits and the gods favour us because of you. Others have not fared as well. They will want what we have. We have full granaries and many new animals. The ale this harvest is the finest the alewives have ever brewed."

I heard cheering outside and when I went from my hall I saw Asbjorn and Eystein leading the men north. As I emerged they all cheered and banged their shields shouting, "Dragonheart! Dragonheart!"

I raised my hand, "You go to protect our land and I will follow soon."

The town cheered the forty young men who now looked a little more like warriors than they had a year ago. The married Ulfheonar rode up to me as the column disappeared. They all had their own stad to the south of the town on the slopes of the Old Man.

"Where do they go, Jarl?" Haaken always wanted to know everything.

"To reinforce Arne. We leave tomorrow. Kara and Aiden have dreamed of danger. I have sent for men from Sigtrygg and Wolf Killer. I would have you find as many men who can fight and have arms. If they have neither helmet nor spear then they stay here with Karl One Hand. He will command the defence of our home. We leave as soon as we are mustered."

"You will take all of our men? What if there is an attack from the south, from Mercia?"

"I will send a message to Coen Ap Pasgen for his men to trade with Mercia. They are the best spies we have. I will also send Siggi to ask Thorfinn Blue Scar what he knows."

Haaken said, "Then I had best begin to collect the men." He paused, "Karl One Hand is happy to be here and not fight with our warriors?"

"He knows he cannot fight in the shield wall and this way his skills are not wasted. We have needed someone to train our young men since Rolf was killed."

"Aye Rolf. It is strange how we forget those who were so much part of our lives."

I shook my head, "I never forget. When I sleep at night I think of those who died so that we might be where we are. So long as I remember then they are not forgotten."

"You are right and I am ashamed."

"No Haaken, do not feel shame. You remember them in your sagas and your songs. Perhaps you can put more of our warriors in them eh?"

By the time I had done all that I had set myself it was dusk and I was exhausted yet I had done nothing but speak with people and send messages. Brigid smiled as I trudged into my hall. "I have watched you all day, Jarl. You have worked tirelessly. I am proud of you."

Viking Legend

I kissed her, "And I am proud of you. You never complain. But I will take you to task for one thing."

"What is that?"

"I like not the words you call me; Jarl. It sounds as though you are a thrall still."

"But you are Jarl Dragonheart."

"And I am your husband. Call me husband or my birth name."

She frowned, "Birth name?"

"My mother called me Garth. The boys I grew up with and my father called me Crow but I do not like that name. Call me husband or Garth."

"Then I am your wife?"

"I think the birth of our son confirms that. We are hand-fasted and that is enough for me."

She took my hand in hers. "My religion has a ceremony. If you truly wish me to be your wife then we should have a ceremony. If not, I do not mind but you wish me to be your wife...."

"Do you not need a priest for that? Should I capture one?"

She shook her head, "No, I am sure that Deidre and Macha will know the words."

"Then find them and we will do it this night for I must be gone hence in a few days." It was rare for me to be able to surprise Brigid but I did so that evening. It had been when speaking to Karl that the thought had come into my head. I thought of her as my wife and yet she was not. She was my woman and she deserved more than that.

With Aiden, Haaken and Kara as witnesses, we were married. Deidre and Macha had that self-satisfied smug look which hinted that they had converted me. They had a not. It was a witnessing of a marriage. We did much the same but without the interminable ceremony. We just took each other in front of witnesses and said we were wed. It was that simple. I had not understood any of the words they had said anyway save for Amen which I was relieved to hear for it meant it was over. But I was pleased I had done it for Brigid. She had given up much and this was little enough to return to her.

Viking Legend
Chapter 13

We left my home three days later. Wolf Killer and Sigtrygg came with their men and they each brought twenty. Wolf Killer brought Elfrida and his family to stay with Kara. That made us all happier. Karl One Arm would make sure that they would be safe or he and his new warriors would die trying. Haaken managed to muster forty warriors. It meant we had over a hundred warriors from Cyninges-tūn in addition to Arne's men, those brought by Sigtrygg and my son not to mention those who were now with Ketil. I left Aiden with my wife because I did not want to risk him. His magic would not be needed and I was acutely aware of how weak my defences were. Aiden and Kara would protect my people. I knew that the two of them were now even more powerful than they had been. I knew not if it was the chest or something else but the bond between them had grown.

We picked up another ten warriors as we headed through the Rye Dale, the Grassy Mere and Threlkeld. All had a helmet and a shield and were strong young men. I was happy to take such warriors. Haaken had also had a supply of the twisted nails made. He liked the way we used them. They were now known as horse breakers to my men. Each one carried a leather pouch with them. The Ulfheonar led horses with mail and weapons. We would not ride to war for it was not seemly when our men marched. Snorri had ten boys who rode fast little ponies. They had all seen ten summers and within another two would be ready to train as warriors. They could use a bow and a slingshot. More importantly, they were keen to fight for Jarl Dragonheart. They would act as scouts. Not as skilled as real scouts, their numbers meant we could spread them out over a large area and have advance warning of an enemy.

When we reached Arne's land I saw that Asbjorn had erected shelters for his men and they were working on more for us. It made sense for we could not all fit in the walls of Arne's stronghold. However, it meant we could be seen easily. If the Scots used the river then we would give away our small numbers. There was little I could do about that. I left my Ulfheonar to organise the warriors and I went to speak with Arne.

"Thank you for coming, Jarl Dragonheart. The rumours have been growing. There are some of our folk who live in the northlands. They have been flooding south for many days. They speak of columns of wild, half-naked barbarians who are making their way south."

"Have you seen any?"

He shook his head. "I have had my men preparing defences. I did not wish to risk losing them in the lands of the enemy. I hope I do not disappoint you?"

"No Arne. You did right. It is sad that you people have lost lands and animals but they are alive and your defences mean that they can withstand an assault from without. This is a good stronghold."

Viking Legend

We are protected here by the two rivers. However, if they come further east there is nothing between here and Ketil to stop them. They could flood down the valley towards Mungo's Dale and your lands would be threatened."

I nodded, "It is why the Romans built their wall. I have sent men to reinforce Ketil and his castle is well protected. They have to come past us to reach Ketil. It is the gap between you that they will exploit." I glanced around at the men he had within his walls. "How many warriors can you spare?"

He rubbed his chin, "These walls can be held by farmers and fishermen."

"I will need warriors to stand and break the backs and the will of this enemy. How many warriors can you supply? I want no farmers. They would be slaughtered. I need those you would stand alongside in a shield wall."

"Twenty."

"That includes you?"

"It does."

"It is not enough but it will have to do. Have your men ready to move at a moment's notice. I want to stop this King Alpín mac Echdach before he has travelled too far. If he gets into the hills we will not be able to control his movements. It is here in the river valleys where we stand our best chance."

By the time I reached our camp, it was chaos but of the organised variety. My jarls and Ulfheonar organised the many different warriors. I waved Snorri over. "The Scots must be close. Refugees have been coming here for some days. I want you and Beorn to take the scouts and patrol between here and Brougham. This is where he will strike."

"Jarl, it is not for me to question you but why not move the army further east if we are to try to stop him?"

"Because he could then land here. If his aim is to take what we have then it is not this fort he wants but the farms, their crops and their animals. It is the families who will be enslaved. We have to be ready to move quickly."

"Why not use the wall then?"

I felt as though someone had slapped me on my face. "Of course. The Romans used the wall and we can move along it quickly! Thank you, Snorri." I turned and shouted, "Ulfheonar!"

They all came running. The urgency of my voice drew them. Wolf Killer and Sigtrygg needed no invitation; they had both been Ulfheonar. Standing expectantly around me, they waited for my words.

I took out my sword and marked a cross in the soil. "Here we are." I put another cross south and east of us. "Here, twenty miles away, is Ketil. We are here to stop the Scots from rampaging through our land but Snorri has pointed out that we can stop them further north. We can use the Roman Wall. They have to cross it to get to our lands. I have seen their ships and they will not use them. They will use the gaps in the wall. It is a line ten miles long which we would need to watch." I put another line from my first cross east. "Before dawn, we march the army to the wall. Snorri and his scouts will ride north to find the Scots. Each one of you will have twenty warriors with you. You will have half a mile of the wall to watch. The Romans used small turrets every quarter of a mile. You can use them for archers and as markers for our lines. We will be spread thin but I want each of you to have your men build a fire. You light it when you see the enemy and then we all congregate at the point of the fire."

"We will be exposed to their whole army. That will mean twenty or perhaps forty facing an army that could be in the hundreds."

"Aye, Wolf Killer but we will be on top of a wall. You all have bows and javelins. You hold them off. This is not like standing in a shield wall where the weight of numbers can force you back. The Romans put ditches before their walls. They will head for the gaps and will not have brought ladders. Help will be no more than half a mile away. If the fire is lit when they are sighted then warriors can be at your side before they arrive. Anyone who is attacked will have sixty warriors within a short time. Once we see him and know whence they come I intend to send to Ketil to bring his men north. With the extra men from Windar's Mere and Ulf's Water, we might have enough to throw him back across the river."

"And how many men does he have?"

"I know not Sigtrygg. Snorri and Beorn will have to discover that."

They nodded. None was afraid despite the daunting prospect of having to hold off a whole army with just twenty men. "Make sure you have enough food and water for at least three days. I will see Arne. He can hold the wall nearest to his town."

By the time I had sent messages to Ketil and visited with Arne, it was dark. I headed for my camp. Haaken awaited me with a bowl of stew and a horn of ale. "Come Jarl Dragonheart, you need to eat. The plan is a good one and you have done all that you can."

"Is it? I did not get the impression that everyone was happy."

"It is time that we all learned to stand on our own feet. They have a responsibility and they will have to lead. They are all Ulfheonar. They can lead. Just because you do not stand by their side with your wolf banner does not mean that they cannot fight." I nodded and began to eat. "We have divided the men. You have the warriors who we picked up on the way. There are ten of them."

"And which section did you think I should guard?"

"None. Wolf Killer thought that you should be mounted and wait in reserve. That way you could be the first at any breach."

I smiled. It made sense and my son has shown that he had a keen strategic mind. I put down my empty bowl and drank the beer. "Perhaps this unwanted attack may prove to be the iron which makes us stronger. If we survive this then we will have leaders who have survived fire, steel and blood. That will make them stronger."

"We will be stronger, Jarl. It is our enemies who underestimate us. They see weaknesses which do not exist."

I was woken by the noise of men moving out in the dark. Audun Thin Hair's son, Leif, handed me a horn of beer and some bread and cheese. He

Viking Legend

was one of the men we had picked up while heading north and would serve with me. "There is no hurry, Jarl Dragonheart. The men are with the horses and we have time aplenty." He spread his arm around. We are the only ones left in the camp."

"Thank you, Leif Audunson."

"We are all honoured that you chose us to fight alongside you. I have grown up listening to my father tell me tales of your deeds. To be this close to a legend is beyond my wildest dreams. I hope that we do not let you down."

"If you do as I command, stand firm and survive then you will not be letting me down! I want no reckless acts of bravery trying to impress me! Is this your first battle?"

He looked a little sheepish. "It is Jarl."

"Then here is some advice from someone who fought in his first battle when he was a little older than the pony riders. If you strike with your weapon do not hold back. The man you fight will be trying to kill you. Use anything at your disposal to kill him: your shield, your sword, your dagger, your helmet, even your teeth. And if you are hurt then keep on fighting and try to kill him. You fight for those around you too. We are one band this day!"

He nodded and I saw fire in his eyes. I hoped that his helmet, shield and sword would be good enough. He was a farmer and they did not value weapons as much as warriors did.

The temporary shelters were left. It looked like a ghost town. I put on my cochineal and donned my helmet. I handed Leif my wolf standard. "Carry this for me. Today you shall be my standard bearer. Let the enemy know who it is they fight."

Mounting my horse, I led them east through the dark towards the thin white line that marked the sun. We all carried spears. I knew that most of those I led also carried a bow. If I was being realistic that would be where their skill would lie. I did not think they would be the greatest of swordsmen. Our job was to get to the danger and relieve until the rest arrived. It would not need heroic deeds; just men willing to bleed for the cause.

By the time we reached the Roman Road dawn had broken. I turned, "We will ride up and down this road watching for smoke. Keep a good eye out and shout when you see any. If you see a rider then tell me too." I shrugged, "My eyes are different from you, young men."

The journey across the land to Din Guardi had hardened my rear but I knew that I had had enough of the backs of horses. It took almost half a day to ride to the eastern end of our line and then journey back to Arne. We walked rather than trotted. Speed was not important. We had just begun a second journey when Beorn rode in. "We have found them, Jarl. Or at least we have found two of the columns."

"Two?" That upset my preparations. I had planned on facing one enemy army. We would not have enough men to stop them in two places. The Norns and their threads were tricky creatures.

Viking Legend

"Aye. One is just a mile or so from here and the second is two or three miles east of us. They are heading for the two gaps. One is close to the deserted Roman fort and the other is just a mile or so west. I think they plan on getting through the gaps quickly."

That made sense. Putting all of his men through one gap would slow them up and make them vulnerable to a counterattack. I closed my eyes to picture where my men were and where they would strike. I opened them. "Are they both equal-sized columns?"

"I know not Jarl. I saw one but it was two of the boys who reported the other. The one I saw had some horsemen and the banners of King Alpín mac Echdach."

"Ride to Vermund, Ulf and Finni. Have them take their men to reinforce Eystein the Rock. Today they will have to be the rock upon which this unknown column falls. Then tell the others what is happening."

He rode off. I turned to Leif. "Ride to Jarl Arne and Erik Ulfsson. Tell them to take their men to Sigtrygg. Warn them that the Scots are coming their way. They must hurry. Time is of the essence."

I had been downhearted when I heard of the columns but now I knew that I was foolish to do so. We would not have to wait for a signal fire. This way I could bring my men together before the attack. I led my tiny column of men to join Olaf Leather Neck.

The wall to the west of the high Roman fort was made of turf. It was still an obstacle but the wooden towers had long fallen to dust. The stone ones, the turrets, still remained. They would have to become the strong points for this attack. Snorri and two of the boy scouts rode up as we headed to the turf wall just a hundred paces from us. "Jarl, we have seen King Alpín mac Echdach and his army. They are heading for Sigtrygg."

"I know, Beorn told me. Ride to Haaken, Wolf Killer and Asbjorn. I am reinforcing Eystein and Sigtrygg for there are two columns coming this way. They must be the bridge which joins our two flanks." He nodded and rode off. I turned to the two young boys. "What are your names?"

"I am Beorn Beornson."

"I am Cnut Thordson."

"Well, Beorn and Cnut today I give you a task. If you succeed then you will save my men and I will be in your debt." I saw them sit a little higher. "Ride to Ketil at Brougham. It is on the road which goes to the south and east. Tell him that Jarl Dragonheart has need of as many men as he can spare. Tell him where to come."

"Aye Jarl!"

"May the Allfather protect you."

I turned my horse and kicked him in the flanks. Time was something I could not buy. I had cast the bones and now I would see which way they fell. Olaf turned as we galloped up. I pointed to the north west. "There is a column coming from the north. It is led by the King of the Scots. Take your men to Sigtrygg. They are heading for the gap in the wall by him."

Viking Legend

"Shall I send a message to Asbjorn the Strong?"

"No, for there is another column heading for Eystein."

He shook his head, "It is never simple is it, Jarl Dragonheart?" Turning to his men he growled, "Follow me and we shall find glory this day."

I led my men ahead of him to join Sigtrygg. I could see them preparing to light the fire as I rode up. "Hold Sigtrygg. There is no need for fire. Let us leave that. We might need a fire to cover a retreat."

"But see yonder, Jarl. The banners of the enemy. They come and they are heading for here."

"And I have sent for reinforcements. Olaf, Erik and Arne will be here before the enemy." I lowered my voice. "A second column attacks Eystein."

"I see horsemen here."

I dismounted and turned to my men. "Dismount, tie the horses to those trees and stand behind Jarl Sigtrygg Thrandson's men." I took out the bag of twisted nails. "Here give these to the rest of the men and have them sow them thirty paces from the wall. They will discourage the horsemen."

They hurried to the clearing before the gap. It had been the gate when the wall had been in its glory and the road was a good one. The enemy would hurry to make the gap and the horse breakers would come as a shock to them. Leif rode in and dismounted. "They are following me, Jarl."

I looked beyond him and saw Erik's men running to join us. "Good. Take my banner and place it on the wall. Today you mark my position."

I took my spear and hefted my shield around to my front. For the first time in a long time I would be fighting with warriors I did not know. Sigtrygg's men were good warriors and many had mail but they were his oathsworn and not mine. The gods were testing me again. I looked at the defensive position we held. The two stone turrets which stood at either side of the gap were vital. Olaf Leather Neck and Erik Ulfsson arrived at the same time.

"Erik put your archers in this tower and any mailed warriors in the gap. The rest can go next to the right-hand turret. Olaf, put your archers in the right-hand turret, your mailed man in the gap and the rest next to the tower and use your horse breakers in front of the ditch."

I saw the enemy column begin to deploy into line. Our presence must have come as a shock to them. I clambered up the side of the turret to afford a better view. There were two groups of twenty light horsemen on the flanks. I would not worry overmuch about them. I had fought them and knew their weaknesses. The centre appeared to be a mixture of one or two men with mail and a large number with swords, axes, shields and spears. I estimated that there were well over a hundred but it was difficult to estimate for they were not in ordered lines. It was like a herd of animals milling about.

"Sigtrygg, when Arne comes I want his mailed men with me in the gap the rest can support your left flank."

"You will be in the gap?"

"Aye. It will be where the fighting is the hottest. We have to stop him at the two gaps. If we can do that then Ketil's extra men might just make the

Viking Legend

difference but we have a whole day, at least, to hold out." I looked up at the two turrets. Each held five archers. "You archers must keep up a rain of arrows. Find flesh!"

"Aye, Jarl Dragonheart!"

I went down the steep bank to the gap. There were just twelve warriors there. I was gratified that the bank was steep for that would make ascent hard for the Scots. The men stood aside as I descended. "Today you fight alongside the sword which was touched by the gods. Soon we will have more warriors but for now we must hold this gap. We do not retreat. If we fall then so be it! They will have to climb our dead bodies to enter our land."

They all cheered and began banging their shields. I pointed to those who had the best mail and warrior bands. "You seven stand with me and you five have your spears over our shoulders." I pointed Ragnar's Spirit at my banner fluttering on the wall. "They will come for me. Let us show these barbarians how Vikings fight and die!"

I stood in the centre. "Your name?" I asked the man on my left.

"I am Gunnar Gunnarsson."

I turned to my right, "And you?"

"Thorir The Slow."

I laughed, "That is good for the three of us will not move this day." I had sheathed my sword and taken my spear up. I tapped my shield with my spear. "When they see this wolf then they will come for me. That is what I want for I have the best armour. The two of you should be able to kill many Scots this day."

Gunnar said, "Today Jarl Dragonheart, we will fight as your oathsworn. If you fall we fight to the death."

"Then I will make sure that I do not fall for my people need warriors with courage such as yours."

I heard Sigtrygg's voice from above. "Jarl Dragonheart, they come!"

"Ready." At that moment spears appeared above our shoulders as Arne's breathless men joined us. I did not count them but took comfort from the hedgehog of spears which bristled above. It was a wall of metal which would deter all but the bravest of warriors.

I saw that this King Alpín mac Echdach was a cautious man. The warriors who hurtled across the ground before us were not his mailed warriors. They were his wild men from the mountains. Half-naked with painted bodies and faces they bore small shields and fire tipped spears. Their intention was to shatter our spears and break our will, allowing the better warriors to march through after we had been weakened. He was aiming all of his men at the gap. His horsemen on the flanks would exploit any weaknesses. The Roman ditch before the wall was not as much of an obstacle as it had been but it still provided another obstacle in addition to the turf wall.

The wild warriors were bunched together. The archers in the turrets managed to bring down many of them but they hurdled the dead bodies and came on. When they found the horse breakers it was as though they were

Viking Legend

stopped in their tracks. They were either barefoot or had thin-soled leather footwear. The nails tore into them. The press of men was so great that many were simply trampled to death by those behind. The effect was to thin the numbers who reached us.

It was as I had expected, they came for me. They came angry for many of their friends had died in the attempt to reach me. It was not a wedge but three warriors ran at me with others at their sides. They were eager for the glory of killing the Viking leader. I knew that I would be struck and I braced myself. I lifted my spear above my head for I saw that two of those who faced me had square shields. They hit my shield as I punched forward with my spear. As I stabbed down one of the fire tipped spears shattered against my shield and a second slid along the side of my armour. I withdrew my spear from the body of the first warrior I had killed and punched it upwards into the second man I knew that I had punched too hard when I saw it emerge through his side. As he fell he broke the spear. I swung the broken haft sideways at the third man. I hit him so hard on the side of his head that he staggered and Gunnar ran him through.

I drew Ragnar's Spirit. I was always happier with my sword in my hand. They came at me still but they came individually. We had broken up their first line with arrows, stones, spears and horse breakers. I knocked aside the first spear and swung overhead to hack through the warrior's neck. The archers in the turrets began to release at the press of men before us and as the Scots raised their shields I stabbed and slashed into unprotected middles.

I sensed that the pile of bodies before us was making them waver. "We charge and knock them back! Now!"

It was my command and I led my men by two quick steps. I felt Gunnar and Thorir hurry after me. Thorir belied his name. I swung my sword sideways and ripped through the throat of a surprised Scot. Another tried to ram his fire tipped spear at me. It shattered on my armour and I turned my head to him. He must have seen my red eyes for the first time. I howled and he screamed and tried to run. I laid open his back to the bone. That was enough and the rabble before us fled.

"Back to the gap!"

Along the two sides of the wall warriors banged their shields and shouted, "Dragonheart!" Over and over. We had not won but we had made them think.

I turned to the men who had fought alongside me. "You are heroes all. Wait here while I spy out the field."

I made my way up the turf wall to stand next to the turret. Sigtrygg took off his helmet and grinned, "It is some time since I saw Dragonheart fight and I had forgotten how ferocious he is."

"We were lucky he did not send in his best warriors. Next time he will." I looked to where the Scottish King was speaking to his leaders. "I think he may well try to attack Olaf and his men. Have a small force ready to support him."

Just then Snorri rode in. "The Northumbrians and Scots have turned our flank, Jarl. Wolf Killer is retreating here. They follow still."

Viking Legend

My strategy was in tatters. We were now outflanked. I had begun to believe we might win but the weird sisters had other plans for us. "Had we lost many warriors?"

"No but they came with mailed men and Finni's warriors had little armour. They broke through and some ran."

I detected criticism in his voice. "Do not be too harsh on them. This is the first real battle for some. Tell the men to fall back and form a line behind Olaf."

He rode off.

"Sigtrygg, some of your men will have to form a line at right angles to Olaf and his men. The Northumbrians come."

I descended to the gap. I would have to come up with a better plan now that we were outflanked.

Chapter 14

The men made way for me. They were exultant. Olaf came to the turret above us. "Olaf you will be attacked soon and the Northumbrians have flanked us. Be ready to bend your line. Sigtrygg will send men to help you."

He waved his sword, "They have not hurt us yet, Jarl! They are wild men with no skill!"

I pointed with my sword where the Scottish were being organised for another attack. "They will hit us on two sides. Watch them!"

I stepped forward and picked up some of the fire-hardened spears the Scottish had used. As weapons they were useless but as a barrier, they might slow the enemy down. I rammed a half dozen so that the haft faced the enemy. They would not cause a wound but they would slow them down. They would also distract the enemy and that could sometimes be the difference between success and failure; victory and defeat.

The first of Asbjorn's men appeared to my right. I heard Olaf and Snorri organising them. "Those with mail in the front rank. Those without in the second."

I knew, without looking that there would only be one or two with mail but they would join Olaf's two mailed warriors. We did not throw away lives needlessly. I saw the Scottish warriors as they lumbered towards us. This was no mad rush. This was a measured attack. I had no doubt that there had been some conference between the King and the Eorl who led the Northumbrians. They had learned from their first attack against us. The Eorl had used his better warriors and that had caused the breach. This was a coordinated attack and it had almost succeeded. Had I not put the wall to good use we would have engaged the Sots only to be attacked on our vulnerable right side by the Saxons of Northumbria.

I forced myself to plan as the Scots came slowly on. Once darkness fell then our enemies could slip over the wall at more than a dozen points. We had to withdraw and fight them on a better ground. The only way to do that was to hurt them and make them withdraw as they had the first time and then quickly fall back. I shook my head ruefully. I had left Aiden at home. With his mind and his maps, he could have selected a perfect battleground. I would have to improvise and use all of my experience.

The Scots were a hundred paces from us and my archers, in the turrets, began to release their arrows. Other archers began to loose too. We did not have enough nor did we have many boys with slingshots but we were wearing them down. Their shields were not as big as ours and arrows began to strike home. Men fell and disordered the line. It took time to reorder their front and in that time more men were hit. Not all died but a wounded man was still an obstacle. Then, suddenly, the two lines of horsemen hurtled towards us. Would they be foolish enough to try to charge us?

"Ready in case they charge!"

Viking Legend

When the lines were almost at the ditch they turned and rode along the length of the advancing warriors. They hurled their javelins at the men on the wall. Some were taken by surprise and plunged to the bottom of the ditch. They were the ones who were not warriors. All those who had fought before had a shield held tightly before them. Some of the ponies stepped on the horse breakers and threw their rider but the real intent of the abortive attack was to stop the relentless arrow storm on the advancing warriors. The Scottish King had sacrificed some of his horsemen to save those with mail. He was as ruthless as I was. When the riders disappeared, the advancing line was less than thirty paces away and they were ready to fight. To my right I heard a Saxon horn which sounded the charge on our right flank. We were being squeezed between two rocks.

This time there were mailed warriors who faced us. Not everyone in their front rank was so armed but one in three was. The ones in mail would struggle to climb the turf wall from the ditch and they would try to sweep us out of the way by sheer weight of numbers. Once they were through the gap those on the wall could be picked off easily. "Second rank push your shields into our backs in case they try to push us from this gap."

"Aye Jarl."

I had a limited view of the enemy for my helmet afforded me great protection but I saw the three mailed warriors heading for me. They had to slow down while they cut down the line of spears and my archers hit another five warriors. Although not mortal wounds they slowed them down. There were five less for us to fight. Suddenly the rest ran and I braced myself with my left leg forward and my sword held behind me. I took two spears on my shield and I felt the blows as the warriors crashed into us. My arm shivered with the shock. The third spear slid upwards and over my shoulder. The other two spears from behind had helped me. I stabbed up and forwards with my sword. It had a sharp edge and was longer than any Scottish sword. They had thought they were safe.

I saw the warrior on the right throw his head back and scream as my sword ripped up between his legs and into his stomach. I twisted my blade as I withdrew it and punched with my shield at the same time. The pressure of the men behind meant that the front row of the enemy could not use their spears. Our own spears darted forward and found flesh for the Scots wore open helmets. The other two mailed warriors fell dead. They were replaced but I saw that these warriors had no mail and, like the others, their spears were not held high enough. They slid up off my metal rimmed shield. My own sword sprang in and out as quickly as I could move it. Every blow drew blood and warriors fell; some clutched wounds others went to their god.

I saw a two-handed axe come towards my head. The warrior who wielded it was in the second rank. I brought up my shield as I stabbed the man who protected the axe man. The edge of the axe bit deeply into my shield. There were many nails and it was covered in leather. I saw him tugging to free it and the action was moving my shield. I stepped forward on to my right leg as he gave a tug and he overbalanced. I leapt from the line and skewered him to the ground. I was suddenly assailed on all sides and I took many blows but I stepped back into the protection of my men. My mail had protected me but I had no doubt that it would need repair and that links had been damaged.

Gunnar asked, "Are you hurt, Jarl?"

To be truthful I had no idea but I felt no blood and nothing felt broken. "Aye, I live still. Are you all with me yet?"

The chorus of "Aye Jarl!" filled me with pride.

The storm about us raged until the pile of bodies before us was a barrier to the Scots. They were losing too many men in trying to climb over their own dead. They withdrew.

"Gunnar, Thorir, take the mail from the dead Scots and give it to those without armour. The rest of you find any more spears and weapons. Make another barrier beyond the dead Scots."

I took off my helmet and as I did so one of the warriors said, "Jarl, your head is bleeding."

I put my hand to the side and it came away bloody. "Thank you I will get it healed after we have sent these savages north."

This time I climbed the eastern bank. I could see that Wolf Killer and my men had driven off the Northumbrians but I also saw that they had taken casualties. Unlike those with me they had not had the protection of the ditch. My son wandered over to me and when he reached me took off his helmet. "I am sorry, Jarl we could not do what you have done."

"I had a better defensive position but we are all in danger." I pointed towards Arne's stronghold. "I intend as soon as it is dark to slip back to the junction of the two rivers. There we can use the two river banks to defend our flanks and we can use Arne's men from his stronghold to aid us with their bows."

"How will we slip away?"

"My Ulfheonar will use our skills to make them think that we attack them. You will lead the rest of the army back. Have any wounded taken over the river and then destroy the bridges."

"But we will be trapped."

"Ketil is coming but we need to buy his reinforcements time. If they cross the bridges then they will spread through our land bringing death and destruction. They have horsemen!"

"Even so..."

"We can use Arne's fishing boats to build an improvised bridge. Trust me, my son."

"I do and I fear that when you are no longer with us then I will not be half the leader you are."

"You will learn. Now make sure we make a show of strength. I leave it to you to tell the others of my plan."

"Aye Jarl."

Viking Legend

As I descended I shouted, "Snorri!" He appeared almost instantly, "When it becomes dark I want the Ulfheonar to come with me and slit a few throats. It will buy us time to withdraw to a better position. Tell the Ulfheonar."

"Aye Jarl! The wolves will feast this night."

Rather than being daunted by the prospect I knew that my Ulfheonar would relish it.

When I reached the gap, I saw more warriors wearing mail. It would give them confidence if nothing else and the sight of so many mailed warriors might make the enemy think we had been reinforced. Glancing at the sky I saw that it would be dark within the hour. Would they risk another attack?

I had a sudden idea. I began banging my shield and chanted, "Ulfheonar!"

The men with me took up the chant and it began to spread to the east and west. My Ulfheonar led the chant and it grew in volume. I felt reckless and I began to walk towards the waiting Scots. I continued chanting and the warriors behind me followed. The warriors who had been facing the Northumbrians also followed us and we began to spread out across the dead Scots who littered the ground. I stopped and the line spread to the left and right of me. When we were one line of just fifty warriors I stopped chanting and held up Ragnar's Spirit. Everyone stopped. We were silent and then I heard the flap of my standard as Leif waved it over my head.

I shouted, "This is Ragnar's Spirit and it is the sword touched by the gods. Today it will lead us to victory." I changed to Saxon. "Is there one amongst my enemies who will face me in single combat?" There was silence. "Is there none who will face me? Are you afraid of one man with grey in his beard?" I saw men looking at one another but the legend of my name and my reputation daunted them. I laughed, "You are women!" I changed to Norse, "Let us eat, I am hungry!"

My men all laughed and they followed me as we turned our backs on our enemies. It was a gamble but we had humiliated them. I could not see them charging us. I glanced to the west and saw the sun dipping. Soon it would be dark and they would retire to their camp and lick their wounds. They would plan a gory and grisly end for me. I had no doubt that they thought they would win. They outnumbered us and we had barely held them. As we entered the gap and my men cheered me I said, "Light fires! Ulfheonar prepare for war. Wolf Killer you know what to do."

Beorn Beornson rode in on a pony which was almost on its last legs. "Jarl Dragonheart, Jarl Ketil and his men will be here by noon tomorrow!"

"You have done well! Now rest. I want you to return to him in the morning with a message."

By the time the fires were lit it was dark. Wolf Killer took the bulk of the army with him. One or two moved around the fires as did my Ulfheonar. We had ten men who would stand watch to give the illusion that the whole army was still there and to feed the fires. We used the kindling we had prepared for our signal fires. The fires burned brightly and gave the illusion of a huge camp. I sat with my warriors and we sharpened our swords.

Viking Legend

"This is my plan. We let the enemy talk about the day and plan their attack tomorrow. When it is dark of night we will kill their sentries and bring terror to their camp. Beorn and Snorri, you will cut loose their horses and drive them through the gap. Take as many as you can to Wolf Killer. We can use them on the morrow."

"Aye Jarl."

Haaken looked around at the small number of warriors. "Think you this will be enough?"

"It will. We have done this before but this time we stay close together. When we hear the horses galloping then we give the wolf howl and escape. They will be confused and think they are under attack from a larger force. The Scots have yet to experience a night attack by the Ulfheonar."

"Then this will be enough."

We rested although all of us had nerves stretched to breaking point. Even though we had done this before each time we did it there was a risk. All it took was one missed footing and a warrior could slip and be captured or killed. They just needed to be lucky; we had to be perfect.

Some of those we left as sentries had placed food on the fires to cook and the smell of cooking meat drifted over to the north. The Scots would think we were feasting. I doubted that they would be eating as well. Those who had fled to the fort had brought their animals with them. We slipped out of camp, invisible in our black cloaks. Because we were close together, thirty paces separated us, our task was made much easier. Erik and Vermund killed the first two sentries and we headed towards the horse lines. Their other sentries were spread further apart than we. The horses were to the north and west of the camp. The Scots did not want to be upwind of the horses. There were three guards there and they died silently. We left Beorn and Snorri to untie the beasts and we entered the camp. We were coming from what they thought was their safe side.

We moved like wraiths. They had no tents but slept on the ground. A party of six warriors all had their throats slit at the same time. They died without a murmur. We could hear the noises of men sleeping, snoring and farting. We heard those who talked in their sleep and we heard the men who told such talkers to shut up. Those who slept alone died instantly. We passed others lying close together. We took no chances. I wanted to be in the heart of the camp when we gave the call of the wolf.

We divided into two when we came further into the camp. I had my seax and I went with Haaken, Asbjorn and Eystein to the six men who slept in a circle with their feet to the fire. I drew my seax across the throat of a snoring warrior. The air from his throat seemed to sigh. The man next to him opened his eyes as he heard the sigh. I rammed my seax through his open mouth and pinned his head to the ground.

We were in the centre of the camp and I saw a huddle of warriors sitting around an open fire and talking. They looked to be leaders. I sheathed my seax and drew my sword. It was at that moment that we heard the howl of Snorri.

Viking Legend

We all lifted our heads and howled. Then, howling, we ran towards the leaders. There was pandemonium. They did not see us. We were coming from the wrong direction and we were dressed in black. I swung my sword two handed at the warrior who turned as he heard me run towards him. My sword bit deeply into his middle. The other leaders took shelter from what they thought were ghosts or wolves. I took out my seax as we headed south. And then we were in the dark heading for our lines. Men's white faces appeared before us as they woke and panicked at the strange and eerie sounds. We slashed left and right as we ghosted through the camp. We were unseen and they died without knowing who had slain them. When there were no more warriors before us I stopped and turned, sword and seax in hand.

One by one my men joined me. I could hear the cries and shouts in the Scots' camp as they searched for us. I saw Eystein limping, "Are you hurt?"

"A lucky blow with a sword. I will live."

We hurried back to our camp. The men we had left as sentries looked up as we entered. "It is time to leave." The ten men picked up their pieces of cooking meat and began to lope off west. Snorri and Beorn reined in. They each had five horses. Snorri pointed west, "Ten horses rode that way. We will pick them up on the way."

We mounted the horses and headed for our camp. If nothing else we had denied them sleep, killed a couple of leaders and terrified them. The most important achievement had been that we had extricated our men from a difficult position and we would live to fight another day.

Wolf Killer and Sigtrygg stood with swords drawn as we galloped up. Sheathing his weapon my son said, "We heard the howls and the battle. We were worried."

Sigtrygg shook his head, "I was not worried. I have been a wolf in the night and know that the advantage always lies with the Ulfheonar."

As my son led us into the lines of sleeping warriors he said, "How you survive when all around you are enemies I shall never know. I was Ulfheonar but I would fear to do what you do."

"It is because we are so few that we succeed. In our cloaks and black armour, we are hard to see. We look like shadows and when you awake from a sleep you see what you expect to see. You hear howls and wake to see black shadows. You think it is wolves and the wolf still terrifies men. And now, my son, my men and I need to sleep. Tomorrow will be a long day. I want the men with mail in the front two ranks. Sow the ground before us with any horse breakers we still have and then use old spears driven into the ground. We need to break down their attack."

"What if they choose not to attack but head down the valley to the farms?"

"Then they will meet Ketil and we will fall upon their flanks. The god Icaunis will help us now. With a river on two flanks the two kings fight Vikings and has to defeat Icaunis. We are in the strongest place which I could devise."

Viking Legend

Nodding, Wolf Killer said, "Arne has gone to his citadel to ready fishing boats and to bring archers. He says he will use the fishing boats to fetch the archers. All will be ready by dawn."

We sat around the fire and my warriors looked downhearted. We had fallen back. I was so tired that could have slept standing up. I nodded to Haaken. We had known each other so long that I did not need words. He stood and began to chant his new saga. I had not heard it all but I had heard fragments. It was the tale of the death of Magnus the Foresworn.

The Saxon King had a mighty home
Protected by rock, sea and foam
Safe he thought from all his foes
But the Dragonheart would bring new woes
Ulfheonar never forget
Ulfheonar never forgive
Ulfheonar fight to the death
The snake had fled and was hiding there
Safe he thought in the Saxon lair
With heart of dragon and veins of ice
Dragonheart knew nine would suffice
Ulfheonar never forget
Ulfheonar never forgive
Ulfheonar fight to the death
Below the sand they sought the cave
The rumour from the wizard brave
Beneath the sea without a light
The nine all waited through the night
Ulfheonar never forget
Ulfheonar never forgive
Ulfheonar fight to the death
When night fell they climbed the stair
Invisible to the Saxons there
In the tower the traitors lurked
Dragonheart had a plan which worked
Ulfheonar never forget
Ulfheonar never forgive
Ulfheonar fight to the death
With Odin's blade the legend fought
Magnus' tricks they came to nought
With sword held high and a mighty thrust
Dragonheart sent Magnus to an end that was just
Ulfheonar never forget
Ulfheonar never forgive
Ulfheonar fight to the death
Ulfheonar never forget
Ulfheonar never forgive

Ulfheonar fight to the death

When he finished my men cheered and banged their shields. They asked for a second rendition. Haaken looked at me and I nodded. The song was like food for their hearts. When he finished a second time I nodded my thanks and rolled into my cloak. I was so tired that I did not dream at all. I fell into a black hole and it was only when Leif shook my shoulder to wake me that I crawled from the darkness into which I had crept. "It is almost morning, Jarl Dragonheart, and the enemy approaches. They know now that we have moved."

"Thank you Leif and thank you for carrying my standard. You put yourself into danger."

"I was following you, Jarl and I was honoured to carry the standard." He grinned, "They call me Leif the Standard now. It is a noble name."

"And you have earned it." I noticed that he was wearing one of the Scots' mail byrnies. I was glad. Carrying the standard meant he could not wield a sword. He needed all the protection he could manage. He handed me a horn of ale and I drank greedily for my mouth was dry. It was only when I handed it back that remembered we had few supplies. "That was the last eh Leif."

He nodded, "Sorry Jarl, but there is water aplenty."

"True and by this evening we all either lie dead or be drinking Arne's stad dry."

"Then I hope he has ale in abundance."

I was stiff as I rose. I had taken many blows the previous day. They would soon ease but I walked like an old man as I sought my leaders. Sigtrygg, Wolf Killer and Arne were with Haaken close to the front to our lines. I could see that they had managed to find some broken spears and stakes to make a crude barrier. I was just pleased that these were Saxons and Scots we fought. They had few bows. We had a tight defensive position but nowhere to hide if they decided to shower us with arrows.

"So we have until noon to hold out." I sounded more confident than I was. We had fought hard the previous day and unlike the enemy had no fresh warriors.

"If Ketil does as he promised."

"I know you do not know him Wolf Killer but he is reliable. He may be young but he has held off three seasons of attacks and, with our help, he has beaten them all back. He will come." My son nodded. "How many do we estimate?"

"There are more Saxons than Scots but we think there are over two hundred and fifty of them. We all need to kill at least two men each."

"Horse?"

"There are thirty Saxon horsemen. They are to the south of their lines watching the road."

"Then they expect us to be reinforced. That is not good."

Viking Legend

Snorri ran up. He had been beyond our lines and he made his way back through the traps and stakes, "Jarl Dragonheart, their leaders come. They wish to talk."

Wolf Killer said, "It may be a trap."

"It may be but anything which delays the start of this battle aids us. We need Ketil. Snorri you and Beorn cover us with your bows. I will go just beyond the stakes. That is well within your range if there is to be treachery. Come son, and you Sigtrygg, let us see what they wish." I turned, Leif, bring my standard!" We took off our helmets to show that we meant peace. The red cochineal had run giving my face a ruddy complexion. I wondered what they would make of that.

As we made our way towards the four men who approached us with palms outward I saw that my men had done a good job. I knew that there were horse breakers and I was looking for them. I could barely spot them. An enemy who did so and tried to run would find it much harder.

The four of them stopped thirty paces from our lines. They were all dressed in mail and three of them were younger than I was. The fourth looked to be a little older than me. All four had open helmets in their hands. The older warrior spoke in Saxon; it was a language we all understood. "I am King Alpín mac Echdach." He held his hand to his right, "And this is Eorl Aethelfrith, King Eanred's man."

I nodded and remained silent. They had asked for this meeting and not I. I saw a look of annoyance cross the King's face. I had not deferred to him. He did not like that. "You fought well yesterday but you are outnumbered now and your backs are to the river. When we attack you will all be slaughtered." Still we remained silent. Sighing he went on, "Here are our terms: surrender Jarl Dragonheart to us so that King Eanred may punish him for his treacherous murders and the violation of his home." Wolf Killer started forward but I restrained him. The King went on, "Then you will all bow your knee to me and accept me as your overlord. Do that and you shall all live and keep your weapons." He smiled as though this was the most reasonable offer a man could make. He went on, "And before you answer know that King Eanred himself is coming with a mighty host. You are all going to die if you refuse my kind offer."

I nodded and turned to my son and Sigtrygg, "Does this sound reasonable to you?"

Wolf Killer laughed, "This man calls himself king and yet he leads a ragtag army of half-dressed and wild savages. I would as soon bow to a pig and bare my arse to his warriors than acknowledge him as king. In fact, I have a mind to take my warriors and conquer this piece of scrubland called Alt Clut!"

One of the warriors with the King was obviously a Scot for he started his hand towards his sword. I hissed, "Think hard my friend. I have an archer behind me and if you draw your sword at this truce then you will die before your King and the Eorl here."

Viking Legend

"Hold Kenneth. This Viking is right. This is a truce and there are rules." The warrior's hand came away from his hilt. "So you all wish to die?"

I laughed, "We are Vikings not followers of the White Christ. If we die with a sword in our hands then we go to Valhalla. Do you think death bothers us? And remember Alpín mac Echdach that we are the warriors who sent your men fleeing when they raided Thorfinn Blue Scar, we managed to surprise King Eanred's strongest castle and last night ten men terrified your whole army. I will not make the same offer to you. You attack us and you die. You do not attack us and we attack you and you die. You flee and we will follow you. We are Vikings and we are afraid of no man!"

He had no answer to that and he turned on his heel and left.

Once we were back in our lines Sigtrygg said, "Reinforcements?"

"It will be the fyrd. They are less well trained than even our bondi. They are numbers that is all. He wants to frighten us with a mob. The best warriors they have are here already. That is why they were successful yesterday. It was their eorls and their oathsworn who fought and died. This shows that he is worried. He would not have negotiated if he thought he could win. There is doubt in his mind."

"Will he wait for King Eanred?"

"I hope so, son, for that means Ketil will be close. Did Beorn Beornson leave before dawn?"

"Aye."

"Then Ketil knows our situation." I smiled, "He is as good at ambush as any Ulfheonar." I pointed to the river, "And with Arne's archers we have an extra weapon that he knows not of. However, just to make sure I will make a blót in the river. Where are the ponies we captured last night?"

Snorri pointed. "They are by the river drinking."

"Good." As I approached them I saw one white pony. It was lame and stood forlornly alone. It should have been destroyed already for it could barely stand. *Wyrd*. It was meant to die and would serve my purpose.

As we approached the small herd the other ponies moved away and the white one looked at me. It raised and lowered its head. I looked into its eyes and knew that this pony had a warrior's heart. Had I had Aiden with me he would have held its head and read its mind. I could not do that. The beast, would know, however, that it was going to a better place and serving a noble cause. All of my Ulfheonar had followed me and those others close by gathered for they knew that something important was about to happen.

I drew my seax and put my left arm around the neck of the pony. I spoke softly as I led it to the water. It hobbled on its three good legs. "You are in pain, my friend, and I shall end that for you. Your sacrifice will help us to win this day and for that you will be remembered. When you are in the presence of the Allfather then tell him that we need his aid this day if we are to drive our enemies hence. You are noble and I will make this swift. You have had enough pain in your life."

He raised his head and whinnied as though he understood.

Viking Legend

I took him into the sluggish river so that the water came to my chest. I spoke loudly so that my men and the gods could hear. "Allfather and great god Icaunis I give you a blood sacrifice to ensure that we defeat our enemies this day. Take this fine beast and welcome him to run free with the others in Valhalla." The pony raised his head as I drew the seax across his throat. The blood spurted and splattered me. Its body fell into the river and the current took it west towards the sea. It was a good blót. The animal had not fought me. Those who had seen it all cheered. Arne's archers on the far bank took up the cheer and it seemed to echo across the Eden valley.

I waded from the water. My helmet and my armour were covered in the blood of the pony. This was a good sign and my men banged their shields as I walked past them to the front lines. Wolf Killer walked next to me with his hand on my shoulder. "The gods favour you, father. The pony wanted to die. There was no struggle. That was a good blót."

We will know by the end of the day."

Viking Legend
Chapter 15

It was late morning when their horns sounded and they began to advance. Perhaps that meant King Eanred had arrived. We could not tell for the land to the east was hidden to us. There was no sign of Ketil yet but that did not worry me. If I could not see him then our enemies could not. I stood with my leaders in the front rank. There were now fifty of us with mail. Some, like Leif, had taken the mail from dead Scots. It was a more formidable line than we had had the day before. The two rivers protected our flanks. We stood with a line of interlocked shields and fresh spears. Arne had ferried them over during the night. Our problem would come if they broke through our mailed line for behind us we had just fifty warriors and they had no mail. If we failed, and I prayed that we would not, then they would be ferried to the safety of Arne's citadel. The Scots would be denied their corpses. Of course if that happened then they would flood into my land and my people would suffer. We had to make sure that we did not die.

I had Wolf Killer and his men to my right and Sigtrygg and his oathsworn to my left. The centre was made up of Ulfheonar and those who had claimed mail. Haaken had not been happy about that for he wanted my Ulfheonar in one block.

"They will fight better alongside the best that we have. Would you rather we put them together? Would that not be the weakest part of the line. This way we have strength all the way along the line."

"But I would protect your right side, Jarl Dragonheart, as I always have."

"And you will but there will be another warrior between us. Gunnar Gunnarsson fought well yesterday. He deserves the honour."

And so we stood and we waited. Our front was narrow and they were using a boar's head wedge to come at us. This gave two points to probe us. It meant that Wolf Killer and Sigtrygg would bear the brunt of the first attacks. Perhaps they were wary of attacking me. Our second ranks had not only spears but javelins. They would hurl their javelins and then use their spears to form a barrier. The archers beyond the river would release their arrows once the enemy were fifty paces from us. They might not kill those with mail but any without mail would be hit. This time we had forty archers. They might make all the difference.

The two wedges came on slowly, warily watching the ground before them. My warriors had placed the stakes and spears to show the archers when they could loose. As the wedges were broken up by the spears the arrows fell. They made a terrible noise as they clattered and clanged off helmets and mail. The steep angle of the arrows meant that some even penetrated metal links and soon the advancing Scots and Saxons had lifted the shields above their heads. Few fell but many were hit. As the ones with mail passed through the arrow storm more men were felled as those without armour were hit. They lifted

Viking Legend

their shields high above them. They were like the grains of sand on the shore. No matter how many we killed their ranks were filled by others.

Behind us, the men with the javelins prepared to throw them. Some threw them high while those, who had the skill, threw them horizontally. I saw one Scot clutch at his stomach as a well-aimed javelin went beneath his raised shield. His place was quickly taken but the fallen body was yet another obstacle to those who followed. I saw the leading warriors all wore boots and they stamped as they marched. The horse breakers were crushed into the ground. They were now ineffective as a barrier

I saw the wedge tighten as they prepared to charge.

"Ready! They are about to charge!"

Because many at the rear of the two wedges were still negotiating bodies and stakes they did not have as many men charging as they might have liked. When they struck us, it was with little effect. They did not have the weight of mailed men behind them. I saw Wolf Killer spear the leading warrior who faced him. He threw his body contemptuously to one side and then brought his spear sideways into the open helmet of a second. They were holding. The enemy line now began to fill in the gap between the two wedges. I saw that Leif was still waving the standard back and forth above my head. It seemed to draw the enemy to me. That was good. That was what I wanted.

The clash of arms and the shouts of the dying and the wounded filled the air. I concentrated on the mailed Eorl who came towards me. He had a wild boar painted on his shield and from his helmet fluttered four feathers. His mail looked to be well made and he had a sword which was almost as long as mine. I held my spear at waist height for a pair of spears were on each of my shoulders. We both jabbed forward at the same time. I took his spear on my shield but perhaps he was distracted by the two spears which faced his eyes for he failed to lower his own shield. My spearhead bit into his mail. He was not wearing a leather byrnie beneath for I saw the look of pain on his face as my spear struck flesh. I withdrew it and stabbed again quickly. He was not expecting the blow. At the same time, the two warriors behind me stabbed forward and their spears hit his helmet above the nasal. He fell back. I pulled back my arm and hit him a third time. This time my spear went beneath his byrnie and tore up into his unprotected body. He fell backwards into his warriors and his oathsworn.

The warriors of the Eorl gave a roar of anger and hurled themselves at me, keen to avenge their lord. They fought angry and that is never a good idea. Their wild strikes got in the way of each other. I took the flurry of blows on my shield all the while stabbing with my spear. On the third strike it broke and I drew my seax for we were too close to each other for swords. Their angry fury-filled faces were before me and they were cursing me in Saxon. I cursed back, "Follow your Eorl you women who feared to face me last night! I am Jarl Dragonheart and I fear no man!"

I ripped my seax horizontally three times in quick succession and three men had their throats cut and fell in a blood heap at my feet. The press of men

Viking Legend

behind meant they could not raise their hands. I stabbed to the left and to the right until I had enough space to draw my sword. It was then that I could swing. I stabbed forward and made a warrior jump out of the way. That allowed me to sweep to my right and my sword bit into the side of a warrior who was busy fending off Gunnar Gunnarsson.

As I brought my sword round again I saw that there were no mailed warriors before me. We have broken their first line.

"Push! We have them!"

Perhaps it was just we in the centre who had had the success but we began to hack into warriors without armour. Gunnar Gunnarsson was chanting as he slew, "Dragonheart! Dragonheart! Dragonheart!" It seemed to help his rhythm.

The men before us could not stand against such a weight of armoured men. They had no warriors behind them to hold and to protect with their spears. As they backed into the stakes and spears they fell and were skewered where they lay.

I heard a horn sound three times and the whole line began to fall back. We were not strong enough to pursue and so I called, "Hold and reform."

I looked down our line and saw many dead warriors. These were men who had come with us to fight the Scots. Some of those who had just acquired mail lay dead but the bodies before them showed that they had died well. Many Scots were piled up their bodies. Wolf Killer and Sigtrygg stood and raised their swords in salute but many of their oathsworn lay dead.

"Strip the enemy of mail and remove our bodies to the rear. This is not over. Water and food. One man in every two fetch food and water."

I turned and saw Snorri approaching. "We are running short of arrows, Jarl."

I nodded, "They have done their job. Any sign of Ketil?"

"It is still before the time he said he would arrive but look yonder," he pointed and I saw the banner of King Eanred. He had his oathsworn with him and behind came a column of armed men; it was the fyrd.

The enemy might have been wavering but now they were being reinforced. It would give heart to the others. I took off my helmet and handed it to Leif. I gave him my shield too. "Watch these. You did well. Make sure you have food. This battle is not yet over."

He smiled and rubbed his shoulder. "I thought that working on the farm was hard enough but this is harder than harvesting the rye in the dale."

"And when you go back your arm will be so strong that you will complete the task in half the time!"

More than half the men who had fought were not warriors but farmers. Warrior blood coursed through their veins but I knew that the ones who had died had been the farmers and not my warriors. I walked around my lines talking to as many as I could. I spied Asbjorn and Eystein. Eystein's lower leg. The bandages were bloody. "Have that cauterized. I cannot afford to lose my rock."

Viking Legend

"I will do so after the battle."

"You will do it now that is my command. Asbjorn take him. I will talk, while you are gone with my young cubs here!"

Asbjorn led him away. I saw Rolf Eriksson. He now had a short mail byrnie and sported a scar down his face. "Will Hlif like that scar do you think, Rolf?"

He looked confused for a moment and then shook his head, "I have not thought of her for some time. You were right, Jarl. I was a foolish young man. I am sorry."

"We can only get wisdom when we are older if we make mistakes when we are young. You and your comrades have done well. Have you lost many of the crew of *'Odin's Breath'*?"

Rolf's face became serious, "Five have died and two lie across the river, wounded."

"Do not grieve for them. They will wait for you in Valhalla. You will have many more tales to tell them."

Another of the cubs, Rollo Thin Skin, asked, "Will we win, Jarl Dragonheart? They have been reinforced."

"Have they breached our lines yet?"

"No Jarl."

"Then there is your answer. So long as we fight for each other then we will never be broken. When our enemies fall they believe they go to a heaven where all is peaceful and no one fights. We go to Valhalla. That is why we will win."

Rolf said, "And because we are led by the Dragonheart who wields the sword which was touched by the gods. The whole world has heard of you and fears you."

"No Rolf, the world apart from our land fears me. I would hope that none of you fear me."

Rollo said, "When I was growing up and I misbehaved my mother said that the Dragonheart would come in the night and punish me. I was afraid of you. I thought you could change into a wolf. When we heard the howls last night it brought back all those memories. Even though I know you just wear the cloak I am still in awe of you and a little afraid."

"Then fear not for my wolves only bite and kill when our enemies are around. We will drive them hence. Fear not."

I spoke to each group of warriors. Those who were Wolf Killer's men and Sigtrygg I did not know as well as those from my own settlement but I was pleased that none were disheartened by the reinforcements.

Haaken shouted, "Jarl, they come."

I strode back to our front line. Leif handed me my helmet. Before I donned it, I studied their attack. King Eanred had placed his oathsworn ahead of his other warriors and they were being backed by the fyrd. They were heading towards our right side. The Scots had a smaller warband and they were coming in one large block of men led by his mailed warriors. The two wedges

Viking Legend

had failed. He was using sheer weight of numbers to try to defeat us. We had but forty-two men in mail and that included me. We had enough arrows for a short time only.

"Move back towards the rivers I want a solid line flanked by the water. Icaunis will protect us."

"Aye Jarl."

As we moved back it gave heart to our enemies who thought we retreated. They came on faster. As they neared the spears and stakes I saw that the warriors at the front hacked at them with their swords and axes. It removed them but it blunted their weapons. The destruction of those flimsy defences seemed to give them the taste of victory and they cheered and began to run at us. That was a mistake. They did not keep their shields tight together and our archers hit more of them.

We had fewer spears now as many had shattered. I had the few which remained given to those in the second rank. "Press your shields into our backs!"

This time the attackers had more momentum and would hit us harder. The nearer they came to us, however, the narrower became our frontage and they began to barge into one another. They struck our line but many were unable to bring their weapons to bear. As most had spears as weapons there was a huge crack which rippled down our line as they struck shields and armour and shattered. We did not bend and the spears broke. The spears in our second rank, in contrast, had the freedom to punch at head height into the open helmets our enemies wore. The enemy were so packed together that they could not get their heads out of the way in time.

I held my sword at the side of my shield and I sliced forwards and up. I felt it grind against the links of the mail byrnie. I pulled my hand back a little and punched harder. This time the links I had weakened broke. And my sword found flesh. I leaned into the strike and kept pushing. I could feel him trying to get his own sword out but the press of men was too much. Next to me Gunnar had been hit in the side of the head by a spear and his cheek was bleeding but that just seemed to make him more determined than ever. He head-butted his opponent and as he reeled backstabbed him in the throat.

The warriors we fought might have been good warriors but there was neither order nor leadership to be seen. We kept our shields locked; they were bigger shields than those of our enemies. Our swords were better and sharper. We fought together.

Suddenly a huge war hammer came from over the heads of the front line of their warriors. It swung at our front rank and I heard the crunch as it hit the skull of a warrior to my left. I was splattered with blood and brains. I stabbed at the warrior before me and my sword slit along his face. He reeled back and the warrior with the hammer stepped along to the gap so that he could get to me. He swung his hammer at me. I barely had time to lift my shield and take the blow. A spear darted from beneath me and I felt it hit my mail and then my leather byrnie. I brought my sword down hard and it bit into the shaft and

Viking Legend

then cut it. The hammer blow was so hard that it briefly numbed my hand. It was time to take the offensive.

"Gunnar, Eystein, on my command punch with your shield and then stab with your sword. We need space."

"Aye Jarl."

I saw the hammer being raised again. "Now!"

The boss of my shield caught the warrior in front of me on the nasal of his helmet. His nose erupted on blood, bone and cartilage. More importantly, his head flew back and smacked into the warrior with the hammer. I stabbed into the bare throat of the warrior with the broken nose and, as he fell, stepped forward to hit the hammer man with my shield. Already overbalanced he began to flail his arms as he fell. I brought my sword diagonally across his neck so hard that his head hung, briefly, by a flap of skin before the gory mess fell amongst those behind him.

I had accidentally created a wedge. I decided to exploit it and I hit the next warrior with my shield. My warriors emulated me and the heavy metal bosses of our shields pushed the Scots and the Saxons back. Any blows they struck were taken on mail. The warriors in our second rank kept up the pressure by thrusting through the gaps. Although they caused few deaths they distracted the enemy long enough for our swords to wound and kill.

I noticed that the arrows had ceased to fly over our heads. They had run out of arrows. It was down to less than seventy men now to fight the combined Scots and Saxon armies yet, incredibly, it was they who were going back. When I began to stab and hack into warriors without mail I knew that their best warriors had fallen. Eanred's oathsworn had been thrown away. I spied crudely made weapons ahead and knew that they were the fyrd. If we could wreak havoc with those then they might flee.

Then I heard Beorn's voice. He was on the far right of my line. "It is Ketil and his men. They are attacking the Northumbrians!"

I shouted, "Now is the time! On my warriors! One more push and we will have them at our mercy!"

All of our words were in Norse and I knew that the enemy had no idea what I had said. They could tell, however, that we were going to attack for their shields came together as they tried to weather the storm of our blades and shields. Had they had bigger shields then they might have held us. If they had worn mail or had helmets which were better made then their resistance might have been stronger. As it was I brought my sword over my head and smashed it down on a Scottish helmet. The warrior had no padding and the blow would have cracked his skull but his helmet was so poorly made that I split the helmet in two and then his skull.

Our opponents tried lifting their tiny shields when we raised our swords and then we used our shields. We were relentless. We smashed our way through their lines. And then Ketil and his warriors struck the flank of the Northumbrians. They quite literally tore through the poorly armed fyrd who fled. It was not just one or two it was the whole force who threw down their

Viking Legend

weapons and ran to the rear as fast as they could. My accidentally formed wedge now began to cut through the two halves of the enemy warriors. There was no longer any order or leadership. Their eorls and chiefs lay dead.

Then the horn sounded three times. We knew what that meant. They were retreating. The last warrior I slew was a greybeard. Perhaps he had had enough of life or could not face the dishonour of retreat. Whatever the reason he tried to strike me with his sword. I held up my shield and heard the clang of his sword. When it came away it was bent. I swung my sword hard and high. His shield was smaller and my sword shattered it and drove on into his shoulder. He was a brave man and even as he dropped his shield he swung again at me with his bent sword. I blocked it and said, "Go to your god!" I stabbed him in the throat and he died, sword in hand, instantly.

And then it was over. My men wandered the field giving the warrior's death to those too badly wounded to run. All of the others ran. Arne and Ketil found many over the coming weeks lying, as they did on the roads north and east. Some made it twenty miles before they died. The two armies' road home was marked with the bones of their dead.

I took off my helmet and walked to the river. As after most battles, warriors clasped those with whom they had fought shoulder to shoulder or spoke quietly to those who were wounded. I left those who had fought with me doing just that and I went to the river to bathe and to thank the pony whose sacrifice had ensured victory.

"Thank you Allfather and Icaunis. Thank you white horse from the north."

I put my whole head under the water and felt the cool river water rush across my face. I rubbed my face to remove the cochineal and the blood-spattered during the battle. When I rose I felt cleansed. I turned and saw Haaken and Wolf Killer approaching. They too were bloodied. We had been so close to our foes that it had been impossible to avoid such gore. Eystein limped behind. His bandaged leg was no longer bloody.

"That was hard fought." Wolf Killer did as I did and immersed his head in the river.

"Aye," I remembered the warrior who had been struck by the war hammer. He had been standing close to Eystein on my left. "Who was struck by that war hammer?"

"It was Thorir the Slow. He knew nothing about it. He had just slain two with one strike. He is in Valhalla."

Haaken said, "There are many in Valhalla."

I looked at him, "Ulfheonar?"

"No Jarl we all live to fight another day."

Eystein put his hand for me to help him up, "And our young crew of **'*Odin's Breath'*** are all better for these three days. They have stood in the shield wall and are not broken. They know what it is to be a warrior."

I turned to Wolf Killer. "I thank you for your support in this battle. This is far from your home. I will not forget the sacrifice your men made."

Viking Legend

"We are all one family and one people. We fight all who are enemies. Had we not come then who knows, we might have been next."

We headed back to the lines where the bodies of the enemy were already being stripped. Snorri stood while Beorn tended to a wound he had suffered. "It is a pity we could not pursue them Jarl."

"Aye. I will see Ketil. He can use the captured horses and follow the Saxons. We will march north tomorrow and make sure that King Alpín mac Echdach has left our land Wolf Killer and Sigtrygg can return to their homes." They both nodded, "Take the men from the valley with you. I will just take the Ulfheonar and the crew of *'Odin's Breath'* with me."

I saw Leif still clutching my banner. He was leaning on it as though it was the only thing keeping him upright. I walked to him. "You did well Leif the Banner. Should you ever choose to go a-Viking I would happily have you in my crew."

"And I will take you up, Jarl but after this slaughter, I would get back to my father's farm and feel the good earth in my hands."

"Aye, you have been on a journey and you need to think about that journey before deciding what to do next."

Ketil headed to me. His men were still searching the bodies for treasure. "I am sorry that we were late, Jarl. We found some horsemen who were heading down the valley. It took some time to kill them."

"I thank you for that. Where were they going?"

"We questioned one who was wounded. They were heading for your home, Cyninges-tūn. King Eanred had heard of it from Magnus. He sought to punish you for your attack on his home by attacking yours."

I nodded, "Then this is not over between us. We have captured some horses. I would have you and your men follow Eanred and make sure they return home."

He nodded, "With the horses we took from the raiders I can mount all of my men. This was a great victory Jarl. You defeated two kings. Men will speak of this for years to come."

"I could not have done it alone. I had jarls on whom I could rely and warriors who were as brave as any in Valhalla."

It took until dark to finish burying our dead. We built pyres for the enemy dead. Arne's people brought us food and we ate surrounded by the bone fires of the Scots and Saxons. When Arne's farmers collected the ash, they would have richer crops. They would benefit from the sacrifice of my warriors. We had buried forty of my warriors in two barrows and twenty from Sigtrygg and Wolf Killer in a second. Some of those who died had been in their first battle but for others, this was one of many. There were greybeards who would not return home. Haaken sang us two or three verses from the song he composed. It was not finished but it honoured those who had fallen.

Wolf Killer led the warriors who were heading south. Ketil had left before dawn to pursue Eanred. The battlefield felt lonely as I led my Ulfheonar and the young crew north. Over half of the young men now had mail and all had spare helmets and swords. They looked burdened as we marched north but none would leave behind the evidence that they had been in a battle.

We found the first Scottish bodies by the wall. One had had a stomach wound and he lay, looking almost alive, against the turf bank of the wall. Two others were on the other side. None had treasure. Their own men had taken it. We found others every mile or so. Snorri spotted the horse droppings. They were still fresh and told us that King Alpín mac Echdach was not far ahead. He would probably outnumber my small band but I wanted him to know we were not afraid of him and were happy to follow him.

By the middle of the afternoon, we had reached the Esk. We had left behind the land which Arne ruled for me. Beyond the wooden bridge lay the land of the Scots, where Alpín mac Echdach ruled. I took the decision. "We will cross."

Haaken smiled, "You seek more glory, Jarl?"

"No Haaken, I am putting down my mark on this land." There was a village just five hundred paces from the bridge. "We take the village and we burn it. Then we destroy the bridge behind us. This will leave a message for King Alpín mac Echdach. He can do as he wishes to the land north of this river but the south is ours and he ventures this way at his peril."

We headed for the village. I heard a shout and the villagers began to flee. Some of the young warriors broke ranks to pursue them. "Stay in line." By the time we reached the huts, almost all the villagers had fled. They had left a few animals and their huts gaping wide. One old man stood there in the centre holding an ancient sword. I sheathed my own and took off my helmet. I walked up to him, "You would fight us all, old man?"

He shrugged, "I have lived long enough and I would rather die fighting than be captured and enslaved. Come Viking. I will show you that we can die as well as you."

"No, this is not your day to die. Nor will you be enslaved. Go to your king and tell him that Jarl Dragonheart warns him to stay north of the Esk. If any come south they will never return."

The old man lowered his heavy sword. "I can go?"

"You can go and you have my word that you will not be harmed."

He smiled, "I know that you are never foresworn. Even those who hate you say that you speak the truth. Thank you Jarl Dragonheart."

He put his sword on his shoulder and trudged north.

"Gather the animals and drive them south. Search the huts. They usually bury their coins in pots in the ground. Find soft earth and seek them."

With my Ulfheonar to guide them, it did not take the young warriors long to discover the pots with the coins, amulets, pendants and precious stones they had hidden.

"Fire the huts and bring kindling and brands to the bridge."

The huts were well alight and the smoke drifted north as a smoky message for the king. When all of my men were across the bridge and the kindling laid in four piles I set fire to them and walked to my land. The autumn rains had

Viking Legend

been light and the bridge was dry. Soon it was a raging inferno. I waited until the middle section fell hissing into the Esk before I followed my men south. We camped well south of the battlefield for we did not want the spirits of the enemy dead to disturb our sleep. When we rose there was the first flurry of winter snow. As we passed the col into the land of the Grassy Mere I knew that winter would soon come. The gods would put a wall of snow and ice around us to protect us and we would be safe from our enemies until the spring.

Viking Legend
Epilogue

Although my warriors had been hurt and there were homes now without men Cyninges-tūn and the other settlements had prospered during the summer and the harvest had been a good one. Our trades had gone well and we had all that we needed for the winter. Our granaries were full. We had preserved meat and the extra animals we had collected meant that we would not go hungry even if we had another wolf winter.

As Yule approached I gave thought to the winter celebration. Brigid would want to commemorate the birth of the White Christ. I had seen little of my daughter since my return. She had been in the house of healing, along with Aiden, treating the warriors who had been wounded. For my part, I spent all of my time with my wife and my son. I was, therefore, shocked, when I went into her house of healing and saw her and Aiden embracing.

They gave me a guilty look and then Kara came over to me and kissed my cheek. "We should have told you, father."

"Told me what?"

"That Aiden and I have lain together."

"But I thought Angharad told you that you would lose your powers."

Aiden said, "She was foresworn, Jarl. Kara is more powerful now than ever."

I stared at my daughter. She looked different somehow. "Is this true?"

"My mother became more powerful when she married you and carried my brother did she not?"

I nodded, "Yes but..." Then I saw what was different. "You are...?"

"Yes, father I am with child. Aiden is the father. Our child," she placed her hands on her womb, "is already becoming powerful within me. She will be a volva with such power that we know not what she will be capable of."

"It is a girl?"

They both nodded. "It is a girl."

Aiden said, "Forgive me for not speaking before, Jarl. It just, well it just happened."

Kara held his right hand in her two. "It was *wyrd*. We were in the sweat hut. Mother told us that it was meant to be. Aiden wanted to tell you immediately but you were preoccupied with our enemies and you had your journey below the sea before you."

"You knew that I would have to descend below the ocean?"

"I dreamed. Mother told me you would be safe." I saw in her eyes that she sought approval. "You are not unhappy, are you?"

I realised that my face must have been serious. I smiled, "I am sorry. Of course, I am happy. Aiden has always been as a son to me and now he is. Will you two be wed?"

"There may be a time for that. We will dream. Perhaps the spirits will tell us."

I smiled, "I think, that this is one decision that I will make. You will be wed at Yule on the first day of the new year. I do not issue many commands but this one I shall. It is the will of jarl Dragonheart that you be married."

They looked at each other and nodded. Kara came and hugged me. "And who are we to argue with the Viking legend that is Jarl Dragonheart."

The End

Viking Legend
Glossary
Afon Hafron- River Severn in Welsh
Alpín mac Echdach – the father of Kenneth MacAlpin, reputedly the first king of the Scots
Alt Clut- Dumbarton Castle on the Clyde
Bardanes Tourkos- Rebel Byzantine General
Bebbanburgh- Bamburgh Castle, Northumbria
Beck- a stream
Blót – a blood sacrifice made by a jarl
Blue Sea- The Mediterranean
Bondi- Viking farmers who fight
Bourde- Bordeaux
Bjarnarøy –Great Bernera (Bear island)
Byrnie- a mail shirt reaching down to the knees
Caerlleon- Welsh for Chester
Caestir - Chester (old English)
Casnewydd –Newport, Wales
Cephas- Greek for Simon Peter (St. Peter)
Chape- the tip of a scabbard
Charlemagne- Holy Roman Emperor at the end of the 8th and beginning of the 9th centuries
Celchyth- Chelsea
Cherestanc- Garstang (Lancashire)
Corn Walum- Cornwall
Cymri- Welsh
Cymru- Wales
Cyninges-tūn – Coniston. It means the estate of the king (Cumbria)
Dùn Èideann –Edinburgh (Gaelic)
Din Guardi- Bamburgh castle
Drekar- a Dragon ship (a Viking warship)
Duboglassio –Douglas, Isle of Man
Dyrøy –Jura (Inner Hebrides)
Dyflin- Old Norse for Dublin
Ein-mánuðr- middle of March to the middle of April
Faro Bregancio- Corunna (Spain)
Fey- having second sight
Firkin- a barrel containing eight gallons (usually beer)
Fret-a sea mist
Frankia- France and part of Germany
Fyrd-the Saxon levy
Garth- Dragon Heart
Gaill- Irish for foreigners
Galdramenn- wizard
Glaesum –amber

Viking Legend

Gleawecastre- Gloucester
Gói- the end of February to the middle of March
Grenewic- Greenwich
Haughs- small hills in Norse (As in Tarn Hows)
Heels- when a ship leans to one side under the pressure of the wind
Hel - Queen of Niflheim, the Norse underworld.
Here Wic- Harwich
Hetaereiarch – Byzantine general
Hí- Iona (Gaelic)
Hjáp - Shap- Cumbria (Norse for stone circle)
Hoggs or Hogging- when the pressure of the wind causes the stern or the bow to droop
Hrams-a – Ramsey, Isle of Man
Hywel ap Rhodri Molwynog- King of Gwynedd 814-825
Icaunis- British river god
Itouna- River Eden Cumbria
Jarl- Norse earl or lord
Joro-goddess of the earth
Knarr- a merchant ship or a coastal vessel
Kyrtle-woven top
Leathes Water- Thirlmere
Ljoðhús- Lewis
Legacaestir- Anglo-Saxon for Chester
Lochlannach – Irish for Northerners (Vikings)
Lothuwistoft- Lowestoft
Lundenwic - London
Mammceaster- Manchester
Manau/Mann – The Isle of Man(n) (Saxon)
Marcia Hispanic- Spanish Marches (the land around Barcelona)
Mast fish- two large racks on a ship for the mast
Melita- Malta
Midden- a place where they dumped human waste
Miklagård - Constantinople
Nikephoros- Emperor of Byzantium 802-811
Njoror- God of the sea
Nithing- A man without honour (Saxon)
Odin - The "All Father" God of war, also associated with wisdom, poetry, and magic (The Ruler of the gods).
On Corn Walum –Cornwall
Olissipo- Lisbon
Orkneyjar-Orkney
Penrhudd – Penrith Cumbria
Pillars of Hercules- Straits of Gibraltar
Ran- Goddess of the sea
Roof rock- slate

Viking Legend

Rinaz –The Rhine
Sabrina- Latin and Celtic for the River Severn. Also the name of a female Celtic deity
St. Cybi- Holyhead
Syllingar Insula- Scilly Isles
Scree- loose rocks in a glacial valley
Seax – short sword
Sheerstrake- the uppermost strake in the hull
Sheet- a rope fastened to the lower corner of a sail
Shroud- a rope from the masthead to the hull amidships
Skeggox – an axe with a shorter beard on one side of the blade
South Folk- Suffolk
Stad- Norse settlement
Stays- ropes running from the mast-head to the bow
Strake- the wood on the side of a drekar
Suthriganaworc - Southwark (London)
Syllingar- Scilly Isles
Tarn- small lake (Norse)
Temese- River Thames (also called the Tamese)
The Norns- The three sisters who weave webs of intrigue for men
Thing-Norse for a parliament or a debate (Tynwald)
Thor's day- Thursday
Threttanessa- a drekar with 13 oars on each side.
Thrall- slave
Tinea- Tyne
Trenail- a round wooden peg used to secure strakes
Tynwald- the Parliament on the Isle of Man
Úlfarrberg- Helvellyn
Úlfarrland- Cumbria
Úlfarr- Wolf Warrior
Úlfarrston- Ulverston
Ullr-Norse God of Hunting
Ulfheonar-an elite Norse warrior who wore a wolf skin over his armour
Volva- a witch or healing woman in Norse culture
Waeclinga Straet- Watling Street (A5) Windlesore-Windsor
Waite- a Viking word for farm
Withy- the mechanism connecting the steering board to the ship
Woden's day- Wednesday
Wulfhere-Old English for Wolf Army
Wyddfa-Snowdon
Wyrd- Fate
Yard- a timber from which the sail is suspended
Ynys Môn-Anglesey

Viking Legend

Historical note

The Viking raids began, according to records left by the monks, in the 790s when Lindisfarne was pillaged. However, there were many small settlements along the east coast and most were undefended. I have chosen a fictitious village on the Tees as the home of Garth who is enslaved and then, when he gains his freedom, becomes Dragon Heart. As buildings were all made of wood then any evidence of their existence would have rotted long ago, save for a few post holes. The Norse began to raid well before 790. There was a rise in the populations of Norway and Denmark and Britain was not well prepared for defence against such random attacks.

My raiders represent the Norse warriors who wanted the plunder of the soft Saxon kingdom. There is a myth that the Vikings raided in large numbers but this is not so. It was only in the tenth and eleventh centuries that the numbers grew. They also did not have allegiances to kings. The Norse settlements were often isolated family groups. The term Viking was not used in what we now term the Viking Age beyond the lands of Norway and Denmark. Warriors went a-Viking which meant that they sailed for adventure or pirating. Their lives were hard. Slavery was commonplace. The Norse for slave is thrall and I have used both terms.

The ship, '***The Heart of the Dragon***' is based on the Gokstad ship which was found in 1880 in Norway. It is 23.24 metres long and 5.25 metres wide at its widest point. It was made entirely of oak except for the pine decking. There are 16 strakes on each side and from the base to the gunwale is 2.02 metres giving it a high freeboard. The keel is cut from a piece of oak 17.6 metres long. There are 19 ribs. The pine mast was 13 metres high. The ship could carry 70 men although there were just sixteen oars on each side. This meant that half the crew could rest while the other half rowed. Sea battles could be brutal.

The Vikings raided far and wide. They raided and subsequently conquered much of Western France and made serious inroads into Spain. They even travelled up the Rhone River as well as raiding North Africa. The sailors and warriors we call Vikings were very adaptable and could, indeed, carry their longships over hills to travel from one river to the next. The Viking ships are quite remarkable. Replicas of the smaller ones have managed speeds of 8-10 knots. The sea-going ferries, which ply the Bay of Biscay, travel at 14-16 knots. The journey the 'Heart of the Dragon' makes from Santander to the Isles of Scilly in a day and a half would have been possible with the oars and a favourable wind and, of course, the cooperation of the Goddess of the sea, Ran! The journey from the Rhine to Istanbul is 1188 nautical miles. If the 'Heart of the Dragon' had had favourable winds and travelled nonstop she might have made the journey in 6 days! Sailing during the day only and with some adverse winds means that 18 or 20 days would be more realistic.

I have recently used the British Museum book and researched about the Vikings. Apparently, rather like punks and Goths, the men did wear eye makeup. It would make them appear more frightening. There is also evidence that they filed their teeth. The leaders of warriors built up a large retinue by paying them and giving them gifts such as the wolf pendant. This was seen as a sort of bond between leader and warrior. It also marked them out in battle as oathsworn. There was no national identity. They operated in small bands of freebooters loyal to their leader. The idea of sword killing was to render a weapon unusable by anyone else. On a simplistic level, this could just be a bend but I have seen examples which are tightly curled like a spring. Viking kings were rare it was not until the end of the ninth century that national identity began to emerge.

The length of the swords in this period was different from in the later medieval period. By the year 850, they were only 76 cm long and in the eighth century, they were shorter still. The first sword Dragon Heart used, Ragnar's, was a new design and was 75 cm long. This would only have been slightly longer than a Roman gladius. At this time the sword, not the axe was the main weapon. The best swords came from Frankia and were probably German in origin. A sword was considered a special weapon and a good one would be handed from father to son. A warrior with a famous blade would be sought out on the battlefield. There was little mail around at the time and warriors learned to be agile to avoid being struck. A skeggox was an axe with a shorter edge on one side. The use of an aventail (a chain mail extension of a helmet) began at about this time. The highly decorated scabbard also began at this time.

I have used the word saga, even though it is generally only used for Icelandic stories. It is just to make it easier for my readers. If you are an Icelandic expert then I apologise. I have plenty of foreign words which, I know, taxes some of my readers. As I keep saying it is about the characters and the stories.

It was more dangerous to drink the water in those times and so most people, including children drank beer or ale. The process killed the bacteria which could hurt them. It might sound as though they were on a permanent pub crawl but in reality they were drinking the healthiest drink that was available to them. Honey was used as an antiseptic in both ancient and modern times. Yarrow was a widely used herb. It had a variety of uses in ancient times. It was frequently mixed with other herbs as well as being used with honey to treat wounds. Its Latin name is Achillea millefolium. Achilles was reported to have carried the herb with him in battle to treat wounds. Its traditional names include arrowroot, bad man's plaything, bloodwort, carpenter's weed, death flower, devil's nettle, eerie, field hops, gearwe, hundred leaved grass, knight's milefoil, knyghten, milefolium, milfoil, millefoil, noble yarrow, nosebleed, old man's mustard, old man's pepper, sanguinary, seven year's love, snake's grass, soldier, soldier's woundwort, stanchweed, thousand seal, woundwort, yarroway, yew. I suspect Tolkien used it in the Lord of the Rings books as Kingsfoil, another ubiquitous and often overlooked herb in Middle Earth.

Viking Legend

Slavery was far more common in the ancient world. When the Normans finally made England their own they showed that they understood the power of words and propaganda by making the slaves into serfs. This was a brilliant strategy as it forced their former slaves to provide their own food whilst still working for their lords and masters for nothing. Manumission was possible as Garth showed in the first book in this series. Scanlan's training is also a sign that not all of the slaves suffered. It was a hard and cruel time- it was ruled by the strong.

The blue stone they treasure is aquamarine or beryl. It is found in granite. The rocks around the Mawddach are largely granite and although I have no evidence of beryl being found there, I have used the idea of a small deposit being found to tie the story together.

There was a famous witch who lived on one of the islands of Scilly. According to Norse legend Olaf Tryggvasson, who became King Olaf 1 of Norway, visited her. She told him that if he converted to Christianity then he would become king of Norway.

The place names are accurate and the mountain above Coniston is called the Old Man. The river is not navigable up to Windermere but I have allowed my warriors to carry their drekar as the Vikings did in the land of the Rus when travelling to Miklagård. The ninth century saw the beginning of the reign of the Viking. They raided Spain, the Rhone, Africa, and even Constantinople. They believed they could beat anyone!

There was a King Egbert who did indeed triumph over King Coenwulf. He founded the power base upon which Alfred the Great built. It was also at this time that the Danes came to take over East Anglia and Yorkshire. The land became, over the next 50 years, Danelaw. Its expansion was only halted by Alfred and was finally destroyed when King Harold defeated his brother and King Harald Hadrada at Stamford Bridge in 1066. Until Alfred the Danes were used as hired swords. They fought for gold.

I used the following books for research

British Museum - 'Vikings- Life and Legends'
'Saxon, Norman and Viking' by Terence Wise (Osprey)
Ian Heath - 'The Vikings'. (Osprey)
Ian Heath- 'Byzantine Armies 668-1118 (Osprey)
David Nicholle- 'Romano-Byzantine Armies 4th-9th Century (Osprey)
Stephen Turnbull- 'The Walls of Constantinople AD 324-1453' (Osprey)
Keith Durham- 'Viking Longship' (Osprey)

Griff Hosker July 2015

Viking Legend
Other books by Griff Hosker

If you enjoyed reading this book, then why not read another one by the author?

Ancient History

The Sword of Cartimandua Series
(Germania and Britannia 50 A.D. – 128 A.D.)
Ulpius Felix- Roman Warrior (prequel)
The Sword of Cartimandua
The Horse Warriors
Invasion Caledonia
Roman Retreat
Revolt of the Red Witch
Druid's Gold
Trajan's Hunters
The Last Frontier
Hero of Rome
Roman Hawk
Roman Treachery
Roman Wall
Roman Courage

The Wolf Warrior series
(Britain in the late 6th Century)
Saxon Dawn
Saxon Revenge
Saxon England
Saxon Blood
Saxon Slayer
Saxon Slaughter
Saxon Bane
Saxon Fall: Rise of the Warlord
Saxon Throne
Saxon Sword

Medieval History

The Dragon Heart Series
Viking Slave *
Viking Warrior *
Viking Jarl *
Viking Kingdom *

Viking Legend
Viking Wolf *
Viking War
Viking Sword
Viking Wrath
Viking Raid
Viking Legend
Viking Vengeance
Viking Dragon
Viking Treasure
Viking Enemy
Viking Witch
Viking Blood
Viking Weregeld
Viking Storm
Viking Warband
Viking Shadow
Viking Legacy
Viking Clan
Viking Bravery

The Norman Genesis Series
Hrolf the Viking *
Horseman *
The Battle for a Home *
Revenge of the Franks *
The Land of the Northmen
Ragnvald Hrolfsson
Brothers in Blood
Lord of Rouen
Drekar in the Seine
Duke of Normandy
The Duke and the King

Danelaw
(England and Denmark in the 11th Century)
Dragon Sword *
Oathsword *
Bloodsword *
Danish Sword
The Sword of Cnut

New World Series
Blood on the Blade *
Across the Seas *
The Savage Wilderness *

Viking Legend
The Bear and the Wolf *
Erik The Navigator *
Erik's Clan *
The Last Viking

The Vengeance Trail *

The Conquest Series
(Normandy and England 1050-1100)
Hastings
Conquest

The Aelfraed Series
(Britain and Byzantium 1050 A.D. - 1085 A.D.)
Housecarl *
Outlaw *
Varangian *

The Reconquista Chronicles
Castilian Knight *
El Campeador *
The Lord of Valencia *

The Anarchy Series
England 1120-1180
English Knight *
Knight of the Empress *
Northern Knight *
Baron of the North *
Earl *
King Henry's Champion *
The King is Dead *
Warlord of the North
Enemy at the Gate
The Fallen Crown
Warlord's War
Kingmaker
Henry II
Crusader
The Welsh Marches
Irish War
Poisonous Plots
The Princes' Revolt
Earl Marshal
The Perfect Knight

Viking Legend

Border Knight
1182-1300
Sword for Hire *
Return of the Knight *
Baron's War *
Magna Carta *
Welsh Wars *
Henry III *
The Bloody Border *
Baron's Crusade
Sentinel of the North
War in the West
Debt of Honour
The Blood of the Warlord
The Fettered King
de Montfort's Crown

Sir John Hawkwood Series
France and Italy 1339- 1387
Crécy: The Age of the Archer *
Man At Arms *
The White Company *
Leader of Men *
Tuscan Warlord *
Condottiere

Lord Edward's Archer
Lord Edward's Archer *
King in Waiting *
An Archer's Crusade *
Targets of Treachery *
The Great Cause *
Wallace's War *
The Hunt

Struggle for a Crown
1360- 1485
Blood on the Crown *
To Murder a King *
The Throne *
King Henry IV *
The Road to Agincourt *
St Crispin's Day *
The Battle for France *

Viking Legend
The Last Knight *
Queen's Knight *
The Knight's Tale

Tales from the Sword I
(Short stories from the Medieval period)

Tudor Warrior series
England and Scotland in the late 15th and early 16th century
Tudor Warrior *
Tudor Spy *
Flodden*

Conquistador
England and America in the 16th Century
Conquistador *
The English Adventurer *

English Mercenary
The 30 Years War and the English Civil War
Horse and Pistol

Modern History

The Napoleonic Horseman Series
Chasseur à Cheval
Napoleon's Guard
British Light Dragoon
Soldier Spy
1808: The Road to Coruña
Talavera
The Lines of Torres Vedras
Bloody Badajoz
The Road to France
Waterloo

The Lucky Jack American Civil War series
Rebel Raiders
Confederate Rangers
The Road to Gettysburg

Soldier of the Queen series
Soldier of the Queen*
Redcoat's Rifle*
Omdurman

Viking Legend

The British Ace Series
1914
1915 Fokker Scourge
1916 Angels over the Somme
1917 Eagles Fall
1918 We will remember them
From Arctic Snow to Desert Sand
Wings over Persia

Combined Operations series
1940-1945
Commando *
Raider *
Behind Enemy Lines
Dieppe
Toehold in Europe
Sword Beach
Breakout
The Battle for Antwerp
King Tiger
Beyond the Rhine
Korea
Korean Winter

Tales from the Sword II
(Short stories from the Modern period)

Books marked thus *, are also available in the audio format.
For more information on all of the books then please visit the author's website at www.griffhosker.com where there is a link to contact him or visit his Facebook page: GriffHosker at Sword Books or follow him on Twitter: @HoskerGriff or Sword (@swordbooksltd)
If you wish to be on the mailing list then contact the author through his website.

Printed in Great Britain
by Amazon